Brian Thompson

Bad to the Bone

VIKING

For Joel Kaye

VIKING

Published by the Penguin Group
Penguin Books Ltd, 27 Wrights Lane, London W8 5TZ, England
Viking Penguin, a division of Penguin Books USA Inc.
375 Hudson Street, New York, New York 10014, USA
Penguin Books Australia Ltd, Ringwood, Victoria, Australia
Penguin Books Canada Ltd, 2801 John Street, Markham, Ontario, Canada L3R 1B4
Penguin Books (NZ) Ltd, 182–190 Wairau Road, Auckland 10, New Zealand

Penguin Books Ltd, Registered Offices: Harmondsworth, Middlesex, England

First published in Great Britain by Viking 1991
1 3 5 7 9 10 8 6 4 2

Copyright © Brian Thompson, 1991
The moral right of the author has been asserted

Set in 11/13½pt Lasercomp Sabon
Printed in England by Clays Ltd, St Ives plc

A CIP catalogue record for this book is available from the British Library

ISBN 0–670–83641–9

1

It's an enterprise economy, for those who still have any. In July of last year some enterprising soul who worked for a security vault in Knightsbridge thought of a way of emptying forty steel deposit boxes of their contents without leaving so much as a scratch on them. Making his way from the building, he paused to kick a protesting customer in the groin and then drove in his own car to Battersea. There he abducted a woman in a second car and disappeared in a puff of exhaust. He was a Greek Cypriot with a house in Brookman's Park worth a third of a million.

'I know Yanni is innocent,' his wife told us on the six o'clock news. She looked relaxed and informal. Behind her head was a bowl of cut flowers and a row of books on antiques. We had just seen the girl her husband had abducted. She acted excitable and laughed a lot. If you were charitable you might put this down to hysterical relief. But my bet was Yanni had made her day. He had left her tied up with her tights in Epping Forest and blown her a kiss before parting.

'People do not escape the consequences of a crime like this,' the most junior Home Office minister assured us. And that is why we part our hair in the middle – to show just how solid and imperturbable we are, how Victorian in our rectitude.

Or then again: we part our hair in the middle to demonstrate a current truth, that the rich can do more or less anything they choose and be anything they say they are. This particular prat was often on television. His haircut had disturbed me more than once. There was a child molester down our street when I was a lad who likewise favoured a central parting. The hair oil ran off his scalp like raindrops. He could give points to Benny Hill for obnoxiousness. Fashion changes with the times.

Next day, untidy men from the tabloids with ashtrays for brains began the work of sifting through Yanni's dustbins and photographing the girl who delivered the morning papers. Maybe they offered her a grand to say she had slept with the robber. She was all of twelve, so I suppose it occurred to some hotshot. The man who had been kicked in the groin learned from his son that Mother was having it off with a neighbour, the president of the local badminton club. This was not on the news. It was just something the kid felt he had to get off his chest.

Yanni's wife made a second television appearance.

'I beg of you to give yourself up,' she said, smiling straight down the lens of the camera. She looked terrific. See you in Brazil, Yanni, her gold bangles and impudent nipples seemed to be saying. She brushed thick honey hair back from her temples. By cocking my head to one side I could read the titles of the books she and Yanni browsed.

People put all sorts in deposit boxes. For some of our citizens, also with a spirit of enterprise coursing through their veins, they are a working necessity. On the local news, there was a nice little follow-up outside the security vault premises. The keyholders stood in line to go down and check their holdings. I wouldn't say they were drenched in the sympathy of the general public. Their faces lacked that certain something, principally an open and frank expression. Some of the dodgier customers had sent along their mothers and daughters. I recognized a couple of briefs. These mixed with a few genuinely distraught duchesses and ancient old men in Rifle Brigade blazers. Nobody was that keen to be interviewed. Down there, under the pavement, the disgracefully rich, for whatever reason, had stashed loot only to be guessed at – jewels, stamps, currency, gold, love letters, firearms, negatives. What Yanni had done was hardly like robbing a bank. Good luck to the plucky Greek, the world seemed to be saying. The depositors were out there on their own.

But then, I was an unreliable witness – a detective sergeant of the Hampshire police with a divorce and maintenance orders out against me – a lazy and incompetent officer with a record of insubordination. The very morning Yanni filled his pockets, in this life charged full with responsibilities and duties, I was rolling around on the bed with Dawn, wife to Edgar, cricketer, numismatist, and Detective Inspector. A graduate entrant destined to go far, and already with a firm foothold on the faces of his junior officers.

'A graduate of Strathclyde,' Dawn remonstrated, pushing me off and sitting up with her head in her hands. The mattress bounced.

'But a graduate all the same. Don't be such a snob. What was wrong with Strathclyde?'

Sweat ran down her back. It made her blonde hair cling to her neck in rats' tails. Her breasts were warm and wet with it. I rolled on to an elbow and licked her spine.

'What a bastard you are,' she said.

She bounded from the bed and walked through to the en suite bathroom. It gives an idea of the problems she faced. Edgar set great store by the good things in life. On his front lawn was a well-established weeping willow. At the back he had a barbecue pit. On the patio, which he preferred to be called a terrace, was a fine wrought-iron pub table with an umbrella fit for a howdah. Screwing Dawn round at her place was like living in a colour supplement. In the shower, she arched her back and the suds ran down her just as they do in the glossy leaflets.

'I always feel humbled when I come round here.'

'Piss off,' she said.

3

It was hardly past ten in the morning. The kiddies' cereal bowls were still on the kitchen table. Edgar was at a crime conference in Basingstoke. Those of his neighbours who had retired were mowing the lawns, buzzing about with infinite attention to detail. My car was outside, pointing like a gigantic neon sign at the upstairs windows. They knew I wasn't there to sell double glazing.

I joined Dawn in the shower and we clung together like tree frogs. The water ran off us on to the cork floor and hid under a baby-pink rug. A Spanish ragamuffin looked at us reproachfully from a print on the wall. Dawn bit my neck.

'What am I doing, messing with trash like you? God, you're flooding the goddam bathroom, you pig!'

We tumbled out of the shower tray still locked together and crashed to the floor.

'Tell me I'm crazy,' she gasped.

'You don't need any of this,' I panted, meaning the marriage and all its works, its willows and barbecues.

But secretly we both knew the house and its flourishes were all she had ever desired. She was right – she *was* crazy. Downstairs the washing machine chuntered pleasantly and a reproduction case clock clucked in the hall. Their King Charles spaniel sat watching the front door, ready to grass me up to Edgar, should he return. In the cupboard under the stairs, Master's cricket bat leaned against His golfclubs. Everything was just as the ads say it can be, if only you can empty your mind of doubt and unease.

'I must be mad even to let you in the house,' Dawn shouted. We skidded along cork tiles on which Edgar had lavished eight coats of button polish. My head hit the lavatory bowl with a clunk. Dawn sat on me, riding to a close finish, her fists clenched in my hair.

Edgar came in exactly a moment too soon.

'That is my bathroom floor!' he roared.

*

4

In the language of the police serials, I was well and truly stitched up. The Head of CID disliked Edgar almost as much as I did, but for less profound reasons. Edgar had once or twice corrected his grammar. But on this occasion an appeal to fellow-feeling was pointless. The boss read out a long list of my errors and omissions compiled by the graduate cuckold and added one or two of his own. Then there was silence. Look out of any window in the south and you see a mute aeroplane, laconic, silver and unstoppable. Its faultless logic – to arrive – has a mocking quality all of its own.

'Well,' Bert said glumly, 'what do you want to do?'

After consultation with the Federation rep, I resigned the force, as they say. The unspeakable business of Edgar's floor had already been communicated to my ex-wife's solicitors, and some legal knots were slashed through there. The house was sold and the monies divided. Lengthy legal wrangles went up in a puff of smoke. I was on my ear.

I moved to a room in a house run by two scruffhounds, next to a launderette which doubled as a house of assignation. A huge, good-natured girl called Trace ran a little business in the flat upstairs, giving pleasure, of a kind, to pensioners. They dropped in their washing and then tottered up for a bit of a bounce. Trace made them a cup of tea and listened to their ramblings about the Dover Castle garrison, when beer was fourpence a pint and the Hun was at the gate.

My landlords were called Steve and Eric. I lived at the front, on the ground floor. At night I could hear them singing. Eric was knocking sixty and a bit given to musicals and light opera. Steve was a Roy Orbison fan. They cooked catastrophic meals and drank sherry and orange juice until their brains shrank. Once a week they asked me round, four paces from my hell-hole to theirs – a room painted dark blue, giving on to a yellow kitchen.

'It's like living in the armpit of a Rugby League shirt.'

'Oh well, if you don't like it, you know what you can do, dear.'

5

But Eric was actually the more tender of the two. He kept a scrapbook on the Duchess of York, whom he described as a poor lost soul. We sat around drinking sherry and orange juice, watching television.

'Get her,' Eric would observe, of Nick Ross, or Michael Buerk.

Steve was inclined to be sullen. Karate and kung fu had failed him. He so wanted to give the world a flying scissors in the balls but was honest enough to see that opportunity was everything. Once in a while he would resume his weights and his Bullworker, but his desire for revenge on life was balanced by a certain dizziness. He used a lot of hair gel and sported a Freddie Mercury moustache.

'I would rather be me than some clapped-out copper.'

'Good for you, Stevo.'

'Who goes around pretending all this shit is none of his making. You're part of it, man. You're law and order, or you was.'

'Were, dear,' Eric cooed.

'Was,' Steve said spitefully. 'All this cynicism. Gets up my nose. I love this country, but it's been ruined by yuppies and police. That is my opinion. Furthermore, the usual thing in marital matters of the sort you got yourself into is that the offending party does a bunk. Clears off out of it, moves to another town.'

'Suggest one.'

'Yeovil,' he said, recklessly. We none of us knew exactly where that was. Eric tutted. He was knitting a cardigan and peered over half-moon glasses.

'You're lucky little Edgar didn't bash your head in.'

'We were both sworn officers of the Crown, Eric.'

'That does make a difference, I'm sure.'

'The point is, you partook of the status quo, and now you are unwilling to pay the price. Except through snide jokes and that.'

I examined Steve carefully. Maybe there was a vein of shrewdness in there somewhere. He pointed a grubby finger.

'I bet that Edgar has told all the blokes you put away in your time where you live and that. I shouldn't be surprised to find them come round and kick your effing head in.'

'Edgar is a graduate of Strathclyde.'

'Har har,' Steve said, meanly.

Did *he* put the word out, or was he right that it was Edgar? In all events, a couple of weeks later I was set upon in Tesco's car-park and kicked senseless. Middle-aged women with Spanish tans watched impassively. I had three stitches put in my right ear and was detained in hospital while they tried to find my relocated liver. Nobody came to see me. It goes without saying, the police made no enquiries.

One of the nurses was called Andrea. She was tall and skinny, with a nose like a parrot. The world is a small place; her mum was Dawn's cousin.

'What a terrible man you are,' Andrea said. 'If they'd kicked you any harder, you'd be dead by now.'

'I thought I was.'

She lingered a moment by the bed.

'Dawn chopped up Edgar's cricket bat with the garden spade.'

Her oppo, the little Indian nurse, giggled. They had been dying to tell me that. But there weren't many other jokes. The pain of passing water was excruciating. I could just squeeze out enough to fill the bottom of a kidney bowl before feeling the ward spin. On nights there was a large and sombre Jamaican sister, who shook her head and gave me peppermints to suck. She held court at the nurses' station to two jolly but whispering orderlies. Sometimes she – and they – flew away down long telescopic tubes, dwindling to a dot and then rushing towards me again. I was in bad shape, and unwilling to be discharged.

*

I was sent home in an ambulance one bright morning, along with a punk who had drilled a hole through his hand with a Black & Decker, and a genial old man who sang me the song that Rick told Sam never to play again. As well as knowing the words, he could also bash it out on the old accordion, the old tit-trapper.

'I've heard that bloody song in every seaport in the world,' he told me. 'That, in my opinion, is fame. So don't talk to me about rock and roll.'

The house was empty and, after the blissful order of the men's surgical ward, it was dull and oppressive. The bedclothes had vanished from my sagging divan, and my possessions were stacked against the wall. Where there had been a coffee table now was Eric's ironing board. There was a mountain bike leaning against the fireplace. I had forgotten the smell of the place, compounded of dust, Steve's embrocation and toiletries, and chip fat. I made a cup of coffee in their kitchen and sat staring out of the window at the ruined patch of grass where Steve was wont to do his sunbathing. Across the fence the panel-beating firm was at it hammer and tongs. Some homecoming.

My landlords were, as I half expected, ready to say farewell for ever. Eric had a thing about violence. It put him clean off his knitting.

'And in any case, you weren't getting anywhere with us, were you? I mean you weren't exactly improving yourself.'

Steve had taken up the weights again, and the floor resounded with muffled thuds. Eric glanced at the door.

'Steve has a friend, Roy the swimming-bath attendant. He's looking for a place. We said he could have your room. Steve's a bit upset. He says you're bad news. He'd rather not have dealings.'

'Give me a week to find somewhere else,' I pleaded. 'Or couldn't you pass me on to friends? Just for a while. I need to think about what to do.'

'Who do we know who'd put up with *you*?' Eric asked, with unanswerable melancholy. 'All this smart-arse talk. All this cooking on the front burner rubbish. It's hard enough, us being what we are. I suppose you've been told before you're incurably facetious?'

'Yes.'

'Well, I'm not sure it's helping you along life's thorny way. Really I'm not.'

His gaze was tender. But later that night I was summoned to their parlour. They had come up with an idea. Someone they knew had a railway carriage in the form of a summer-house, out in the sticks somewhere.

'A railway carriage,' I said with foreboding.

'All the rage, dear. The place is miles from anywhere, up a farm track. It would be like a holiday. You could do a bit of sunbathing, get a tan and that.'

'But a railway carriage, Eric.'

'Total bon ton. You could write a book. And you'll like him. He's a perfectly harmless old queen.'

'So take your sense of the ridiculous and sod off,' Steve concluded.

Hilary Watson turned out to be a real charmer, the authentic article from the thirties, miraculously preserved, like the swallow-tail butterfly, or Oxford bags. He lived in a wonderful house of flinty brick, with sagging window apertures and a ruined roof. In winter he retreated to a back room and spent more or less all day in bed, reading and listening to a Walkman someone had given him. But in the summer months he came out like Brock the Badger. He was a painter of landscapes and a botanical illustrator. When I first set eyes on him he was sitting on a rusting wheelbarrow, drinking Margaux and squinting at the sunlight. The kitchen table was leaning drunkenly in knee-high grasses. His plat du jour was on a white dish – a round of chopped ham fresh from the tin.

9

'Quite the most difficult thing to do when you are old is to alter petty circumstances. I mean, you could put me if you chose among the Trobriand Islanders, should they still exist, and I don't suppose I could stop opening tins of the wretched stuff. I would have them sent out from Safeways. I can truthfully say I would not give you a thank-you for a coconut.'

'Would you paint any differently?'

'Shouldn't think so. I'm not at all a Gauguin. No, I think I should paint from memory out there. This is a dear old place, you know. The Trobrianders would think me very odd.'

'Do you sell many of your paintings?'

Hilary shot me a glance.

'I don't think that's why one paints, is it?'

I had offended his sense of decorum. His expression indicated that he thought me very crude.

'I find all policemen very tiresome. I know you are no longer one, but you are a cynic in that mould, perhaps. A young cynic is almost always some form of impostor. Eric has said something about that aspect of your character. But says you are to be trusted. We shall see.'

The railway carriage was mounted on crumbling and deathly grey sleepers. You could easily roll a bottle diagonally across the sloping floor. The interior was encrusted all over with chicken shit and little grey feathers. I spent the first few days there scraping and scrubbing with a wire brush. Some of the chickens who used to live there could read and write, for the walls were decorated with some quite disgusting graffiti, as well as drawings of pert bums being pierced by massive fleshy daggers. Cemented to the floor by the fowls were copies of magazines printed in Denmark for the German market, or perhaps the other way round.

'We used to have parties,' Hilary explained, with a vague wave of his hand. 'It was all very tedious. People have a devil's own job enjoying themselves. I much preferred the chickens. They came later, of course.'

'What happened to them?'

'A really delightful man was rearing them for table. It was a business arrangement. It fell through, as these things always must.'

I used to watch him come out in the mornings in his yellow pyjamas, squinting at the light and stretching his canvases and paper with trembling hands. He drank tea from a jamjar, or perhaps he was drinking the water he used to clean the brushes. His cat, Wallace, sat on the rickety table, too shagged out for anything but the occasional blink.

'You may well wonder why I do not invite you to the house. I shall, in due time. But two things you don't need as you grow old are sleep, and company. I'm sure you're a famous chronicler of life as we know it today, but that's a pleasure I shall defer to some point in the future. We must meanwhile preserve a landlord–tenant understanding.'

That suited me. He lived on chopped ham, washed down by Margaux and camomile tea. I lived on Indian tea and vegetable curry, a dish I have found to be a great solace as well as easy to prepare. For the rest, I sunbathed and watched a lot of ants and other insect life getting on with it in the grass. Occasionally Wallace the cat would saunter over and give me a weary inspection.

And then, one fine day, the pace quickened.

2

When I first saw her she was wearing a blue halter-neck and a wrap-over skirt. Her arms and legs were very brown. She sat at the table out there in the grass, reading a newspaper and from time to time bending to scratch her ankle. It seemed like the action of an angel, a heavy, strong and faintly surly angel. Pigeons were cooing in the wood and the light was like champagne. It was truly as though she had dropped from heaven.

Close to, she was big. Everything about her was big, solid, sculptural. She was a Maillol. Her expression was calm and unsmiling. I could easily imagine her not brown and warm, but green, fashioned from unyielding bronze. She was magnificent.

'Hilary said there was a madman about,' she said, as I made my entrance across the dewy meadow. I gave her my jovial side, my bright morning.

'Good old Hilary,' I said. 'Where is he?'

She laid down her dish of camomile on the leader page of the *Guardian* and lit a cigarette.

'Do you have any coffee in your little hen-house?'

'The finest powders, garnered from the four corners of the warehouse.'

I put her age at thirty-eight. Her voice was educated, practised. Maybe she was an actress. Maybe she was Titania, Queen of the Faeries. There were little sharp lines about her eyes that had not come from being merry with strangers in the early morning.

'I'd like some coffee,' she said, resuming her reading.

While I was making it, Hilary came out all dressed up for the occasion in belted slacks and a cyclamen shirt. Stephane Grappelli, without the fiddle. She said something and he glanced towards the carriage. Although he could not know I was watching, he made a face and stuck out his tongue. Righty-ho.

I shaved and changed my shirt before making a second entrance with two mugs of Asda's own.

'Shall we introduce ourselves?'

'This is my daughter,' Hilary said. 'Her name is Judith.'

'And you,' Judith explained, 'are the bent policeman.'

'Not bent.'

'Nobody resigns just because he's caught in bed with another officer's wife.'

'You tell me.'

'There were other matters.'

'For example?'

She came straight to the point. Wasn't I the one who had stolen a pound of grass used in police evidence against a certain Wolcott Brain, described in the Press as a black baron of drugs? Hadn't Edgar held that little pistol to my head? I was startled; but after a moment's reflection, realized she must have talked to somebody like Steve to get that nugget of information. As it happened, I was not the one who lifted the grass, although widely suspected at the time. It made a good story with the lads and set the long-suffering Bert by the heels for a month or two. Wolcott's brother carried the tale round all the clubs in the guise of a rap. The most readily available rhyme for grass featured prominently. She may have heard of the case that way. All the same, and to please her, I dimpled prettily.

'We're not talking major dope here. Wolcott grew it in his garden, but it makes a good story. What are you, his brief?'

'Judith is an entrepreneur,' Dad said fondly. 'She has irons in many fires.'

'She knows a hell of a lot about me.'

'Is there really that much to know?' she murmured. I flattered the remark by laughing at it. Hilary laughed. We all laughed. I was helping her over a sticky moment. Something weird was going down.

But then again, she smoked, and drank coffee and bought newspapers, and for this I forgave her much. It had grown to be tedious swilling camomile with Hilary and chatting about what Wallace got up to in the days of her youth. And she just might be Hilary's daughter. They shared the same snooty airs.

'Wolcott was a right-on bloke. Maybe you know him.'

She shook her head.

'I don't get my grass from some council-house garden.'

'It's sent round by Harrods van, is it? I'm trying to make a connection, that's all. Maybe we've met?'

'Eric and Steve told me all about you,' she confessed. 'Eric sends his love, by the way.'

'How are things working out with Roy the baths attendant?'

'Not good,' Judith said. She rose from the table. 'I'm going to sunbathe.'

As she went, she tossed her lighted cigarette away in the grass, something I would never do in front of Hilary. The gesture somehow made her much less likely to be his child, leaving aside all other considerations. He seemed to read my thoughts.

'Her mother was a strange creature, a reforming daughter of the clergy. From Shropshire, where they are a bit slow on the uptake. She thought my problems were just those of self-discipline and facing up to responsibility. Judith's turned out rather well in the circumstances, don't you think?'

'Plenty of self-possession there,' I hazarded.

'Oh, masses. She eats men like you for breakfast.'

'We've just had breakfast,' I objected, reasonably enough.

'You look thoughtful, dear heart,' Hilary said. 'Is it because of this Wolcott business? I've told you, she's my daughter. We have no secrets. It's a very amusing story. You really mustn't look for difficulties before they arise. Take her as she is.'

'As she is, or as she is advertised?'

'Ha ha,' Hilary said, without mirth. All the same, he ducked his head, as at a thrust from a fellow foilsman. I studied him in the new light Judith cast over things.

'I never really asked you – how do *you* know Eric and Steve?'

'I should have thought that was obvious.'

'They don't seem your type.'

'My, my, we are in a suspicious mood today.'

His adjective, not mine; but as soon as he uttered it, I recognized what had been floating in the air like thistledown. For some reason, warning bells were going off in my head. At times like these, in the cockpits of airliners at any rate, the bells and everything else that is being said and heard are recorded in a black box. That's how it is in airliners.

But one thing was certain – she liked to sunbathe. Prone, she could not be seen from the carriage. But from time to time she sat up as plump and naked as a peeled orange. With occasional excursions to the house for books and mineral water, she stuck out in the sun all day long. Some of the time I suppose she slept. So did I, some of the time. It was a comfort to drop off knowing that a few yards away there was this lioness in the grass, sleek as Wallace but a whole sight more interesting. She made enough impression on me to cause me to wash out most of my clothes, something the damn cat had not been able to achieve. The day passed in buzzing holiday somnolence.

That night I was invited to the house. Judith cooked supper and the table was carried in from the ruined garden. It was lit with candles. Hilary's books gave off a pleasant peppery smell and the wine fumed in my head. At the conclusion of the meal Judith took out her skins and some resin and rolled a great joint. We sat round the table like happy families.

15

'What do you do, if I may ask?'

'She's a tart,' Hilary said.

'I have a flat in Knightsbridge.'

'And you whore for a living.'

'That's one way to put it.'

'Good class of people?'

'D'you mean do they take off their socks? Yes.'

Outside, an owl hooted in the looping branches of a chestnut tree. I passed the spliff to Hilary, trying to make sense of all this nonsense. I judged we were all as drunk as each other. Over dinner we had talked, not without some hilarity, about water-colourists and drinking clubs and poetry editors. If she had now said she made children's programmes for radio I would have found it more believable. If she said she had a play running at the Donmar or imported Peruvian arts and crafts, I would have believed her. Judith watched me with a slight smile on her face.

'If it helps, I don't actually walk the streets. I don't even work the hotels.'

'Terrific.'

'I read English at Oxford. Does that help?'

'As it happens, no. I have a bad record with graduates.'

'But you're very well informed all the same. You know a lot about poetry editors.'

'Ah, but that's straight crime,' I quipped.

Hilary gathered himself for an explanation.

'He is a buffoon with some unawakened seriousness in him, Judith. Wallace tells me he reads Russian history for his relaxation. Of course, with these and some other disabilities, we may well ask why he ever became a police officer.'

'I was asked to make up the numbers.'

Hilary flapped at me with an old man's disdain.

'I'll tell you why, shall I?' he said. 'You're a child of your time. This is a repressive age. Some people can't take it, and for others it is the very embodiment of what their heart desires. It tells them something they wouldn't otherwise admit to – I mean that they *are* repressed. They kiss the flag with fervour, hoping it will poison them.'

'Pretty deep for me, Hils.'

'You're not so difficult to understand.'

'And I thought we liked each other.'

The mood was turning a little more indigo. The neighbourhood owl gave a sardonic toot. Hilary, in reaching for his wine, slopped some over his wrist.

'Oh, I don't make my likes and dislikes known quite as easily as that. You're amusing – or at any rate your predicament is. Judith works harder. Wallace is nobler than either of you. I like what you've done with the carriage, that much I'll grant you. But you're too woolly to be likeable, my dear.'

When I left, the moon was full, beaming down on lunatics and lovers everywhere. The extreme stillness and the damp of the grass reminded me of scout camps in those far-off days when everybody wanted to be a Phantom pilot and drive a beaten-up MG. No one I knew achieved even the second of these dreams. I sloped into the railway carriage and took a large belt of whisky. There was enough light coming through the windows to read by.

Judith's passage through the grass made a soft swishing noise. She climbed up the steps and stood in the doorway a moment, before taking off her skirt. Then she came inside and leaned against the wall. We stared each other down.

'May I see your ticket, please?'

'You let him get to you,' she said. 'That's unnecessary. He does like you, otherwise you wouldn't be here. Going to let me use your toothbrush?'

She cleaned her teeth and washed her face busily in the little stainless steel bowl provided. She took off the rest of her clothes and went outside for a pee. It was Ma and Pa Kettle.

We lay side by side for a while, touching at the hips and along the lengths of our arms. I sneaked a look. Her eyes were wide open. She seemed to be examining the curve of the ceiling and the little sails of cream paint that had been hoisted over the years as the old GWR livery flaked.

'I may look stupid,' I said at last, 'but I know when I'm being set up. This isn't de Maupassant. You haven't got a heart of gold. And you didn't come down here to gather wild flowers and get a tan.'

Her fingers sought and enlaced themselves with mine.

'I can't sleep in the house. It oppresses me.'

'Bullshit.'

'Oh don't be so dull. I wanted to talk.'

'I thought that was usually the punter's line.'

She rolled over and lay across me, her tongue in my mouth. The warmth of her breasts was alarming, shocking. Her free hand reached for me and yanked. It was a little parody of lust. She laughed.

'Oh honey,' she said, 'you get me so excited.'

She laughed again, and kissed my throat before rolling back.

'Come on. Don't be such a wally.'

'I'm all goosepimples,' I said gallantly.

Judith lay passive as I kissed her spilt breast. Her breastbone, for all the sunbathing, gleamed silver in the moonlight. She reached up lazily and pushed me away. We resumed our study of the flotilla on the ceiling for a while. I could hear her tummy rumble, a pleasant and endearing sound.

'Remember Yanni Kyriakides?'

I didn't; until she mentioned the security vault. Then I did. Many possibilities flashed through my mind.

'He's hiding out at your place.'

'Wouldn't that be fantastic?' she murmured.

'He's your secret Latin-American dance partner.'

'Steve's friend, Roy the baths attendant? Has a pal who's a fisherman. This bloke's at a reservoir and finds a lot of papers stuck together, you know, gummed up by the water and so on.'

'From the security vault.'

'You catch on quick,' she said sardonically.

'Who says?'

'That they're from the vault? They are. I've bought them.'

It was my turn to loom over her. Her expression was calm enough, but a bit defensive. I tried to see into her eyes completely. After a moment she looked away.

'You *bought* them? That was good thinking. And I fit into this story somehow, do I?'

'I thought you might like to make some money.'

Enough of this madcap nonsense. I grabbed her wrist and pulled her upright. We sat in the puddle of moonlight with our legs stuck out before us.

'Listen,' I said. 'You have to remember that I wasn't born yesterday. We're talking old sweat here. You're no more a tart than my auntie. You're almost certainly not his daughter either. Maybe the flat in Knightsbridge is true. And maybe you've got hold of some of the gear from the vaults. But stop trying to give me the run-around.'

'Forget it then.'

'That's better.'

I let go of her wrist and she hit me quite hard in the mouth, enough to draw blood.

'I hate a smart-arse.'

'No you don't. You're just a bad loser. Who's behind all this? And stop pouting, Judith. What are we playing here, *Midsummer Night's Dream*?'

'Do you know a man, a politician, called David Nicholas?'

David Nicholas was the junior Home Office minister who parted his hair in the middle, the Home Secretary's flak-catcher and media personality, the man who had promised to bring Yanni to book. 'The papers I bought belong to him.'

'His memoirs. His KGB card.'

'They are love letters. From me to him.'

I looked at her carefully.

'On headed notepaper.'

19

'Yes, on headed notepaper.'

'That's how Roy the baths attendant found you.'

'Yes.'

She brushed back her hair and waited. I was getting there in my own time.

'You're being blackmailed.'

She lay back once more and rolled on to her stomach. Naked or clothed, she could time a line.

I am saving David from being blackmailed,' she said to the pillow.

I got up and lit two cigarettes from the same match, one of those things you always want to do stark naked after midnight in some godforsaken railway carriage out in the woods. I passed her hers. Mine tasted of straw burning outside a pony-trekking stables. I poured two small whiskies.

'Now do you understand?' Judith asked me.

'No. In fact, I don't buy it. I've never met Roy, remember, but if he thought he could put the bite on a junior Cabinet minister, he wouldn't bother with you, beautiful though you are when you're angry. If little David Nicholas could be identified from this junk, you wouldn't come into it. What happened to the new-found spirit of openness we had just a few moments ago?'

'Why won't you just take what I say to be true?'

'I think it's because you take your clothes off in too much of a hurry on a first date. Or is that old-fashioned? What's more, my dear Scarlett, you have an impudent tongue.'

'You're not real,' Judith said, with just the right flattering amount of admiration. I tried to think of a reasonable scenario that could be constructed from this mess of lies.

'Okay, you're muddling along somewhere, maybe Knightsbridge, maybe somewhere else, and you get a call from this muscle-bound oaf who calls himself Roy. When you meet him, his moustache smells of chlorine, he has lats a mile wide, and he wants to sell you something he thinks is yours. He thinks it comes from your deposit box. He's made a balls of ungumming the stuff, he came on the Tube, and he's as camp as a row of tents.'

'We hit it off,' she said.

'I bet you did.'

'And then what?'

'You tell me. I'd have to know what was in the letters.'

'I have told you. They were love letters.'

'But did they say, for example, "that night you had me on the Cabinet Room table with all the others watching told me what we had was special"? Or – "not a word to the PM until we are really sure of ourselves"?'

'He asked me for two hundred pounds. And I paid him.'

'For the sentimental value, as you might say.'

'Yes.'

I patted her on her broad shoulder.

'Good girl. And count me out.'

Criticism made her petulant. Her lower lip jutted.

'Think about it, Judith. A nasty man who is a baths attendant in some hick town you never visit asks money for some letters. You pay up. Not very much – and that makes him either clever or stupid. Which? Did he go away thinking, well here's a week's drinking money for doing sod-all? Or did he smile a secret smile, as if to say this is just the beginning, darling? I'm not getting a complete picture. He asks: you pay. That's your story. Then you come down to this dump and want to offer me money. The bait is all this codswallop about letters and blackmail and saving young David. Seems to me you've already done that.'

'There's more,' she said, after a slight pause.

'I bet there is. What happened next? A retired primary school headmaster found some more letters hidden under a rock on Helvellyn, maybe? Or a pony walked out of the New Forest with a bundle stuffed up his arse?'

'Don't be smart.'

21

'Then don't be coy.'

'You haven't asked me a single question about David.'

'I already know the only two things I need to know about the bloke – he keeps you, and you'd like to see his eyes drop out.'

I was surprised to see wet tears running down her cheeks.

'He was my life.' she sobbed.

The table was back out on the grass. Hilary was tottering about with a plateful of Whiskas for Wallace, and the pigeons were taunting from the tallest branches. The only indication she had ever been here was the sheet wound like a rope on the mattress and her silver screw of resin which she had left on top of the coffee jar. And this flaky story of love and abandon. I looked in vain for my incorruptible male pride, or failing that, my common sense.

Making love to her, plunging as deep as I could into the deepest river, I had arched my back to look into her face. Her cheeks were wet with tears, but she was smiling like a child. She was smiling, it seemed to me in the blue-green light of a country dawn, as might a child at a circus seeing the entry of the man with the huge boots and the electric bow-tie. It was an image I could not shift from my mind, that childish delight, that seemingly innocent pleasure. Everything else about her – how she came into my life, the story she told, the hundred devious little sidepaths to her – was about as reliable as a three-pound note.

When the moment finally came, and the sun rose outside and inside me, I lay with my head on her salty breast and listened to a suspiciously steady heartbeat. After a few moments, she pushed me off and turned her back. A few moments more and she took my hand and cupped it round her with a sort of tetchy impatience. Her flesh was slick with sweat. And then, when I wake up, there she is – gone.

3

The most important thing to know about the Right Hon. David Nicholas, MP, was that he was out of the country. The Home Office referred me to his secretary at the House of Commons who explained that he was taking a much-needed break with his wife and family. It was the parliamentary recess, had I realized? Members of Parliament worked jolly hard. Ministers of State worked especially hard. David needed to recharge his batteries like anyone else. He generally went to Tuscany for this purpose, and no she couldn't give me the address or telephone number. Instead, she gave me her most incredulous laugh, as if at the blind impertinence of the idea.

'It's just that I've found all these documents in Russian in an old tree trunk.'

She thought quickly and asked me to put it all in writing.

The same thing happened with his agent, a man who had taught himself, despite the disability of a native Yorkshire accent, to speak in a hyphenated drawl, in the highest traditions of the Party he served.

'David is vacationing actually, with his wife and family,' Mr Austin Bradshaw fluted and tooted. I explained that I had got the telephone number from a lavatory door in Peckham. But Bradshaw was a pro. He kept up the drawl and suggested I pop him a note, making the verb pop sound about as urgent as rolling a barrel down a one in two hundred incline from here to Paris.

I rang a bloke I knew on the Met.

'That tosser!' Jacko said cheerfully. 'Have nothing to do with him, my son. Give him a wide berth. How's Dawn and her rosies?'

I explained.

'Bloody hell,' he said. 'Bit steep. What are you doing these days then?'

'Living in a railway carriage.'

'Oh yes? Well in that case, pip, pip.'

'Listen, Jacko –'

I paused, leaving him to listen in obedient silence. What was my next line – Do you happen to have a file on chummy? A bit far-fetched. Jacko was far too fly to do anything but listen, probably with his hand cupped over the mouthpiece of the receiver.

'This Nicholas bloke.'

'A right tosser. But aren't they all, eh?'

'I'm a bit involved with him in an indirect way, see? It's nothing bent, just a bit of an involvement.'

'The police are here to help, you're absolutely right to phone in. Not pissed, are you?'

'Wasting your time, eh?'

'Just a bit, my son. What is this, a cry for help? Life kicked you in the cods at long last, has it? I mean d'you want to come and talk, round our place? Sylvia still thinks you're lovely. We've moved, by the way. Got a four-bedroom semi, Barnet.'

'You guessed,' I said. 'I rang up 'cos I was lonely.'

'How'd you meet little David?' Jacko asked all too casually. 'Eh?'

'Your pal the MP. The one you're involved with in an indirect sort of way.'

'Through a girl.'

'Tut tut. The life you divorced blokes lead. Unbelievable. Girls, MPs, bleeding railway carriage addresses. Wossamatter, my old dear? Want to meet? Wanna drink in that place in Orange Street? Six, six-thirty?'

'I'll catch you in Barnet sometime.'

'For sure,' he said, and I knew he was scribbling down a note about what had been said. He gave me his number in Barnet and took my address.

I had, in short, made an almighty rollocks of the whole thing. It hadn't helped my case that in the background to my end of things was the huge booming acoustic of a public baths.

I was right about Roy in one respect – he wore a moustache. But a sorry straggling thing it was. He was one of those loners you meet in motorway cafés, with a narrow skull and lantern jaw, round-shouldered and dejected. He did not give the impression of a blackmailer imbued with a spirit of enterprise. He did not give much of an impression either that he could save lives or even keep order in a public swimming bath. I watched him from the viewing gallery and cafeteria of his place of work. The pool was being run by a hearty girl with swimmer's shoulders. Big Sandy marched up and down the glistening pavements, a pea whistle bouncing against her splendidly firm breasts. These had been drawn to my attention by an habitué sitting near by.

'Say you have your lungs,' this old-timer explained. 'You have your lungs, like, and what swimming does is to improve those lungs. And the heart? Does wonders for the heart. More to the point, you meet a nice class of person.'

He was called Sid, and had been taught to swim by his pals in 42nd Field Engineers. He showed me a photograph of himself and Nobby Clarke from Keighley. It was taken at a tram-stop near Gizeh, immediately before descending into the stews of Cairo.

Roy knew Sid. In his weary way, he knew them all. I came prepared to swap insults with some muscle freak, but Roy was at odds with all that. When his shift was over, we went for a drink in a pub near the leisure complex. He walked with the demeanour of a con exercising: unhasty, unexcited, weary. He

25

smelt of chlorine and wore a large sticking-plaster on the nub of his chin. Maybe he was learning to dive.

The pub he chose was much frequented by bikers. A brindled Alsatian roamed restlessly round the tables. Some of the lads were playing pool. That week's almighty joke was to fart as you leaned over the table. It broke them up every time.

'I was doing the woman a kindness,' he said. 'I thought she might like her letters back, that was all. You could hardly read anything except the address. Headed notepaper and that.'

'What *could* you read, Roy?'

'I don't know. Can't remember.'

'Was it all personal correspondence, billets-doux?'

He was ready with a little French of his own.

'It was all papier mâché.'

'You didn't separate it out.'

'There was a number, a phone number. I just rang the woman.'

'What a surprise.'

He looked surprised himself.

'How come?'

'To find it was Hilary's daughter.'

The remark went in at Roy's ears and sloshed around for a moment or so. At last he closed his mouth. He frowned, perplexed.

'What has Hilary been telling you?'

'That Judith is his daughter.'

'Never!' Roy said, with just enough exclamation, just enough delight for me to hear, like a ghost, the voice of his dear, dead old Mum.

'She's not his daughter?'

'Hilary? We're talking about the same Hilary, are we?'

'The railway carriage in the woods.'

There was a grotesquely fat girl in attendance with the bikers. When one of them recognized me and called me by name, this clown pulled down her jeans and, bending over, mooned us, to cheers from the pool players. Roy studied her mottled blue and white arse, nibbling at his lip.

'He's been pulling your leg,' he said doubtfully.

'You'd never seen her before?'

'A perfect stranger.'

'How much did you ask for the gear?'

'None of your business.'

'Okay, Roy. Now let's stop pissing about, there's a good lad. Where did the stuff come from?'

'Out the reservoir.'

'Try again.'

'It come from the reservoir,' he said.

'You told her some bloody silly story about fishing it out with a lightly baited eight hook. So now you tell *me* the truth, all right?'

'She can't have her money back,' Roy said, with stupid obstinacy.

'Tell me, or I'll take you outside and tear your balls out.'

He shrugged. He was on firmer ground now.

'Once a copper always a copper, eh? We found the gear on the path, or just off. There's hawthorns there. People go back for a crap and that.'

'Who's we?'

'Me and a friend of mine.'

'It was out in the open.'

'It was in the hawthorns.'

'But not concealed.'

Roy shrugged again.

'Was it planted?' I asked.

'We found it, man. It was just loose, scattered around.'

'You said it was papier mâché.'

'Yeah, her bit was.'

'There was more?'

'There were no more letters, if that's what you mean.'

'What else, then?'

'Piss off,' Roy said.

I sat staring at the sticky rings of beer and lager on the table in front of me. Roy felt slightly more at ease. He even tried a wan smile. And his instincts were good. If he wasn't telling the truth, and I *was* being set up in some way, he was hardly likely to be the linchpin of the operation. Maybe he had done his work in finding the stuff. Maybe he had just worked that out for himself. He was in this what he was best at in life: a sacrificed pawn.

'Photographs, negatives?'

'Where?'

You can never be sure about these things, but I felt Roy was giving off harmless vibrations. His aura was good. Or perhaps I trusted him because he drank low-alcohol lager and bought his shoes from Oxfam. Before I left, he had cheered up considerably, and explained at length about the connection between cholesterol and peanuts.

Real heroes would have driven to London and beaten on the door of the flat in Knightsbridge. But then real heroes have the petrol money. I lolloped back to Hilary's in the ageing Renault, wondering why it smelled of dog all the time. I stopped at a Happy Eater for a portion of chips with all the other miserable punters. The weather was breaking and hailstones the size of golf balls had been witnessed in Kent. The Happy Eater's customers were in a frenzy of reflection on this and the other major issues of the day.

'Well, I wonder what it is you want from your fellow countrymen?' Hilary demanded. 'Should they all have been sitting round reciting Gerard Manley Hopkins and welcoming the stranger at the door with a snatch or two of *Don Giovanni*? I should rather like to see a hailstone the size of a golf ball, actually. What an appalling snob you are. Of course, it's your professional background.'

'I'm in a ratty mood, Hilary.'

'You don't say.'

'Who is Judith?'

'My daughter.'

'Try again.'

'I think I'll stick,' Hilary said lightly. 'You have nothing to fear from her. On the contrary, I believe she has been rather accommodating. She cooks very well too, wouldn't you say?'

'Listen, you geek, I'm being set up by someone. You, maybe.'

'If only I could spare the time.'

'Did Judith really have a thing with this David Nicholas?'

'Oh yes.'

'She's his type, is she?'

He hesitated, then when he saw my expression, smiled a tiny rueful smile.

'Life is so complicated.'

'Brilliant, Hilary.'

It was perfectly true that I had come home in a ratty mood. For one thing, the summer was coming to an end and with it the feeling of being on extended holiday. While it might suit my landlord to play the hermit in the woods, the prospect of spending the short days of winter keeping company with him was not an appealing one. That was one consideration. Then there was the fact that the only work or money offered to me in over three months had been by Mystery Woman. As to that, the bells were still ringing in my head. Her story was a rusty sieve. Talking to Roy the baths attendant about almost anything would be purgatory, but substantiating Judith's tale through him was like trying to sculpt frog-spawn. And now here was Hilary telling me life was complicated. I must have continued to communicate wide-ranging exasperation. He sat down at the table with an old man's weariness. He examined the grave marks on the back of his hands and yawned. Then when he saw me grinding my jaw, he sighed.

'Mr Nicholas is married. His wife is Lord Perslade's daughter and there are two lovely kiddies. There's a his and hers BMW, a house in St John's Wood, a cottage in Wiltshire and of course the lovely old Tuscan farmhouse. Lydia Nicholas writes children's books. Her husband is his genial self on television at least once a month. The Prime Minister finds him attractive in his raffish way. He has a distinctive hair style and that seems to help advancement in this day and age. There was only one way a girl like Judith could fit in with all that. He made her his tart.'

He had been painting from pencil sketches. The water-colours were laid on with curious assurance, as by someone quite other than this dickering figure who sat arranging their edges. He looked up at me sideways with a curious expression of sympathy.

'Look,' he murmured. 'I didn't ask you to come here, and I didn't arrange for her to meet you. Why not leave it at that? Let it rest. You form no part of any conspiracy, or anything like that. I mean, in the end everything touches the edge of everything else, but you don't have to know any more than you do already.'

'Just spit it out, Hilary. Don't bother with the delicacies. I'm hooked. You have me wriggling on the end of the damn hook. So just get on with it.'

'Very well,' he snapped. 'Try·this for size. Little David likes to do things to women that no decent woman could contemplate.'

There was no trace of a smirk. He was warning me off, pure and simple. But I had the memory of her skin against mine, the gasp of gratification that comes not just out of the throat, but from the whole room, the world, the universe. We stared each other down like Japanese wrestlers.

'Give me a clue,' I said in a dry voice.
'Games.'
'A clue that I can understand.'

'He likes to express his sexuality in unusual ways.'

'I didn't think there was an unusual way left.'

He flapped his hands at me.

'How very amusing. You're what passes for normal. You make it your style, is that it? Then so be it. I believe she asked you if you would like to make some money. You refused. Gesture – and response. That is surely the end of it?'

'You were saying, about little David.'

'Yes, well, do you see I am rather *angry* with you now. You're a provincial boy who likes books, and old things. The Nevsky Prospekt under twenty degrees of frost back in eighteen whatever it was. The snow falling on the roof of the Peter and Paul. I wouldn't bother myself with anything else. I'm sure we fall well below your threshold of interest.'

'Oh piss off. Pour me a glass of wine and get to the bloody point.'

I'd annoyed him sufficiently to make him go inside. I heard him tottering about the rooms and rummaging. Wallace the cat sat sneering at me. When I gently pinged my fingernail against her nose, she rode the punch better than any heavyweight of the last thirty years. High overhead, a cargo of tourists came winging in from the North Atlantic. Of course, in the States these moments would have a better orchestration. Over there, I would be so goddam hot for the story I would bite the head off the cat, just for something to do.

He returned with a faded salmon pink folder. Glowering at me, he withdrew the contents and pushed them across the cluttered table. I stood up almost at once, feeling the sweet stuff rise up my throat to my teeth. The world paled.

The folder contained ten by eights of fun time with a junior Cabinet minister. If I had not slept with Judith the previous night, I might have concluded that here were police photographs of somebody her weight and age who had been cut up by a garden hedge-trimmer and thereafter disembowelled with bayonets. Her mouth was gagged with her own knickers. The gore and tripe was arranged on her body with pathological exactness: a Breughelish detail – in some of the pictures Wallace lay curled up beside the horror, her eyes blinded by the flash. There were compositions in which Judith lay bound with ropes on dusty warehouse floors. In some, what was undoubtedly her own blood trickled from her mouth. I kicked back the chair that stood behind me and Hilary flinched.

'She permitted all this shit?'

He smiled sadly.

'She loved him, do you see?'

You do get inured to it as a policeman, a detective, principally because you are always the representative, crass as you might be, of order, from which we all derive our idea of ordinariness. No matter how bent you might be as a copper, you are still on the side that is nominally sane and decent. You go home to carpets without bloodstains, and eat meals that haven't shared the fridge with severed limbs. In bed you might fancy a bit of a change, but never with babies or indignant animals. In my time I had met all these things. By the very circumstance of being a police officer, you are filled up with a sense of sex as utter futility. Dressing up as Mae West or Martin Bormann, wanting to find the girl with breasts bigger than seal pups, or the man who could have modelled for the Cerne Abbas giant – all that stuff does not end but begins in disillusion. What little David liked doing with a few pounds of butcher's offal and a complaisant model was not against the law. If that was all he liked doing.

Nor did I need Hilary to remind me that every Bill Sykes will find his Nancy. The question was, whose side was Judith on? The question was, I found myself asking through rare tears, whether he was right and for Judith, this was love.

Hilary poured more wine with an unshaking, scrupulous hand.

'They were at Oxford together,' he murmured. 'That's easily

checked. She brought him here a few times, even in those days. And even then he was barking mad. He is a man who likes to abuse women. It doesn't steal over him when the moon is full. It's part of him. Judith could cope. She is very intelligent. You will have discovered that.'

'She's not your daughter, of course.'

'More's the pity. Her actual parents were horrors, I'm sure it wouldn't profit you to know how or why.'

'She brought him here.'

'Yes. A great many people have come here, over the years.'

'When did he become a politician?'

'In the annus mirabilis of 1979, when else? I don't think he was too keen for a while to remember all the larks he'd had here. But then, somehow or another, they met again. As I say, he married this woman of unimpeachable ordinariness and fathered his two delightful kiddies on her. But perhaps there can only be one Judith for a man like him. I have followed his career in the newspapers. Every so often, he is profiled as the coming man. I doubt it. It's a very difficult secret to keep, you know.'

I had this sudden and sickening recollection of the conversation with Jacko. Hilary studied me carefully. He was waiting for me to make the obvious and screaming connection with the security vault robbery.

'He kept his copies of the photographs in a safe deposit box?'

'I imagine.'

'Along with her letters?'

'He's altogether third rate,' Hilary said, with a slight smile.

'Are these some of the photographs?'

'No. These are mine.'

'And why have you got them?'

'The question is, where are the ones from his safe deposit box?'

'Bloody marvellous!'

33

He toasted me across the rim of the glass.

'They'd be ten times more explicit, of course?'

'Oh yes,' Hilary said. 'There wouldn't be all this fuss otherwise, would there?'

I went for a walk in the woods.

Yanni does the vaults. In among all the swag he finds letters and photographs incriminating a Home Office minister with a woman easily identified by her personalized stationery. He is a man already loaded down with loot – gems, cash, bonds, Christ knows what. Money doesn't come into it. The only possible use he can make of these two bimbos and their guilty secret is to assist him in the strong and now urgent desire he has for foreign travel. Short of working in the Passport Office itself, David could not be a more valuable mark. Once he sees what he's got, Yanni can put the bite on him in under thirty seconds, an untraceable call. The Minister is called away to the phone and fails to return to the dinner-party guests whom he has been holding in thrall with many an insider's yarn about Number Ten. The air around his head seems to thin to an attenuated whisper of molecules. He is discovered in the downstairs loo, throwing up his wife's *boeuf en croûte*.

Next day, Yanni phones again – and again the day after. By now, Nicholas is looking as though he's worked down a lead mine all his life. Wifey is getting worried. The coming man of British politics is sweating through the front and back of his suit, never mind his vest and shirt. He is talking in his sleep. The children are in tears. Whenever the phone rings nowadays, Daddy tries to crawl under the sofa.

For want of a cigarette I pulled a stem of rye grass and chewed its green and innocent succulence. I tried to think of it from her point of view. Say Yanni applies the cosh to *her*, too. If she and Nicholas occasionally took lunch in that oh so discreet wine bar in Holland Park, she must be camping out there now like someone trying to get tickets for Centre Court. Where *is* little David, what is he doing about it? Can he really and truly be thinking of helping Yanni evade the course of justice? He's clever, he's sexy, they think the world of him in the constituency, but can he really swing it for some Greek crook to get away scot-free? Is this the true shape of the world?

However it was, Yanni has long gone, baby. And here we are all of a sudden with gays tripping over the same stuff out on the reservoir, and Judith pitching me a story about saving Mr Nicholas from disgrace. And me, looking into her eyes and seeing the laughter there, the hapless childlike pleasure as the man in the big boots comes staggering into the ring. But according to my scenario, the circus had already left town. Unless Yanni was an idiot, he already had Nicholas on tiptoe in a lake of shit, the stuff bobbing at his chin. I didn't come into it.

Through a screen of beeches, I saw Judith's car lurching down the pot-holed lane. The sunlight flicked off the windscreen with cruel insouciance. When she got out of the car and saw me walking towards her, she held her plump arm over her eyes to shade them and I was reminded again of the child she had once been. A thought was forming in my head that was to become a commonplace where Judith was concerned. This, I thought to myself with a grim lack of confidence, had better be good.

· ·

4

'As Hilary told you, we met at Oxford. He was very bright.'

She considered what she had said with a slight frown, dashing away flies as luscious as blackberries the while. We sat side by side on a fallen log in the woods. Impossibly green grass grew under our feet. Above us, through the canopy of the trees, the sky was turning that dangerous armour-plate colour and the air was menacingly still. We were at the prelude to an almighty storm.

'He was quick,' Judith amended. 'Ambitious. Scheming, once he had you in his power. Witty. Attentive. But calculating.'

'You went to bed.'

'Yes, we went to bed!' she snapped. 'We sweated, we slobbered. What does that tell you? Of course we went to bed. I was nineteen and two stone overweight. I was very unhappy, and not very bright.'

'Do me a favour. Let's leave bright out of it.'

She had already smoked three cigarettes and was trembling slightly, as if her heart were somersaulting. She held her hands in her lap, legs slightly parted and the huge juicy flies crawled over her exposed knees. I could smell the electricity in the air.

'He joined everything, was seen everywhere,' she said. 'He was one of those people who have their invitation cards ranged neatly along the mantelpiece. I mean this is right from the beginning, the first week of his first term. That sort of thing counted a lot with him. He toasted teacakes on the gas fire every day at four. His tea was so much nicer than anyone else's. That sort of thing.'

'I'm getting a vivid picture.'

'I used to listen to him read his essays. He likes music, good music, what he calls serious music. I had never heard any. We listened to that, but in a systematic sort of way, as a means of educating me. It was all so new. At home I had been doing dope and living in a black tee-shirt, everything black. I cut holes in my stockings and burnt the back of my hands with cigs.'

'I bet he liked that, too.'

She glanced at me.

'He was considered a real catch. Odd, certainly, but also very sweet at times. Plenty of people who knew us said I was corrupting him.'

'Tell me about your real parents.'

'My real parents were arseholes. What has that got to do with it?'

'I don't know. Tell me.'

'They don't come into it,' she said. So for a while we just sat there like babes in the wood, thinking about the peculiar smell of burnt bread and – maybe – Mahler on the turntable as people ran up and down the staircase outside. Judith stirred.

'You're incredible,' she said in a wobbly voice. 'What do you want to know?'

I put my hand over hers and waited some more.

'Dad liked to rub himself against little Judith for a bit of fun. Mum was the quiet type. It wasn't wrong, it was healthy. It was clever of Judith to make it happen.'

'Where was this?'

'Bracknell. She died. He's still alive. He worked as a bus inspector. I knew what he was doing, and she knew he was doing it. But nobody said anything. We kept ourselves to ourselves, as he used to say. He plays bowls now, and goes on coach trips to the Holy Land with the church. At least the bloody vicar sees some good in him.'

'What's his first name, what's he called?'

She flung my hand away and stood up, pushing back her hair with trembling fingers.

'You think you're so smart,' she said. 'But you're just pure fucking ignorant.'

She had fallen into a role at Oxford, all too familiar from her childhood. She was the subservient and acquiescent party – it was all her fault. Everything was her fault. It was her shame that Nicholas was as he was to her; not his. As with her father, she was the guardian of somebody else's secret – her body was a secret that she undressed alone. When Nicholas went to the Union, or disputed over the teacups with the hotshot dons, it was in the company of more sophisticated women. Her father, in his time, had whispered little stories to her of the women he had ogled, of how if you stood in the right place on the shuddering platform of the bus when the miniskirts went upstairs, you could catch a right eyeful.

'But then,' he had said, with a little yellow smile, 'I always come home to you, don't I?'

She was not surprised therefore to hear Nicholas use the selfsame phrases. In her second year, she moved out of college and found rooms in a crabby Jericho terrace. It was a place in keeping with her idea of herself. Opposite the lodgings was a pub, where she drank with the punks and scored for amphetamines. They were harmless kids with an interest in impressing each other. She fitted in. There was a gay boy, Keith, who was given to writing her poems. She taught him how to use make-up and dress like a woman. But always she would be on the watch for Nicholas to visit her from the world of light. He had discovered a use for the word amusing. Keith was amusing. Having her crawl across the dank carpet and beg to please him was amusing.

'It's making you sick, isn't it?'

She asked the question with an irritating sense of triumph. It was not so much a question as an assertion. But I knew she was also afraid I would say yes.

'Hilary says you loved him.'

We had come through the wood to the railway carriage. Spots of warm rain began to fall.

'You must have loved your wife once,' she suggested. 'Have I asked you why, or for what? You probably married about the same time. It was something going on in another part of the forest. You got engaged, chose a ring, got married, saved up for a house. Anything.'

We went up the rickety steps into the carriage and she began to light the butane cooker and make tea. She knelt on the floor, watching the harsh blue flame.

'You're a spectator,' she said, surprising me. 'I think I am too. But David's a player. It's going to hurt you, but I got to like it, what he could do to me in perfect freedom, without reproach. If you like, I took a pride in it. He never asked a single question – tying me up, all that shit. He just did it. Can't you see?'

'Still want me to help you?'

'Yes,' she said, after a long pause.

'Then I have to know what was in the letters.'

'Nothing,' Judith said, choked. 'Just words.'

'Look, I don't want to harm you. I want to help. I don't want to know more than I have to, either. But you're not telling me the whole truth.'

She looked up from the floor, aghast.

'You think I'm making all this up?'

'About your father, about Nicholas? Of course not. About the blackmail angle? Everything else? Maybe.'

'Boy, you really take the biscuit. The letters were just letters. They were love letters, yes, but *you* could have written them. Anybody could have written them. The point is, they were on my notepaper.'

'The point is, they were in the deposit box along with little David's art studies of you as so much meat.'

'Roy just sold me the letters,' she shouted. 'Nothing else.'

'Then you've nothing to worry about.'

'That's right!'

'It isn't a crime to love another man's wife.'

'I hadn't realized that.'

She turned off the flame under the kettle and stood up. We faced each other like enemies.

'You haven't asked me one intelligent question that can get me out of the fix I'm in now.'

'All right then, try this. When did you first meet Yanni Kyriakides?'

For a shot in the dark it was a bull's-eye. She picked up half my furniture – one of two folding chairs from God knew what church hall – and flung it against the wall with enough force to break it in two. She pushed past me and half walked, half ran to Hilary's house. You could hear the door slam in three counties. His face appeared at the window for a comic instant and then withdrew.

I relit the stove and made myself a nice hot cup of tea. Before I could get the milk into the mug the trees and grass were suddenly lit by an acid yellow flash and right over our heads the skies cracked apart.

When you are on the bottom, when your feet are firmly in the mud and you haven't the money to buy petrol for a car you cannot tax; when you count the cigarettes in the packet before lighting one up, and study the small change in your pocket with a baleful hatred – then, who's doing what to whom elsewhere in the world becomes a matter of lesser importance. It's a class act, thinking of others. When you're down and out, the population of the world dwindles dramatically. That's one way of putting it. Another would be to say you find yourself all out of empathy. Now, staring at my eye reflected in the surface of the strong red tea, I made myself ask who gave a toss about her, or Nicholas, or their fateful secrets? What I wanted more than anything else was to leave this sodding valley with its wood pigeons and water-colours, its tarts and vicars, its truths and dares. What I wanted was a nice undemanding job with a flat next to the pub and maybe a goldfish for company. Anything requiring brainwork and application would depend upon whether the pub had a quiz machine or no.

The thunder and lightning polka'd around for half an hour and begat rain in glassy sheets. I did not hear the car approach and looked up to find Edgar in the doorway. He wore a trenchcoat over his shoulders in the manner of Alain Delon, and he was without his cricket bat. My favourite Detective Inspector, dressed to kill by Dawn and wearing, in addition, an expression of withering disdain.

'What a pleasant surprise,' I managed to exclaim, thinking Christ, what a stonking turn up for the book. One of Edgar's hobbies was amateur dramatics and he held his pose a moment or two, savouring a good entrance. As they say in the sort of stage directions Edgar was most used to at the Wheatsheaf Players, a cruel smile flitted across his countenance.

'How are you doing, chummy?' he asked.

'Just great, big Eddie, just great. As a matter of fact, I'm just off to drinks with the Lord Lieutenant and a few of his rich pals. You haven't come for your free-range eggs have you? They don't do them here any more.'

Outside, God's ASMs were banging the tin foil with wild enthusiasm. Lightning lit the green gloom. Edgar shrugged off his trenchcoat.

'You're clinging to the drain cover, but you haven't slipped through,' he decided, employing his gift for a vivid phrase. And he had spooked me, no doubt about that. I had an irrational alarm at having forgotten how fit and clean-cut he could look.

'How about you, boss?' I asked. 'Let me guess. Since you bought Dawn the touring caravan things have cheered up between you. She's even taken to seeing your mother in a different light – and of course, the sex is better than ever.'

He was one of those men who can actually make the muscles of the jaw tweak. He looked for somewhere to sit down and then remembered he had stumbled over a broken chair out there in the grass. So instead, he leaned against the wall and folded his arms. He crossed his legs, standing one bench-made brogue on end, the polished cap resting on the floor.

'Keep going, arsehole,' he said comfortably.

'What do you want, Edgar? I'm a busy man.'

'I heard you got a kicking a while back.'

'You heard about that, did you? Where were you on the day – lose your invitation?'

'No, I was happy to stay on the sidelines as an interested bystander. But that's not why I'm here. No. It's about another matter.'

'Fire away.'

'Roy Kinnock,' he said.

Since I was sure he had been about to tell me Dawn was pregnant, my relieved laughter came out a bit gusty.

'Now are you sure you've got that name right? Want to check?'

'This one wears a white tee-shirt, white ducks, a whistle. This one works at the baths and is bent as a butcher's hook. Roy.'

'What about him?'

'You saw him yesterday.'

'Oh him! I'm on your wavelength now. We met for a social drink, for sure, yes.'

'What did he offer you?'

'A half of low alcohol.'

He did not smile, but looked around him, taking things in with a shrewd graduate's glance.

'You live in this shithole?'

'It's a holiday property. I'm on extended vacation.'

'You live here?'

'I thrive.'

He nodded absently. But it seemed he could, after all, time a line.

'We pulled your mate Roy this morning, attempting to pass stolen goods.'

'No kidding,' I said, with a dry mouth.

'No kidding.'

He was playing the scene the way he liked to play, leaning against the proscenium arch and having the audience watch and wonder. If he says the word photographs I am going to leap through the window and leg it. I waited. And so did he, the bastard.

'Okay. What stolen goods?'

'Seventeen krugerrands.'

He peered at me in the gloom, and I at him. I don't know which of us looked more uncertain.

'Krugerrands, eh?'

'What did you talk about in the pub?'

'He took over my lodgings. I wanted the room back. That was the business side of it. I think we went on to the crisis in feminist fiction, and I do remember he was very hot on Mexican debt. You know the sort of thing they chat about in that pub.'

'Where'd you get the rands?'

'Me? I won't even buy South African grapes and oranges.'

'Where'd he get them?'

'Search me. But not before you produce a warrant. What is this bullshit, Eddie?'

'I'm going to do you. I'm going to wipe that smile clean off your face.'

'Go ahead.'

'I want to know where you got that gear.'

'Don't be pathetic all your life, Eddie. Take the day off.'

It was a nice calculation: how much more did he know than he was telling me? If Roy did indeed get the rands from the cache out at the reservoir, that was part corroboration of his

43

story about finding the letters. But rands are untraceable. Was Edgar leading me on? Were there other things that Roy was trying to fence that tied the gear to the vaults robbery? Had Edgar even made the connection to Judith?

'You're looking thoughtful,' he said. 'Not much of a life, is it?'

'Charge me with theft and handling stolen goods, or sod off.'

'Dawn, it might please you to know, thinks sexual inadequacy is at the root of your problems.'

'Ah now, she's being too hard on herself there.'

He hit me flush in the mouth and was very excited when the blood flew back into his face. That's what he had come for, that's what he had dreamed about. Nor was I shamming in sinking to my knees. I was wondering whether I had bitten my lower lip in half. Edgar got on to the front foot with speedy sportsman's instincts, and kicked me quite expertly in the ribs, toe-ending me to the boards of the carriage. The mug of tea went skittering. Before I could roll into a ball, he got in the shot he must have visualized a hundred times sitting on the pot of the en suite bathroom. He kicked me in the balls with ferocious energy and laughed when I was racked between throwing up and never breathing again. I tried to crawl. He pushed me over with the toe of his brogue.

'Can you see? Have your eyes fallen out? Your pal Kinnock had some cock and bull story about finding the gear out at Syke Head Reservoir. So I had a little trip out there myself.'

He waited while I threw up. I was blubbering. He liked that. He seized my hair and jerked my head back.

In his hand was a 35 mm negative. He smiled.

'You know what this is, don't you? The fairies left it out there. It and another three rands. Don't you want to know what it is? It's a shot of your new girl-friend, together with a well-known Member.'

He considered that one a real cracker.

'Your chum. I can't tell you how pleased I was to find the negative. You owe me. You owe me quite a lot, apparently. Dawn says I should leave you alone, but then she would, wouldn't she?'

When I reached for the neg he dropped it in the vomit.

'You want to think of me as a figure of fun. You resent my having gone to university. Maybe you both do. You want the world to go round, you want somebody to do the graft, but you don't want to get involved yourself.'

'You're a player, I'm a spectator,' I croaked. Why not? The concept seemed to find favour with him. He preened himself like a bloody parrot.

'What a good head kicking I could give you now. But that would be too easy. So, here's what I have in mind. A grand for the neg, from either of them. You can be my agent. One K, that's not too much to ask. Otherwise I go to the police.'

And that really broke him up. I scrabbled for the little grey and silver square and Edgar stepped aside willingly.

'All I ever want is to remember you like this. The money's not important. Make that point clearly to them. They'll understand.'

I was trying to wipe off the neg and hold it up to my streaming eyes. Edgar retrieved his trenchcoat with an Elizabethan flourish.

'You're an idiot,' he said at the door. 'But bye-bye for now.'

It was not the original, of course; it showed Dawn in a bikini bottom and no top, taken on their famous visit to Majorca three years earlier. I peered at her black breasts and white nipples, her black hair and white loop necklace and – sad to say – I was sick all over again.

And the next hour stayed in black and white. Hilary strapped my ribs, while Judith dabbed at my lip with a bowl of peroxide. Robert Ryan grimacing while Gloria Grahame pouts. We were all holed up in the country cabin on the back road out of town. Outside, the engine of the getaway car cooled under its dusty hood and skunks kept guard for the Highway Patrol. The old doc was plenty nervous, never mind his degree was in gunshot wounds. You had the feeling he might skip at any minute. Gloria was thinking up double- and triple-crosses. Back there in the city, minutes and seconds were ticking away. Burly men who wore their hats to sit at a desk and smoke cigars were putting two and two together.

Meanwhile, I lay on the ruined sofa, Judith's breasts against my cheek. They had discovered me crawling across the hissing grass. Between them they had carried me into the house and Hilary had forced hot sweet tea inside me. Now, as a comforter, we all sat watching television – they sat, and I sprawled, waiting for the world to change back to glorious technicolour. I must have dozed. When I awoke, it was an hour later. Hilary and Judith were out of the room. Someone had turned down the sound on the set and I was watching the news, mute. People came in and out of buildings. They arrived by car or on foot, and left in motorcades a mile long. The buildings they vacated were shelled, or blown up. Flags were flown from flagstaffs, or twitched about on the aerials of speeding Peugeots. Every so often, back to the studio, where the expression on those comfortable and neutral faces made you feel even more certain that things were bad and getting worse.

The door opened and Judith stood silhouetted.

'Why did he do that to you? Why be so savage?'

'I dunno. Has it stopped raining?'

'Hours ago.'

'I want to go back to the railway carriage.'

'Stay here. I'll make up a bed for us. We can talk. I need to talk.'

'You do,' I promised. 'But not in here.'

Hilary appeared at her shoulder, watching me with his habitual half-frown.

*

Perhaps I should have settled for the bed, the incredible warmth generated from her body, and more lies. But instead we staggered back to the carriage. Slugs the size of milk bottles were on patrol outside. She had been in to clear up the mess and left the butane lamp burning. It ran out. Judith found my emergency supply of night lights and lit them all. I went to bed with two sweaters and a pair of needlecord trousers, feeling sick and desperate. Against all advice, I was drinking whisky. It was not the most promising setting for a council of war or, come to that, a court of reconciliation. The little flames burned wanly, as if in a Mexican hovel just after the plucky paisano, the one that stood up to the landlord, has been carried home to die. Judith crawled in beside me, fully clothed and very frightened.

'You can't go on like this,' she said. 'Why did that man beat you like that?'

'He was simply a police officer making routine enquiries. I've told you.'

'Was he really a police officer?'

'Indisputably. His Christian name is Edgar, and he's a graduate of Strathclyde. I haven't asked him how he votes, but you can score one for David Nicholas, MP, I think.'

'You're angry with me.'

'There's more than a hint of that, yes.'

She kissed me on the ruined lip, with the faintest of touches. Her hand brushed back my hair.

'Please. Suppose I was trying to keep you out of it?'

'With this result? You're not trying to keep me out of it, you're trying to keep me ignorant. Not the same thing at all.'

'I never met Yanni Kyriakides in my life. Does that satisfy you?'

It did not. It came nowhere near.

'Roy brings you some letters of yours he's found at a reservoir. They contain nothing but idle words, according to you. You pay him £200 and he's pleased as punch. That's two

47

weeks' pay for him, try to get your mind round that. But scattered in the same location are some krugerrands – little gold coins. These, dear Judith, are slightly more valuable. He pockets them, and is caught trying to fence them. Got the story so far?'

I was beginning to have a case of the hot and cold sweats. Judith took my hand and kissed the knuckles.

'No,' I warned. 'You pay attention. This is final approach. Who do we suppose put the gear there in the first place? We suppose it must have been Yanni. But what a funny way of going about things, eh? He is clever enough to lift all those lovely strongboxes and then he leaves some of the evidence where any fool – and Roy qualifies comfortably there – can find them.'

'I don't understand.'

'Then along comes Edgar. We've got the letters, the little gold coins and now we discover there was also a negative of you and David doing it the way he likes best.'

'The police have it?' she gasped.

'Not the police. Edgar.'

'The police can identify David from the negative? Have you got it? Show it to me.'

'You'll just have to imagine it. Or remember it. And not the police. Edgar.'

She was trembling.

'This Edgar wants money for the negative?'

I rolled on to one hip, not without hearing my ribs groan, and took her face in my hands.

'Now listen to me, Judith. Whoever left the stuff out there in the first place – and forget Yanni – is having a field day. Roy has been arrested, I have been beaten up, you are running around like a headless chicken, and Nicholas is going to have to cough up a grand to a damn police inspector with shit for brains. The only other thing that might happen is a flight of pigs over Gatwick, or water turning into wine in a Brighton restaurant. Now supposing we start on a brand new footing.

It's an old-fashioned idea, but suppose you tell me the truth?'

It seemed simple and predictable. Two weeks earlier, Judith received a negative herself, through the post. No compliments slip, no friendly note. A London postmark. She knew Nicholas had kept such things in his security deposit, and she remembered the vault had been turned over. She thought she ought to tell Nicholas this news, but then remembered the lad was spending a precious three weeks of the parliamentary recess in his delightful Tuscan hideaway. Then she hears from Roy. She panics, buys the letters, acts distracted for days on end. Something bad is going down. Mysterious forces are at work. The stitching is coming out of the teddy bear. Judith drives down to see her old mate Hilary. Hilary has a lodger.

It still stank to high heaven.

5

In the morning she claimed an appointment with her accountant in London. Maybe I made too much of a wry face at that:
she paused in making up her eyes and gave me the hard glance.

'You think that's funny?'

'I think it's sad.'

She threw down the little brush and its tray and pulled a
loose green sweater over her head. Her jeans were airing on
the steps to the carriage. She picked up her cigarette and drew
on it carefully.

'I have an accountant because I have an accountant. His
name is Gerald Waxman, he lives in a wheelchair, his wife is
called Leah. They live in the flat downstairs. You want to
make something of it?'

'Take it easy, Judith.'

'I like you,' she said. 'I would like you to trust me. If you
don't want any more of this, then say so.'

'Any more of what?'

I knew what she meant: watching her walk around with a
floppy green sweater and silver satin knickers, smoking and
making-up her eyes. Or in bed with her, my belly snug against
her broad backside. During the night I had been sick again.
She cleaned me up, undressed me and sponged me with cold
water, crooning the while. In the morning, she made coffee
and boiled me an egg. These were amazing luxuries. I felt a
heel for wondering how and when she earned enough to
warrant an accountant. She was quick to read my expression.

'You find it all thrilling but disgusting, don't you?'

'Suppose we make a pact, not to put words in each other's mouths.'

'But you feel dirty.'

'I feel wonderful. Waxman is perfect. You are perfect. It's a pity this other business has to spoil it, but then we wouldn't have met in the first place.'

I was intending it as only a tiny barb, but I was learning that you couldn't fool with Judith. If she thought she faced the slightest criticism, she got the hump – an expression taught to me by my grandmother and applied by her often (and justly) to my mother. Judith fetched her jeans and shoved her legs into them with considerable humptiness.

'Trust me to end up with a world-weary cynic who screws like a choirboy and smells of soap all the time.'

'I resent the crack about the soap. You're never here long enough to let me smell of anything else. You're always darting off.'

'I am not darting off,' she shouted.

She liked being made angry. Maybe she liked the novelty of it all, the unaccustomed power she could exercise. She hoisted the corduroy bag from which she had produced a change of clothes on to her shoulder. I capitulated.

'Well all right then, when am I going to see you again?'

'When you grow up,' she snapped.

She stuck out her cheek to be pecked. I kissed her with more fervour than she expected and she pushed my hands away from her with a triumphant pout.

'You've just got to learn to trust people,' she admonished.

And with that patent insincerity, she was gone, leaving me to reflect on exactly what it was that Oxford gave people.

I drove to the village shop for cigarettes and a *Guardian*. Though I had not been conscious of being followed, a very familiar bulk loomed up at my elbow when I went to the counter. It was Ted Gerson, a DI from the Met and a friend from way back. There was about as much accident in our meeting as the arrival of the Edinburgh train into King's Cross. We both knew that. But all the same we went through the pretences of a chance encounter. Ted enquired tenderly after my ex-wife, confirmed that he still followed Reading United, allowed that yes, he had put on another stone or so in weight, and thought the end of summer was upon us. We compared time on our watches, blessed the new licensing laws and decided to go for a drink. The newsagent particularly warned us against the Castle.

'Why's that, chief?'

'Because I drink there, Mr Gerson.'

Ted narrowed his gaze.

'It's Mr Bumstead,' he concluded.

'Alec.'

'That's it. Well, Alec, we'll take our sodding custom elsewhere.'

'You do that.'

We left the shop and ambled slowly down the street.

'Who is he?' I asked.

'Someone who's paid his debt to society. How are you making out?'

'Terrific.'

'She wasn't worth it,' Ted rumbled.

He meant Dawn: it was a bad slip. I began to feel a vague dread. Ted cuffed his nose with his thumb.

'News gets around,' he said. 'You're an idiot, always have been. Your missus was an even bigger idiot. But *that* woman wasn't worth it. I haven't met one yet who was.'

As we crossed the road to the Swan, a tractor passed. Ted's restraining hand on my arm was uncomfortably meaty.

'Living in the country doesn't stop you from being run over. And you look as though you already have been, once or twice.'

'Fell down some steps.'

'That can be nasty, too.'

I bought the first round. Ted sat with his enormous back to the room, his heavy head in shadow. I looked more closely at his hands. They were scarred with thorn scratches. The finger nails were cut straight across. He was only my age, but twice as intimidating. Nobody in the pub could mistake him for an insurance salesman or a regional arts co-ordinator. He looked what he was, a dangerous authority figure, steeped in short sharp answers to life's rich pattern. He saw me thinking all this through his pale watery eyes. He sighed.

'Listen, mate,' he said, 'we've known each other a long time. There's no point in havering. We need to talk.'

'Jacko,' I guessed.

'Everything's unofficial, no sweat. It's just a word or two see, nothing serious. You know what I'm saying.'

'Was it Jacko?'

'Jacko's a dreamboat, but he was thinking for you. I don't know what you're up to, but it rang bells in London.'

'I've been out in the cow parsley for the summer, Ted. You're going to have to spell it out, whatever it is.'

His gaze fell far short of being warm and friendly.

'Nicholas,' he said. 'The MP. Your new girl's pal. You were having a few little problems, you said. Want to tell me?'

'Tell you what? It's nothing. You know, something and nothing.'

'No, I don't know,' he said slowly.

I suddenly saw him as Alec Bumstead and his kind saw him, not as a man-mountain rose grower with a lean-to conservatory and a season ticket to Reading United, but as a force, a demiurge. He aligned his lighter with the beer-mat.

'There's no paper on this yet, you know. It couldn't be more casual.'

'Jacko's got hold of the wrong end of the stick,' I said. 'I'm going out with someone who used to know him, that's all. That can't have rung too many bells.'

'Going out? What is this, a fifties revival?'

'We're friends.'

He looked even more doleful.

'This bird, what's her name?'

'Piss off, Ted.'

He had already drained his pint. He set the glass down in the exact centre of the beer-mat and studied the suds that clung to the inside. I found these little habits of his disconcerting. They said about Lenin that he could not begin to think before the pen was parallel to the blotter, and both at right angles to the short edge of the desk. Ted looked up.

'Don't tell me to piss off, you dickhead. Every single move you've made with me so far is saying yes, there is a prob, yes I could do with some weight. Now we're talking about a member of the Government. You and your bird have an interest in him. And so do we. We're paid to. Now don't mess me about. What are you doing with him?'

'Nothing.'

He pulled out his pipe and pouch. Filling the bowl was calm, methodical work. He accomplished it without looking at me once, without so much as acknowledging by a breath or a gesture that I was sitting opposite him; and I knew then for a stone certainty that someone somewhere *did* have a file on Nicholas, and that Judith and I were about to be added to it. Unless she was already a featured item. I found I was furtively wringing my hands, enough to make the knuckles crack.

'Been following the cricket?' he asked, at length.

Once, all those innocent years ago, Ted, Jacko and I played park football for the Sunday leagues and thought the greatest villainy was going over the top for a fifty-fifty ball. In those days, having three coppers play for the pub was a laugh, nothing more. In the summer we played cricket for a police team against ribald village idiots and the occasional touring club side. Birds in those days were looking for marriage the way that thrushes cock their heads for worms. Ted had got

Sandra, Jacko Sylvia, the way worms get thrushes. As Jacko went on, he became a murder squad detective with a patchy record and one or two close calls against him. He was quite well known as a Flash Harry sort. About Ted's career, I realized with a terrible lurch of panic, I knew nothing, except that he had made Inspector very young.

'Look, if I had anything to tell you, I would do.'

He looked at me with mild amusement at last.

'My round,' he said. For the moment I was off the hook. Or maybe he had achieved what he set out to do: he galvanized me into thinking of something to do, something practical. As it stood in the saloon bar of the Swan, where the still waters ran deep, I was getting behind on the game. I thought about it, and had a bright idea.

Sonia Kyriakides lived in a short road off the main drag, if the residents of Brookman's Park think of their principal thoroughfare in that light. Certainly, in the private road where Sonia dwelt the very verge-side weeds were arranged according to some tricked-out notion of an older England. Grandfather's Beard nodded. Butterflies flitted. A respectable silence hung over roofs and gardens refreshed by the previous evening's rain. The men of the community were out making it in the big city where the noise and stress were tremendous and life was tough tough tough. Here, back at base, squirrels ran up trees and wood pigeons furnished the kind of background acoustic beloved of afternoon radio playwrights. The last black face seen here had been Edmundo Ros seeking out a petrol station in the fifties. The last Labour canvasser probably died of exposure brought on by ridicule. Sonia, in a word, had chosen well. I said as much crossing her marble entrance hall. The biggest maidenhair fern in Britain set the place off to perfection.

'What a prick,' she said cheerfully, showing me into a garden room that looked out on to sweeping lawns bordered by fine shrubs and specimen trees. I recognized the location. It was where she had pleaded on television for Yanni to give himself up.

She was shorter than Judith and a year or so older. Her crowning glory was a mass of honey-coloured hair I remembered from her two television appearances. She had humorous wrinkles setting off fine slaty-grey eyes. She mixed me a gin and tonic I hadn't asked for and shoved it in my hand.

'Fire away. But if you want to know have I got the Falcon, no I don't.'

She had not been to Oxford but was straight Camden Town and Greek Orthodox. She worked the Park Lane hotels and was much loved for her brisk, even merry way of doing business. She sent back the room service meals if they didn't meet with her approval and felt free to criticize the prints on the wall above the all-important bed. Americans found her full of zing, a ballsy lady. Arabs were reminded of the aunts they had who escaped to Paris and never came home. They were screwing the family's disgrace. All this from Sonia herself, who could talk up a storm and was also generous with the surprises. When I mentioned Judith and her problems she nodded quite casually. They knew each other. It took a second or two to sink in: Sonia seemed not to notice my surprise.

'What has that airhead been saying? That we were buddies? We were. I love that woman. She could have made a terrific marriage, once or twice. I had some terrific clients, you know.'

'She worked for you.'

'Is that what she says?'

'She claims she was on the game. With you, maybe.'

'On the game!' Sonia shrieked with delight. 'What is wrong with these educated girls, they're not happy until they're pretending to be whores? I would ask her out a few times. Once or twice a year maybe.'

'You were friends, then.'

'I just told you, dummy. She *had* a friend, an MP –'

'– Nicholas –'

'– You know? Then what are you doing wasting time? This Nicholas keeps her, the creep. That's another story. I mean, what do you know about this business? Whoring is for whores. It's hard work. Judith is a dreamer. A dormouse. Have you met him?'

'Not yet.'

'Don't bother! I've met a lot of lousy people in my time, sweetheart, but this one is a special.'

'So I hear. To change the subject a little, I wonder whether you've heard from Yanni?'

Absent-mindedly, she passed me a photograph of Yanni and the kids, mounted in a morocco leather frame. They looked incredibly stupid children.

'They say he cleared three million. Can you believe it?'

'You haven't heard from him?'

She laughed, resonating a vase beside her.

'Forget Yanni. You think he's still in this country? You think he rings me every night to say "sleep well"? Yanni has gone. There's no big money in this for you. Is that what she's been saying? I don't know how you met her, or where you come from, but if I were you I'd get out now.'

'Somebody is blackmailing David Nicholas.'

'Good. I hope they crucify him.'

'Maybe it's you, Sonia.'

'Judith says that? She sends you here to say a terrible thing like that? Look around you. Does all this seem cheap to you? I don't need Yanni. I don't need nothing but what I got. From the beginning it's been like this. The biggest surprise of my life, believe me, was when that dumb Greek did the vaults. Where he is now, who he's screwing, it don't matter. Judith and David – even less do I need their money.'

I believed her. The watery sunlight showed off her garden to perfection and what there was that fell through the windows of the conservatory lit a contented and sardonic face. She rose, smoothing her cashmere dress with a hand heavy with rings.

'I'll give you some help with your life. Ask Judith to tell you about Billie.'-

'Billie who?'

Sonia gave me a sage nod.

'That's what I thought,' she said. 'And remember, I know people who can leave you on crutches for the rest of your life. Billie. You got that name? Now be a good boy and come into the kitchen. I want to show you something.'

She wanted to show me a dripping tap. I went into the garage to find Yanni's toolbox; and the thing to admire in Sonia was that she followed me, in case I stole the garden hose while I was about it. I rummaged around in the fold-out trays looking for a replacement washer.

'Who are you?' Sonia asked in her pleasant, unfussed voice. 'Where do you come from?'

'Just an amateur plumber looking for opportunities.'

'Who beat you up?'

'The husband of a friend.'

She laughed.

'You need lessons in love, plumber.'

My hand closed on something unusual. In among the loose screws and carpet tacks, wood drills and panel pins were three shiny Yale keys on a twist of wire. There is nothing so redundant as a key without a purpose, and yet Yanni's toolbox was a model of efficient storage. I palmed the keys, not without a flash image of myself being crippled for it by large men in some North London lock-up. Sonia stirred slightly.

'Can't you find anything?'

'Here you go,' I said, holding up a washer.

We had another huge gin and tonic while I fixed the tap. She put on a tape of what she called Classical, and we talked for a while about music. She wrote down some of my suggestions on the end papers of a cookbook. By glancing out of the kitchen window I could see the muddy snout of the Renault in the roadway; and to be honest I was loth to say goodbye. She was really a lot of fun.

'You could stay, only I got a dinner party for eight tonight. One of them is a county archivist, can you believe that? His wife is having a nervous breakdown.'

'You'll pull her through,' I said gallantly.

Sonia's smile was a thoughtful one.

'Listen. I'm telling you something for your own good. That girl is trouble. She's a lovely kid, but she's big, big trouble. You stay away from her.'

'Did Yanni ever meet her?'

The good spirits evaporated in a few terrifying seconds.

'Idiot! Dreamer! You get out now, or I call some friends. They work you over, you'll wish you were dead.'

'It was just a conversational remark.'

'Yanni, Yanni! Anyone would think he'd won the pools. I have people ringing me every day offering to help him. I have people who want to invest, or start a company, or sell him a yacht. The man is a crook. He is a thief. What kind of a country *is* this?'

'But you can't remember if he and Judith ever met?'

She pointed a round little forefinger.

'I heard the question. You go home and ask Judith about Billie.'

'And don't come back?'

'You come back, make sure your will is in order,' she promised.

There was a hold-up on the way into London. The accident was on the north-bound carriageway. A Toyota had been crushed between two lorries and a second car had burnt out. All three emergency services were in attendance and some unlucky or foolhardy citizens were clearly very dead. But the going-home bottle had been uncorked back there in the city and nothing could stop or divert it. We on the south-bound lane were stalled as the police erected a contraflow system to allow car commuters their inalienable English rights. Every single

59

driver that passed looked hungrily over his shoulder at the carnage, his attention distracted momentarily from Radio One. Four tarpaulins covered four corpses. The rest of the road was littered with thousands upon thousands of yoghurt cartons. A fireman in a yellow plastic waistcoat stared into my car with disgust and loathing. In the background his crew were kicking yoghurts into the verge.

I reached the Knightsbridge flat towards seven. A few Kuwaiti families were still about on the streets and office workers were lingering in the pubs, but a cool air was rushing in from the park, bringing with it that strange and sombre mood that seems to haunt London these days. Or maybe I was in a crappy mood. I found the flat and rang the bell, my face to a battered grille.

'Yes?' a tinny voice spoke.

'Who is Billie?'

'What?'

'Billie, Judith.'

Silence, and then a squawk as the lock sprang back. I pushed into a dark foyer littered with unopened mail-shots and waited for her to come down and let me in through the interior door. She looked flustered and defensive.

'Listen,' she said. 'Deep down, I know you're a prat but try not to behave like one all the time, okay?'

'Who is Billie?'

She turned on her heels and I followed up two flights of stairs. The flat she had was neat and white and understated. She was listening to Sarah Vaughan and had been reading the *Independent*. On the wall there were a couple of really good prints, alongside some awful ethnic rug he might have brought her back from holiday. Her books were piled up, unshelved. She had the habit of retaining the Sunday papers to read at her leisure. It was altogether, to my eyes, the accommodation of an intelligent and essentially self-sufficient spinster.

'What are you looking for, a cupboard full of whips and chains?'

It had come on to rain again and the peculiar acid smell of wet London pavements seeped in through the open windows. Judith threw her plump arms round me and laid her head upon my shoulder.

'I'm nervous,' she said. 'I didn't believe you'd ever come here. I want you to like it.'

'I like it a lot. What would make it perfect is a shower.'

Just as the sitting-room, so with the bathroom. It was orderly, unglamorous, functional. The shower was just a shower (what was I expecting?), the towels were no more than towels. You could look up through a fanlight and see the lavender and yellow evening sky. There were several bottles of shampoo and conditioner, and a Chinese ginger jar filled with cotton-wool balls. I looked for his razor or his aftershave. There was no trace of him. By the side of the bath was a book of essays by Janet Flanner, open at the piece she wrote on Queen Mary. In the airing cupboard her knickers were stuffed between the hot and cold pipes. Her bras and some tee-shirts rested on the tank. All the washing smelt of fabric conditioner.

In the long mirror behind the door I saw a faintly mad looking person, with juicy bruises and suspicious eyes. I dabbed gently at my ribs, thinking of him, Nicholas, sprauncing triumphantly in front of a fitter, leaner reflection, erect with pleasure at the thought of somebody else's bruises.

When I came back into the cool, white sitting-room she passed me a whisky and water. There were cashew nuts in a glass bowl. She was still as nervous as hell.

'Don't you want to dry your hair?'

'Who is Billie? Your chum Sonia asked me to ask you.'

I noticed she wasn't drinking herself, but she had been.

'You've had a whale of a time,' she said bitterly.

'Oh, you mean I shouldn't have been to see Sonia? I'm not supposed to know about that? Let me tell you, I'm getting chewed up about all these little bits and pieces.'

'I don't know what you're talking about.'

'I think you do. Bits and pieces. I'm having to winkle the story out of you. Every time we meet there's a little something that's new.'

It was too much for Judith. She put her head in her hands, slowly and with the unmistakable weariness of despair.

6

Billie's real name was Wilma, surname Curtess. She was seventeen when she met her first and only MP. Nicholas had been to Leeds for a conference of prison governors and came back to King's Cross by train in (we must presume) an uppity mood. The deal was that he should meet his wife at the station and collect the keys to the car. She would then take the train he had just vacated to see her sister in Peterborough. Nicholas would drive the car home.

'Who says? How do we know all this?'

'The car was terribly important. He could be identified through the car. He kept going on and on about it.'

Wilma, called Billie, lived at Royal Oak. King's Cross was her place of business: the station, the streets round about. She came in on the Metropolitan line about three each day, come rain or come shine. She was there in the first place to score. Later in the afternoon she paid for the habit by pleasuring, if that is the word, dazed Northern punters who could not believe this gawky kid in the one-piece nylon flying suit and laceless baseball boots was saying the things she was saying to them. She paid a British Rail porter fifty a day to rent her the key to an unused office between the main line and suburban platforms. The marks would walk in, accustom their eyes to the gloom and find Billie on the table, naked, scabby legs akimbo. Outside came the tramp of feet and the real world, of sandwiches and the evening paper, maybe a report to write up as the 125 headed for home – all *that* – and here in the dusty dark, the raw horror of the idiot-voiced black girl. The membrane between the two was no more than the thickness of a sheet of green and cobwebbed glass.

Judith was crying as she told the story. Huge pearls ran down her cheeks and along the line of her jaw.

'She was proud of herself, get it? She told him her whole life story.'

Nicholas had taken a hell of a risk in picking her up. The station was at its busiest and people would remember such an encounter, one that ended in a car driving away. He actually asked her to crouch down in the front seat, to which she responded by winding his electric windows up and down and giggling. He turned west down the Euston Road and drove her to, of all places, Ravenscourt Park. There, by his account, they had gone for a walk while he listened to Billie ramble on. It was late spring, and the air was cold. It was still early enough for people to feel safe walking home through the park. He kept her off the paths, for she had playfully unzipped her flying suit and was proffering him her breasts and screaming with laughter at his discomfiture. After a while, he got round to his needs, his special interests. Billie, though young and black and lacking in formal educational qualifications, was not about to be beaten up by a junior Cabinet minister for peanuts. They haggled over the price and the location – she was suggesting a hotel all the way back in the Pentonville Road. And then, according to Nicholas, he came to his senses. The park was stiff with freaks, and there he was in his black melton overcoat and – a nice touch! – sporting his Middlesex tie. He gave her a hundred to be rid of her. What was a hundred, not to have her scream the bloody park down? The only alternative was to kill her. He shoved the money into her hands, walked to his car and drove off.

It was painful, having to hurt her, but somewhere this quicksand had to have a bottom.

'He came here, didn't he? He thought it would be fun to tell *you* all about it.'

Judith was sobbing like a child.

'He came here,' I pressed her, 'because he'd just had a great big adventure, a whiff of the real stuff, and the only other people he could talk to about it would have been a team of psychiatrists.'

'Up yours,' she spat.

'When did you find out the kid was dead?'

She looked up, shocked and amazed, as if I were the greatest criminal detective the world had ever seen.

'He didn't kill her!'

'All right, when did they discover the body?'

The answer was that Wilma turned up two days later, on the Surrey side of the river, opposite the Doves at Hammersmith. She was naked. The police surgeons were uncertain about how she came to be disembowelled – maybe from her short journey down the Thames, maybe not. She had surely been beaten to death. Her clothes – the famous flying suit with the crutch that reached almost to her knees, the baseball boots with the flapping soles – were never recovered. In the flat she shared with her mother, also an addict, they found just eight pounds in cash from a short and hard-working life. As far as Mrs Curtess was concerned, she had gone to live in a drawer at the morgue. The body was never claimed.

There was grand panic at King's Cross but it was unnecessary. All that – the disused office, the porter who liked to peek through a hole drilled in the plasterboard partition – had been told to Nicholas by Wilma on their walk through the park. The police failed to make the connection. A few punters who read about the discovery of the body in the *Evening Standard* went a bit green at the gills, and one of the station porters was on the sick for a few weeks. But in the end everybody, like Nicholas himself, was in the clear. The day her body had been spotted in the mud at Hammersmith was the day of the bomb outrage in Selfridges. The Met were looking for Irishmen. Wilma Curtess sank through the files and bottomed out as an unsolved murder enquiry. She was young, black and addicted. That she was also dead was just part of her sad story.

'So now you know.'

'That's one way of putting it,' I said, the despair sweeping through me.

'I haven't seen him since that night, the night he came to tell me about Ravenscourt Park. It was the breaking point. Say you believe me.'

Because I did not immediately answer she banged the coffee table with the flat of her hand.

'It's the truth, for God's sake.'

'Then who's paying the rent?' I wondered.

She jumped up and walked stiff-legged into the bedroom, slamming the door behind her. I felt unable to follow her, if remonstration were the thing that was wanted: instead, I lay slumped, thinking of Sonia moving about with plates of salmon mousse in the house at Brookman's Park, charming her dinner party of eight. I thought of Nicholas in the room I was in, pouring himself a drink, switching channels on the television, humming, maybe, when his heart was full. I tried not to think of Ted Gerson with the back of his hands criss-crossed with rose scratches, his pale eyes calm and unblinking.

Nicholas had lifted her from a crowd of maybe two thousand people, at one of the busiest places he might ever be recognized. There was bad shit going down at King's Cross right round the clock – he worked at the Home Office, he read the police collations for Metropolitan crime. At six in the evening there was a hurry and bustle that perhaps he thought would disguise his own act of folly. Or maybe he drove her away with the lunatic's sense of immunity from the consequences of his actions. Wilma herself could not have cared less. But she would not have left her pitch without the promise of some serious money, least of all to be taken to somewhere as naff as the Shepherd's Bush area by twilight. Somewhere in that flying suit she had her hard-earned pocketful of twenties. She would not have risked them without confidence. Nicholas knew how to drive the car and wait in traffic without picking his nose: she knew how to handle the rest.

Or did she? I dozed for a while and then switched on the television. William Bendix made his wide-eyed, hoarse, incredulous way through the jungles of Guadalcanal. I watched all the way through, for I could not remember whether he got it in the end. He didn't. He survived, and the marines handed over to the army. There's a line in the film where Richard Jaeckel asks Lloyd Nolan what he feels about killing people. These, Nolan says – meaning the Japs who had fabricated the set on which I was watching him say it – aren't people. Jaeckel frowns, thinks about it, and then is satisfied. Life is deep, and the Sarge has swum down to the very bottom of things. If he says they're not, they're not. It was a soldier's tale.

I needed to know Nicholas. I needed some line to him, some way of discovering the capes and bays of his incredible arrogance that was not already revealed to me by his relationship with Judith. I had unrealizable fantasies of walking up some red road in Tuscany and surprising him at his weight-watching breakfast out on the terrace. There, I would send his coffee down the wrong way with a vengeance. I would terrorize the bastard. Thinking these thoughts was not any easier for the sensation of having Ted Gerson sitting on my face.

When I looked up, Judith was standing in the doorway, wearing a shirt nightie.

'You haven't eaten,' she said, sullen.

'It's too late now. Anyway, I don't eat. I smoke and worry.'

'Let me make you an omelette.'

'You could open a bottle of wine.'

She did: an excellent Californian Sauvignon. We were in that excessively polite mode with each other – generally ending in tears all round. She closed the window and drew down a paper blind.

'I'm frightened.'

'Now you're showing signs of common sense.'

'You frighten me,' she said.

'I wouldn't lose any sleep over me. I'm just the local patsy, remember?'

'You think he killed that girl, don't you?'

'If I do, it's for a reason.'

'Which is?'

'That you do too. And so do others.'

Because it must be something like that. Gerson was interested in him for a better reason than that he was having an affair with Judith. It had to be connected with Wilma, or others like her. It was Nicholas's presumption that the file on Wilma Curtess was dead. He may have been very wrong about that. Had some bored young collator with dandruff on his uniform collar stared in amazement at a computer screen before running upstairs to earn sudden brownie points? It was an easy enough scenario to picture, a list of parked car numbers at the scene of crime and all at once out pops a name accompanied by a huge band chord, ta-dah! The brass upstairs push back their chairs with a whoop of disbelief – David Nicholas, the prat MP? Parked up in a side road at Ravenscourt Park, the night the black tart got walloped?

In time perhaps, some weary footslogger was sent out there for a look round. He strolls about, more than troubled by the itch that comes from piles, and with half his mind on the cost of a holiday for three in Malta. It was going to be two, just him and the missus, but Sharon's boyfriend has dumped on her and so she's coming too. A holiday for three in sunny Malta, therefore; where Sharon will find to her distress that all the disco music is fifties and sixties, along with most of the punters. In between these musings, our man tries to imagine an MP of any persuasion, prat or not, having reason to park down this festering side street, where the mauve Cortinas gather rust and where people move their mattresses to the front garden when they have done with them. Nicholas has been unlucky. Some white community action geezers, pissed off to the back teeth with the neighbours but too liberal to say so, have been collecting car numbers. They want to put an end to sexual harassment by kerb-crawlers but they also wouldn't mind if they could save the area from smack dealers. Nasty white men are cruising the neighbourhood looking for a bit of chocolate; nasty black men are doing dope. It's a test for the liberal conscience. But Ursula says we should do something. And here we have, on the night of a vicious murder, the unexplained presence of David Nicholas, one of the Prime Minister's pretty-boy lapdogs.

Was that the germ of it? Did the germ die there on the street while our man scraped Alsatian shit from his shoe with the aid of a vandalized wiper blade from a Fiat Uno? Or did his carefully worded report, neither too long nor too short, designed down to the last comma to be forgotten, find its way, all the same, through the tubes and tracts of the system until at last it reached Gerson?

'If you're not going to eat, come to bed,' Judith suggested.

'You go. The wine is excellent. I'll savour it some more, shall I?'

'Bastard.'

'Don't push your luck, Judith,' I warned.

'What does that mean?'

'It means we're not going to kiss and make up tonight. I know that's what you're supposed to do after a row, but count me out.'

'We haven't had a row.'

'We haven't had any togetherness either.'

'Talk, then.'

'I can't talk. I'm thinking.'

She shrugged, furious, and went back to bed. This time the door was not banged shut, but closed with an unmistakable care to indicate the end of day's play. I slopped some more wine into my glass and went to look at myself in the bathroom mirror. Sure enough, I had a mad dog expression. And she was right: I should have dried my hair. It rose in tufts like the wild man of the woods.

Of the three keys taken from Yanni's toolbox, one fitted the outside lock, one the door to the stairs and one the entrance to her flat. This I discovered on leaving. It was two in the morning. I headed for the M1 with a raging wine thirst and eyes the colour of tiger piss. The Renault lolloped along, mile after mile, moaning and groaning. At Leicester Forest service station I turned off the World Service, wound down the windows, kicked off my shoes and slept.

As I've said, when we were kids the dream was to fly Phantoms and drive a beaten up MG. This was when we were eleven. At fifteen, the dream was to go out with Mandy Williamson, a girl from the grammar school of stupendous fresh-faced beauty. A group of us would gather on the corner of Cornwallis Road, just to watch her cycle past. Lounging over the handlebars of our own bikes, we would give the moment when she passed all it was worth. The long legs pedalling neatly, the hair blown back from the temples, delicate creases and folds in the pale blue gingham dress she wore, even the gentle hiss of the tyres on the wet road, were discussed at length after she had passed.

She married a mate of mine called Bob Seward. He was a trainee reporter on the local paper and much admired for his belted cotton trenchcoat and the extraordinary precocity of smoking a pipe. Without being able to play a note of music himself, he was on his way to becoming one of the greatest jazz record collectors ever seen in the town. It was a mark of favour among us to be asked round to Bob's dank flat next to the Co-op and listen to his choice of music, while smoke from the famous Petersen rolled across the ceiling. His tastes in jazz were eclectic. Sometimes he would resonate the grimy windows with the thunder of Woody Herman's Third Herd. On more mellow occasions, we would try to follow Bud Powell, while big Bob sprawled in the one armchair, his eyes mild and benign behind National Health specs. He was one of those amiable giants destined to live out his life without apology or explanation.

After he married Mandy we kept in touch by postcard and Christmas greetings. I asked him to my wedding, where he looked utterly out of place, no matter he was the consort of the now fabulously beautiful Mandy. They had a couple of kids already: he was subbing on the *Express* and travelling home at night to Bromley. Then, in his late twenties, he moved north. I had almost forgotten where.

The why of it was cruel: his eldest child died of leukaemia a fortnight after her sixth birthday. Mandy could not cope. They moved to a big house in a dark little Yorkshire mill town to start up all over again. Bob got a job on the subs' desk at a paper serving David Nicholas's constituency.

Mandy had changed most. She laughed a great deal, and sank more than her fair share of Bulgarian wine. The years had drawn out the bones in her jaw and nose, so that she had a faint nutcracker profile. Her hair was wild and dyed and uncombed. She still had the long legs and pert schoolgirl figure, but tempered by a seemingly ferocious intellectual disorder. Her speech was rapid and ironic. From time to time she glanced, as with a habit of years, to see what effect she was having on Bob. Towards him, her tone was almost manically joshing. The openings and avenues she created were politely ignored.

She was secretary of the constituency Labour Party, and knew all about David Nicholas. We sat opposite each other in the kitchen while Bob cooked.

'That pillock! Have you met his wife yet – what a gormless cow she must be.'

'I've never met either of them.'

'Of course, they love him here, don't they Bobs? They think he's just wonderful.'

He turned from the stove, blinking behind lenses that had grown much stronger since his childhood. A very respectable beer belly swagged the fair isle pullover he was wearing. His beard was flecked with grey.

'He has to catch a lot of flak from the little old ladies, being on the law and order side of things. He does that very well. Good looking, if you like that sort of thing. Talks like a country solicitor. Interviews well.'

'Quotes well,' Mandy amended sourly.

We changed subjects. Their surviving daughter was called Honor and she was about to start at Central as an actress. At the moment she was travelling student Europe on an Inter Rail card. Bob made great efforts to lead the conversation here. He was clearly passionate about his daughter if nothing else. He told a few stories about the lack of faith the council had shown in the local rep; and how Honor had toured a one-woman show in the villages – that sort of thing. Mandy kept pouring the Merlot and stayed unnaturally quiet. Once or twice I caught her glancing at her watch.

'You look strained,' she said to me, out of the blue.

'I've looked this way for years, I think.'

'No,' she said. 'This is new.'

Bob glanced, not at me, but her.

The food was delicious. Their kitchen was high above the road and overlooked a Victorian cemetery. The streets outside were cobbled. We ate under a huge Japanese paper shade, watching the trees dance and bruised clouds clash together. Angels with plump arms uplifted shone in the crowded cemetery.

'Does Nicholas have a house in the constituency?'

'He does now,' Mandy said. 'Not here. Down the valley. He has another place in Wiltshire somewhere, his home in London and a farmhouse in Tuscany. In this town alone there are ninety homeless families. We're not talking about individuals, or what that swine would call the intentionally homeless, but families.'

'We're luckier than some,' Bob said gently.

'I hate him. I hate what he stands for and the sort of England he has helped create. What does he know about people?'

'Enough to get a five thousand majority,' Bob said.

'Not for much longer.'

Bob's shrug annoyed her. She threw down her spoon and lit a cigarette. He got up with awful patience, chewing, and fetched her an ashtray. She pushed it away with a petulant gesture. Bob turned to me.

'How do you come to cross swords with him?'

'A woman,' Mandy snapped. 'What else?'

They exchanged glances.

'There *is* a woman,' I said, surprised.

'Then I feel sorry for the bitch,' Mandy said.

She went out shortly after. She was on the management committee of a day-care centre and drove off in a whirlwind of lost minutes, last-second phone calls and demands for petrol money.

'Why should Mandy have guessed there is a woman in the case?' I asked him, over the washing-up.

He considered, looking at the suds running off the plate in his hand. Once, this habit of deliberation had been very appealing. I began to wonder whether Mandy had not had her fill of it. He smiled a wan smile.

'It might have been more of a comment about you, of course. But he has got a reputation as a bit of a lad with the women. His wife is dopey all right, but she's a hell of a looker. It all adds to the spice of things.'

We went upstairs to a serener version of his first ever flat. His records were shelved three deep and the CDs were housed in an old pine bookcase. Had *she* grown the sprawling avocado from seed, or had Honor? At all events, Bob watered it thoughtfully from a pot of cold tea and then lit up the faithful Petersen. The carpet and curtains stank of tobacco.

'Seem to remember you're an Adderley fan,' he rumbled, but appeared overwhelmed by the effort necessary to fire up his Marantz and the Rogers speakers. He was drinking beer to my wine. I was well into the second bottle.

'What is it, Bob? What's biting you?'

'You'll stay the night, of course,' he countered. 'We've kept up with one or two friends from those days. Mandy has a lot of friends who seem to need a bed from time to time. Remember Jonquil Roberts?'

Jonquil Roberts was just a sixteen-year-old with red hair and huge freckled breasts, whose Dad had in his time played football for Plymouth Argyle. All I remembered about her was her father's garage at midnight. I stared at Bob with real dismay. We weren't on the same page at all.

7

After a while, he did play some jazz for me. It grew dark outside and there was singing in the street – the neighbours had come back from a night at the Trades Club. Car doors slammed and there were shrieks of laughter, enough to bring anyone else to the windows in curiosity. Someone called Mike had fallen over the bonnet of someone called Ken's car. His excuse was that he was right puddled. Someone vexed and shrill called Olga scraped him up off the roadway. He took it as an invitation to dance. More laughter. It sounded okay to me, but that was another story from another world altogether. Instead, Bob and I sat listening to a Clifford Brown–Max Roach set in awkward and passive silence. The noise in the street died away.

'There's something wrong with him,' he said suddenly. 'That's what's brought you up here, I suppose. He's bent.'

'Remember, I've never met him face to face.'

He shook his match slowly and when it was out, tossed it on to the coffee table in front of him.

'I don't know what you want. I'd rather not know, either.'

'But you've covered him, his career and so on.'

'The paper has. You can use our library, if that's any help. We've covered him, yes. He's never said anything interesting. But he's highly quotable. You're going to ask me why I think he's bent. So. I'll head you off. This is supposed to be a rhetorical question, remember: what does it matter?'

'He keeps a woman as a mistress, or he did until recently. I've got involved with her.'

Bob examined his nails. He bit cautiously at a shred on his thumb.

'It probably sounds crazy, coming from a journalist, but to be honest I'd rather not know. You can find people in this town who would want to tell you much worse things about him than having a mistress. There are always wild rumours flying around.'

'What wild rumours?'

He shrugged.

'Ask Mandy.'

'I'm asking you.'

'Then don't. There's always gossip. A Nicholas story is news of course. But we are given a full quota of Nicholas stories by his position in the Government and what he does in the constituency. If we found he was eating babies, we wouldn't print it. The paper wants bright, sharp copy with a strong local tag, and he can do that for us. He can come up from London, give us a good photo-opportunity, and tell the readers we're on the right lines and happiness is just around the corner. That's okay, that's all we need. Nobody believes him, but he gets elected. That's the story.'

'He has your vote, does he?'

'You're some comedian. I don't vote. I don't even think any longer. I just sit in here and dream. Most of the time when I'm not at work, I'm in here. Just staring at the wall.'

'Are you kidding?'

I was watching him carefully: he was doing no more than tell me the facts. His expression was sour.

'You're so full of shit. You always were. What did you think you'd find here – good old dependable Bob, stored up like this stuff you're listening to, and just waiting to be played? Did you think I'd hand you the dagger? Grow up. I hate the world. This hasn't just crept over me. I always did. You were just too dumb to see it.'

'Jesus, Bob.'

'Even from the little you've told me about your problem – the mystery girl you're talking about – I can see you don't stand a chance. Nobody saves anybody. People just go down, one by one. You can take that from me.'

He sat drumming his thigh lightly to the beat of the music, looking for a way of qualifying what he had just said. I must have looked as though I wanted to burst into tears, which in truth I did. Melancholy was coming out of him like a bad smell.

'I was horrified when you turned up here tonight. There's nothing left of the past and there never was anything there in the first place. We were just no-hope provincial kids with a bit of style coated over us. The one piece of good luck we were going to have in life we had then – we were taught by people who had fought in the war and still dreamed about it. About Monte Cassino, I mean, or watching the wings fall off Lancs over Stuttgart. It made them serious people. I wish I had paid them more attention. It's too late now. They're all dead. We're stuck with people like Nicholas and we deserve everything that's coming to us.'

'I think there's something seriously wrong with him.'

'Of course there is,' Bob said angrily. 'Do you think I'm stupid? The bloke is a monstrous villain.'

'Then help me.'

He stood, wavering a bit. His hand reached out to steady himself and I saw that he must have drunk four times as much as I had witnessed, long before coming home. I pictured him, in some town centre pub where they knew him all too well. He shook himself like a dog coming out of water.

'You?' he asked with contempt. 'Who are you?'

He walked unsteadily to the door.

'Play anything that takes your fancy. I'll make some coffee.'

To say it was a shock, all this, was to come nowhere near the mark. I sat there blinking my eyes, wondering what the hell had hit me. All down the years I had supposed him to be happy when I was not. I had supposed him to be blessed when I was not. And now here he was, apparently adrift and on fire to the water-line. I followed him downstairs and caught him pouring a Scotch from a bottle taken from a kitchen cupboard.

'I'm sorry, Bob. I shouldn't have come. Or maybe you should have thrown me straight out, after the meal.'

He put his Scotch under the tap and added water.

'I know what you've found out about Nicholas, or I can make a good guess.'

'Yes?' I asked, with a dry throat.

'Yes. And I don't want to be involved. I'm sorry I was tough on you up there.' He hesitated. 'Mandy's seeing the doctor about depression. She's got a thing about our daughter, about Honor. She's jealous. They say they hate each other and so on – I'm in the middle. Whatever the truth of it is, I've had enough.'

'Shall I leave?'

'No, that wouldn't be right either. I don't know what's happened to you since we were kids. But what's happened to me is him. I thought I could live without politics. I paid the price. In this house, I paid twice over. There *is* a file on him, I have a file. And I could nail him – d'you understand? I would be doing myself a favour. But it's all too late.'

The kettle was boiling at his elbow. Out in the backyard someone – she, possibly – had made an ingenious hanging garden from tubs and earthenware boxes. The light from the kitchen shone yellow over the nodding leaves and flowers. The kettle began to scream.

'What kind of a file?' I asked.

'Fuck off,' he said, eyes bright with tears.

Mandy had not returned by midnight, and he showed me to a room I knew to be his daughter's. It was at the top of the house, with a single dormer looking out on to a hill of yellow street lights. Furthest away, a long shallow curve, like a frown, marked the ring road. The cloud had broken, and an ice-cream moon slipped and slid through the sky. Honor's dressing-gown hung on the back of the door. A painted chest contained her bras and knickers, some blouses and sweaters. Her letters were neatly bundled up with elastic bands and jostled with wallets of holiday snaps. Like Judith, she piled her books on the floor round the edge of the room. By the side of the bed was a reading lamp made from a Chianti bottle. The shade was burned. I read for a while from a book on Duchamp. I did not switch the light out until half-past one.

When the door opened, I knew it would be Mandy. She smelled very faintly of brandy and she carried a bottle of Courvoisier and two glasses with her. She stumbled slightly in the doorway and then gathered herself.

'What has he told you? What have you made him say?'

She was backlit by the light on the landing. She was wearing some preposterous ankle-length nightie. Her shoulders were bare.

'Come in.'

She sat down on the bed and kicked off her mules. They skittered across the sanded pine floor. The glasses in her hand clinked together.

'I *have* been to the management meeting, of course,' she said. 'But that's not the only place I've been. I've been on my back in what is called the local beauty spot. On a Debenham's travel rug, in the rain. You're not really surprised, or I shouldn't think you are.'

'Is he married?'

'Of course he's married. At our age, we all are. Though it never ceases to seem the most awful bloody bad luck, does it?'

'Does Bob know?'

'I came up here to ask *you* questions.'

She poured a drunk's measure into each glass.

'I love Bob. I've had Ray – this other bloke – in every room of this house and on the stairs and out in the backyard. Riddle me that. I grew up with Bob, I've been near to death in hospital with Bob holding my hand, I've lost a child of six to leukaemia with Bob. Yes, I should think he knows.'

It was so quiet I could hear the blood's river rushing in my ears. There was an additional tiny sound, a tinkling. She was shaking with silent sobs and the noise I could hear was of her drop ear-rings chiming together faintly, very faintly.

'Is this what happens to people?' she whispered. '*This*?'

'You should have given me a meal and chucked me out.'

'You think you've come at a particular time of crisis? I thought you were more intelligent than that. Why are you here? Why are you hounding Nicholas?'

Horribly, the light on the landing went out. She passed me a brandy and sat rubbing her naked shoulders. The moon tangled in her hair.

'It's all right,' she muttered. 'I'm not going to make a scene and we're not going to be discovered. He knows I'm up here. That's why the light has gone out. He's sick, but you're quite safe. I've already had my fun for tonight. I want to know about you and David.'

I had a flash of intuition.

'Tell me about the two of you.'

'I wasn't his type. It gave him a thrill, the political dimension. But as he put it, I was too nice a person. Or far too eager. That probably means the same thing to someone like him. What do you want to know?'

When I said nothing to that, she leaned her head back against the wall with a weary gesture.

'I knew your wife, you know, to change the subject. We used to go out clubbing together, before she met you. Once she had you in her sights, all that changed. She more or less cut me dead at your wedding. She always had the knack of containment. Good housekeeping, close accounts. She knew exactly who she was. Nicholas is like that. To someone like me, it's terrifying.'

She rocked forward and her glass fell to the floor, rolling away into the dark. I reached for her, and she fell against me, her breath roaring.

'Hold me,' she whispered. 'Please hold me.'

They had met face to face for the first time at a drinks party in the town. She and her friends were trying to organize an arts festival. They were surprised when he accepted an invitation to attend. At that time he was still a back-bencher, though an increasingly prominent one. She was in a combative mood, prepared to fight him – but he had been all charm, all good humour. Half a dozen of them had gone on afterwards to a Chinese restaurant. At the end of a boisterously funny and ribald evening, she found herself driving him back to his hotel. She was quite drunk. In the car-park, she hit a Volvo while reversing into a space beneath a huge chestnut tree heavy with raindrops. As punishment he reached up and shook an overhanging bough, so that they walked in showered with pearls of rainwater and smothered in red candelabra of blossom.

'They must have laughed their hats off at the Crown. For a year we had been trying to unionize their kitchens and now here was Red Mandy staggering in with her tits hanging out, round the neck of the local MP.'

'Maybe they were more surprised at him.'

'He doesn't have surprises,' she said. 'They'd seen it before.'

'Do you know that for a fact?'

'It was pointed out to me later,' Mandy said dryly.

They went to his room and as she put it, fooled around on the bed for a while. They watched the first twenty minutes of the soft porn channel. She was surprised at the slow pace things were going. She mistook it for shyness. Then he started talking about a girl he knew, a really intelligent woman, someone Mandy would like: this girl was only happy in bed if her wrists were tied to the bedposts.

'Did he mention her name?'

Mandy looked at me in desolation.

'That's why you're here, isn't it? I knew. I could see it in your eyes. No, he didn't say her name.'

She had begun to feel very uneasy. He ordered coffee and sandwiches from room service.

'I was drunk, remember. I had my skirt off, all that, and he made a point of bringing the old man who brought the coffee right into the room. He was smiling – it was man to man stuff, that was the invitation. But the poor old guy was ashamed for me. Nicholas tipped him a fiver. And that finally sobered me up. When I tried to leave he smacked me a few times and I hit him back. My blouse was torn. I ran out of the damn hotel. It was nearly two in the morning. When I got home, Bob was listening to *Voice of America*. He explained how we were going to be at war with Argentina over the Falklands, how it was inescapable. I thought he was mad.'

She crawled right into the bed and put her arms round me, her wild unruly hair in my face. I stroked her back, thinking of the girl on the bike turning out of Cornwallis Road, her bare legs gilded by sunshine. The tyres hissed on the roadway and as she passed she glanced over her shoulder with an impudent grin. The pale blue gingham dress, trapped between her and the saddle of the bike, made delicate little tucks and darts.

'That was the end of it, except that a year later someone told me that what I liked, what I wanted and needed from men to get my kicks was to be knocked about. A woman told me this. That I was one of those desperate and unhappy creatures that wants to be tied up and tortured, that Bob was doubtless too soft with me. That I got my thrills from debasing men under the guise of being abused by them. That deep down my problem was fear and hatred. Guess who told me all this?'

'His wife,' I said.

She let out a huge, racking sob, and tried to bury herself. She tried to hide inside me, make herself disappear from sight. I held her tight. Hanging from the ceiling rose in the centre of the room, a mobile Honor had made from coat-hanger wire

82

turned gently in the draught. Little cardboard shapes – of judges, the police, soldiers – swung on the end of cotton threads.

'It's what he does,' I said, helpless. 'It isn't you. It's him. It's what he does.'

'He destroyed us,' Mandy whispered. 'We were just too unimportant for him to worry about. He's probably forgotten it ever happened. But Bob was told about it at work three days later. I tried to understand how he could get away with it, how he could escape scot-free. That bitch was right. Somehow or other, he saw Bob in me. He knew what he could risk. He knew we would say nothing. After all, that's his politics.'

When I came down in the morning, neither of them was in the house. A cereal packet, a bowl and a spoon were laid out on the cracked pine table. Some of the post had been opened and some – the circulars offering unique opportunities for time-share in Portugal, a chance to win £100,000 and all the rest of it – remained untouched. On top of the opened pile was a postcard from Honor. She was in Vienna and had queued for three hours to get a return for the State Opera. A cat I did not even know they possessed sat on the lid of the central heating boiler.

I made myself a coffee, smoked a cigarette while reading the letters and leader page of the *Guardian*, and left.

8

Was he mad, this Nicholas, with his smarmed-down hair? Was he in some way trying to get caught, have his urges arrested and brought to book? Or was Mandy right and did he think he was, as they say, unassailable? And who the bloody hell was Mrs Nicholas – what was her weight and gravamen? All the way back down the A1, which I had chosen over the motorway as being more conducive to thought, I wrestled with an image of the Perslades' daughter, blonde and cool as a daffodil, but with half the brains of one. Who did these people think they were? They seemed to be travelling through life with a sense of immunity from any form of prosecution. And, from what Mandy had said about *her*, they travelled not separately but together. Here is a man who risks his public life not once but over and over – and his wife seems to act as his accomplice. It made no sense.

Except that in one way it all made sense. The political world had been created over anew for the likes of David Nicholas. The old wisdom was out of the window. What was wanted now was fearless – and conscienceless – managers. Where once everybody wanted to live in a stately home and act up like Cedric Hardwicke, now the role model was some smooth dentist, or, if not a dentist, a man with a dentist's manner, sitting on the pot in his en suite bathroom, having thrown away all the sections of the Sunday paper except the Business News. Edgar's instincts were good ones. You could go a long way with the right kind of barbecue pit. David

Nicholas was merely the tribune of such people. It was his job to grind the mustard up there in Parliament for the lads in the City to cut. What his personal character was like did not come into it. He merely had to be nimble with the right switches: lower income tax, fewer social benefits, more freedoms. Understanding freedom to mean opportunity and opportunity to mean exploitation. It was the New Man we were studying here – cunningly and persuasively anti-intellectual, contemptuous of the past, interested in money and, above all, at his best in an ambience of mediocrity.

It was almost some kind of relief to get on to the M25 orbital and join the pack as they swung past thundering lorries bearing such essentials as edible nuts, Perrier water, aquatic plant life and – of course – double glazing apparatus. Seeing your fellow countrymen steaming out of the feeder lanes at ninety miles an hour in their company-owned cars, intent on killing someone if it meant a second's delay on the way home to watch *EastEnders*, puts you in touch with the thrusting society endlessly exclaimed over by Nicholas and the other Cabinet hacks.

It was getting personal. The bastard was fondling one woman in a provincial hotel and trying to get a stand by telling her stories about another. While she, presumably (daft cow), sat at home by the telephone reading Janet Flanner. When I finally got back to the idyll in the woods, Hilary was unamused by my crashing arrival, and exasperated by the shortness of my temper. He also expressed surprise at seeing me at all. Judith was expecting me in Knightsbridge.

'Stuff Knightsbridge.'

'Oh dear,' he sang. 'We are in a shocking mood.'

'Do me a favour. Leave the eccentric old bugger act to one side, will you? It's beginning to get on my nerves.'

'I take it you have been off somewhere playing policeman. All this questing after truth is completely pointless, you know.

What will you end up with – the file on Judith Firestone? Or have you switched targets?'

'We can't all lead the life of the artist.'

'Oh yes,' he said, with raised eyebrows, 'we can. That's just the point. I'm not saying I see deeply – I wouldn't be so foolish. But I do see things as they are. If I see an apple these days, I suppose I am expected to see in it some additional tosh about the Common Market; or the temptation of Eve. I'm afraid I don't. I see an apple.'

'So when you look at Judith, what do you see?'

He waved the question away. He stroked Wallace with energetic passes of his other hand and stared moodily at the empty grate. We were, quite unusually, at our ease inside the house. A faint smell of lime was being transmitted through the crumbling plaster and the ceiling paper hung down in unhilarious pennants. Hilary looked at his mottled hands, seeing hands and mottles. I poured myself a Margaux without much caring whether it made him frown. Wallace escaped from his lap and lolloped out of the room.

'I should never have let you near me,' he said. 'It was a ridiculous mistake. It has led to nothing but trouble.'

'I've been thinking about that. Why *did* you let me near you?'

'I imagine you've an idea you're saying something rather deep now. You happened to come along when I needed some money. It was that simple. Have you dreamed up some other possibility?'

'I happened to come along in the middle of some blackmail scam. There's that to keep in mind, too.'

'Was that how it was? I forget.'

The negligence was just too, too studied. It made me want to get up and kick him, or in some other way bring the real world into this artfully empty environment of old books and crooked steel engravings, damp carpets and exhausted up- holstery.

'Listen to me, you geek. Judith is in real trouble. Not just a little local difficulty, but trouble. You know what trouble is, don't you? I thought she was a friend of yours.'

'She is. But I have never wished to get up on top of her. There's the difference between the two of us. It's a matter of common sense quite as much as sexual preference. Women are the superior sex, and for one reason alone. Their integrity is unbreakable. You can do what you like to them, for as long as you like – or are able – and you won't alter them. You're wasting your time, policeman. When you see the words *sex fun* written on a wall by some poor man offering it, or seeking it, I always think you see the truth about men, and sex. It's a bit of shamefaced fun. Which men are far more likely to get from each other than from even the grossest woman.'

'Trouble, Hilary. We're talking about trouble. Not fun. Danger. I don't give a stuff about your theories of sexuality.'

'But you should,' he said. 'It might save you a lot of misery. You come home from some mysterious errand, in the course of which I suppose you learned more about little Mr Nicholas. But you don't seem to be able to grasp that Judith likes him that way.'

'No,' I shouted. 'No, not true.'

He shrugged with a delicate, foppish lift of his shoulders.

'As you wish.'

'What should I do, then? Nothing?'

'Experience tells me you can always be relied upon to do exactly the wrong thing. But if I were you I would leave things as they are.'

I got up to leave the room. The alternative was to brain him with something heavy. At the door, I had a sudden idea.

'Did you ever meet Yanni Kyriakides?'

He hesitated for only a fraction of a second.

'Really rather a preposterous notion, even by your standards.'

'He never came here.'

87

'He never came here,' Hilary repeated, as if humouring a child.

'But you clearly know who he is.'

'Oh dear, was that a trap you laid for me? Yes, I had heard of him.'

He stood up, rubbing his thighs slowly with the palms of his hands, like a much older man.

'You feel you're being led around by the nose. I rather think you are. But not by me.'

'Is Judith using me, Hilary?'

'Oh, I don't know. What do you think?'

I tramped off to the railway carriage and made a cup of muddy coffee. I felt edgy and impatient. The whole story was getting to be like a phone call you know you should return, but cannot bring yourself so to do. I was stalled. I sat looking out on to the whispering grass, thinking about totally useless matters, like Honor Seward in Vienna, all of eighteen and utterly indifferent to any of this carry-on. Her biggest problem was the weight of dirty washing she was humping round the capitals of Europe, while old men like me appraised her glorious innocence from the anonymity of the café terrace and called nostalgically for another glass. I snatched my mind back.

There was something I could fill in time by doing.

The most secure place for us to meet was in his own home. In fact he suggested that. I left the car a couple of streets away and walked. Every house I passed had its front room lit by the same situation comedy. Big blond bloke, bit over the top but still randy as hell, has his eyes wrenched out of his head by dinky twenty-two-year-old with breasts like button mushrooms. The situation in question was this: she's so young she can't believe what she's doing to the poor guy. The jokes were all to do with what went on inside his trousers. What went on under her skirt and beneath the modesty panel of her Marks

& Spencer knickers – that would not have been funny at all, or not in this neighbourhood. I could hear the studio laughter quite clearly as I passed. My favourite house was one where the room was empty, but lit. The dinky girl with button mushrooms was trying to cook. It seemed the very sight of her with a saucepan in her hand was a megaton of laughs. But at number eighty-seven nobody was listening. Perhaps they were in the kitchen with a saucepan.

It felt strange walking up the path beside the weeping willow. Edgar opened the door before I had time to ring the bell.

'Dawn's not here,' he said, as the prelude to admitting me, 'but I don't want you to think that's on your account. She goes to assertiveness class on Thursday. She knows you're coming and it's no big deal for her. But we agreed it would be better if you did not meet.'

Meanwhile, the bloody spaniel had recognized me and was back on its haunches, growling. Edgar was pleased with that: he showed me into the lounge with the dog yapping at my heels. The television was on. He turned it off with a pang of regret. He had been watching the ribtickler like the rest of the street. He picked up a travel brochure and smoothed it, placing it on the tiled coffee table next to a silver rose bowl I knew to be a golf trophy. A dozen red carnations were poked into the mesh. He sat in the spoonback chair his mother had given him and waved me to a seat on the chesterfield.

'How are you getting on with Mr Nicholas?'

'That's not why I'm here. Mr Nicholas is in Tuscany.'

'Then your tart must pay. The slag must come up with it.'

'You'd risk all this for a measly grand?'

'I'm an honest man,' Edgar protested, laughing. 'It isn't the money, the money is quite unimportant.'

'It's the principle of the thing.'

'It's a means of expressing contempt. I can't keep beating you up. How *is* the old tackle, by the way? Out of order, I sincerely hope.'

It was manic, his laughing good humour in the midst of all this tidiness and dust-free wealth. To show me he was not above a bit of sensuous indulgence, he lit a cheroot. I indicated the travel brochure.

'Is that what you were going to do with the loot? A bit barmy, Eddie.'

'Please don't call me Eddie. I can go to Paris any time I please. As I say, it's not the money. What is important is the deadline. If you don't cough by next Monday, the prints and the negs will go to the Met. It won't get him the sack, but it'll put the shits up him. He'll blame her, and she'll blame you. Got it?'

What a buffoon. I wondered by how much he was suffering from Dawn's assertiveness training. His eyes looked very uncertain.

'I think you've been playing too much cricket, Eddie. The sun has got to your brains, maybe. I came to tell you: you are holding the cacky end of the stick.'

'Next Monday,' he warned.

'Talk to Dawn. Get her to explain about subverting the course of justice.'

'Is that what I'm doing?'

'I have a mate, someone I've known for years, who works for the Met. I'm telling you this for your own good. They are on to Nicholas up there. I don't know how, or to what extent, but they're on to him. You're withholding information, you gormless pillock.'

'What's your mate's name?'

'Ted Gerson.'

'You're bullshitting,' Edgar scoffed. But walked into the kitchen for a can of lager all the same. He looked out of the kitchen window, for once finding no solace in the barbecue pit. He was having trouble with Ted Gerson's name. I watched him bite his lip. He came back in, a little chastened.

'When I send them the gear, that's your tart finished. She's

90

the one you're trying to protect. Maybe I forget the money and just send them the gear. That would do as well.'

'You've never met her,' I protested.

'I hope she rots. I hope her nose drops off. You despise all this, don't you – everything I've built up? You don't have any kids, you don't have a wife any longer, you haven't got a ha'penny to scratch your arse with – and yet you despise me. Your way's better, braver. Bullshit. You're a wrecker. You can only pull down what others have built up. You can't make anything. Maybe you've never made anything.'

'Whereas at least you've made the barbecue pit.'

'Yes,' he said simply. 'That's it.'

I suddenly realized he was – for him – drunk. It produced a flood of emotion in me – I saw him for a real person for the first time. Such is the nature of honest emotions, he immediately read my face. He nodded.

'You were right about Dawn. She's keener on it now than she ever has been. We know some people – Babs and Martin, she's probably told you about them – and we watch blue movies with them. In the garage.'

'The integral garage? With the up and over door?'

'I knew you'd understand,' Edgar said.

'Why in the garage?'

'In case the kids wake up. We watch videos of Babs and Martin doing it. That do anything for you? Happy with that idea?'

'Just wondering where it's leading.'

'I should imagine Martin's next. After you, I mean. He's as ugly as hell, and little. But what Dawn calls kind. He's the primary school head. My prize is Babs.'

'You could be more gallant about it.'

He threw his can of lager at the wall. It bounced back and emptied itself on to the carpet in a scummy froth.

'I don't believe you about Gerson. You're bluffing. I know what I'm doing. You'd better raise a grand by Monday. And I'm not joking.'

91

It was a risk I had to take. The only question was one of timing: could I find out about Yanni and Judith before Ted did, after Edgar had got to him? Because that was the key, I was certain. There was a big piece missing, and Yanni must be it. So, it was a risk, but a calculated one.

'Go ahead. Use the phone now. What do I care?'

He drummed with his fingers on the edge of the coffee table, undecided. Maybe what he really wanted was to clear up the lager from his Berber wool carpet. We had a Mexican stand-off situation. He gave up calculating with a sigh and ran his hands through his floppy hair.

'What's she like, your girl?'

'You've got hold of the wrong script somehow, Edgar. This isn't the best way for you to talk.'

'They're all the same, is that it? That's the point you're always proving. Anything will do. What it must be, to be you. I've thought about killing you, you know.'

'Isn't that a high price to pay?'

'You have taken away my sleep.'

'What about Dawn?'

'Dawn doesn't come into it. Dawn is a woman.'

I stared at him.

'Listen, Edgar –'

'That's your point, isn't it?' he repeated himself drunkenly. 'That one is as good as another in the dark. I wouldn't kill you for love of Dawn. That *would* be too high a price. Love doesn't come into this. It's pure hate. You wouldn't know what that could possibly mean. But you'll find out, mug.'

He waved me vaguely towards the door. The meeting was at an end. He switched on the television again by remote control. The randy but shagged-over blond guy was stuck in the bathroom without his clothes. Innocent little Miss Mushrooms was banging on the door with a tiny fist. She was wearing tennis clothes. He was wearing her shower cap. A recently arrived older woman, possibly her mother, was aghast at the window. The studio audience was in the grip of a collective hernia as the credits rolled.

The spaniel showed me to the door. His expression was harassed by nature, but I thought he showed an extra anxiety in his eyes. Big Eddie was listening to the news, and they could probably hear it in Brittany.

The car radio had this infuriating habit of suddenly falling silent for minutes, hours or days on end. You could be listening to, say, *Harold in Italy* and two days later be startled out of your wits to resume with *Iphigenia in Aulis*. That night, I was driving to London listening to a programme on heart disease, when the radio went into one of its sulks. Right! Now nothing in the world seemed more important than that I should finish listening. I pulled into the side of the road and beat on the panel holding the set. A black kid about the size of the Shell-Mex building opened the passenger door and got into the car.

'Yeah, you better gib me some money, man.'

'Fix the radio first.'

He stared at me and then at the fixtures.

'Is a loose connections. You gib me some money or I break your fucking arm.'

I engaged gear and drove on. The kid was startled.

'Whas dis game?'

'Fix it,' I said. 'You want some money, fix the radio.'

'You asking for big trouble,' the youth promised. 'Next traffic lights, you see you don't get your head busted.'

And so saying, he lifted his buttocks from the seat and pulled down his jeans and some surprisingly crisp white under-pants. A large amount of mauve and lilac flesh was exposed. At the next red light, he got out and stood in the roadway, his jeans round his ankles.

'Help me somebody! This white geezer have been messing wid my body.'

About twenty people crossing the road paused with interest.

But when nobody came to tear the wheels off my car and the light changed to green, the black boy laughed and blew me a kiss before hoisting up his jeans.

I told Judith the story. She laughed politely, but deprecated my characterization of the boy's voice. She found it accurate, possibly, but illiberal.

'You think it demeans the lad?'

'It demeans you, a little. It's not important, I'm not angry.'

'You're not very observant either.'

She frowned. When I came in, she, like Edgar, had been at the bottle. I held out the keys in my hand.

'I let myself in with these. They're not yours and they're not mine. I got them from Yanni's toolbox, in Yanni's garage. In other words and not to put too fine a point upon it, they are Yanni's. So try to think of a quick answer to that one and don't bother about the liberal point of view. I'll take any plausible lie you can come up with, you dishonest, conniving bitch.'

9

Not once or twice a year as she had told me, but every two months or so, Sonia Kyriakides would phone Judith with an offer of work. This was when she had half a dozen girls she could call on for that easiest of exertions, taking a rich old fool to the cleaners. Sonia herself was the uncomplicated and energetic work-horse of the business. On occasion, she became mistress of ceremonies and ringmaster. The girls were called in to create those grand effects she enjoyed planning and executing for certain distinguished clients. They were hardly Jacobean masques, these events, but they did have an absurd high style to them. They were, as Sonia put it fondly, nights to remember for people who matter.

Almost all of the marks Judith met in this way were elderly and dignified Americans. If they had ever truly mattered, it was likely to have been in the Eisenhower era. Their turtle heads peered out at the world today from a carapace of pretty dusty memories. Their dreams and desires were all too easy to gratify. On one occasion she had driven a venerable American scholar to Tintern Abbey and talked to him about the book he was now never going to write. In the evening, someone representing himself as her son arrived. The three had dinner and then went to bed together. The elderly professor pronounced himself enchanted. At breakfast next morning, the boy astonished Judith by revealing he was just what he said he was – an Oxford physics undergraduate with a taste for Romantic poetry. Sonia had recruited him by the simple expedient of going to Oxford and picking him up in a record shop.

Yanni took no part in these shenanigans. He was never called on to impersonate anyone, and for a long time Judith knew him only as the man who nodded hello from the car as Sonia was saying goodbye on the pavement. Then, one Christmas Eve, he phoned the flat. He had been shopping for his children and would like the chance to wish Judith a merry Christmas. He came round with a little watery but romantic snow in his hair. In his hand was a bouquet of emaciated-looking roses, suffocating in their polythene sheath. He smelt of the cold and Jack Daniels, a flask of which he had in the pocket of his fawn wool overcoat.

She made him anchovies on toast. He told her about the children and the marble floor he had just finished laying in the conservatory of his house. It seemed only fair that she should tell him about David Nicholas. Without naming him, she said there was a man, a married man, with whom she kept up a relationship. Yanni merely nodded. He asked if he might watch the early evening news. Staring idly at the carcass of a burnt-out car on the road to Newry, he said he had done as much as he could to the house in Brookman's Park and was thinking of getting a job. He was bored. And so, she realized, was she.

He was a fierce gambler. In the New Year, he asked her out to a casino club of which he was a member. She was suffering from the holiday blues that overcome all women who share their men with a wife and children. David had been incommunicado over the break, except to ring her briefly on Boxing Day. There had been a piece about him in the *Sunday Times* by someone they both knew at Oxford. That, and oh, the Christmas tree he had donated to the local hospital had blown down in a gale. He was phoning from his constituency house in Yorkshire and she could have no idea how poky it was. And Merry Christmas.

There really wasn't much to Yanni. He was huge in frame, genial and attentive, but essentially shy. She was most fascinated by his hands, which were square and strong, with exquisitely manicured nails. He drank quite heavily, with the absent-mindedness of someone who could hold his liquor. He never mentioned Sonia, but spoke often and with great affection of the children. Wherever they went – and she began to see quite a lot of him – he was admired by men and women alike for his simplicity and good nature. She knew that some of those they met recognized him as Sonia's husband, and recognized her as one of Sonia's tarts. But most of the villains and pimps they chanced across proved to like him a lot: and so did she. He dressed expensively. She taught him to forgo deodorant – at any rate, of the kind he wore when she first knew him, the kind that could fumigate a cinema. In the January sales, on a wild impulse, she bought him a pink shirt. He always wore it when they went out together.

His favourite manic bet at roulette was 31 and two of the splits. On the second occasion they played the tables, the number came up on three successive spins, giving accumulated odds on the cloth of 256–1. The chips were black and red striped ponies. He insisted she take the winnings as a little gift. In gallantry, Judith played 16 and all three splits on the next spin of the wheel – and won. They walked away with over eight and a half thousand pounds. He helped stuff it in her handbag as though they were loading up with tissues for a heavy cold. Her protests were waved away. He told her how, for a golden month three years earlier, he had been a hundred thousand up on the house. He lost it all to flat racing and cards. He flew to Düsseldorf every so often to play cards with some fairly dodgy characters who were labour contractors for the Ruhr chemical industry. The boys out there were looking to him as a possible source of muscle in keeping the unruly and sullen Turks on their toes; but he was too gentle and good-natured for the work. He just turned up, drank their beer and gave them his money.

She was enraptured by him. On the first date, she offered

herself; but he refused. The furthest intimacy he allowed himself was to cup her breast in a sort of wonder, like a peasant being offered fruit in winter. From time to time he would come to the flat to cook, or to watch the football on TV. Like a lot of untutored men, he was a great writer of letters to persons in authority. He was indeed Indignant of Brookman's Park. Exasperation flowed from his pen on many a subject. He would compose these letters on Judith's couch, the pad on his knee, her *Chambers* at his side. They were the political expressions of a Mediterranean café owner's son, far from home. As he covered page after page in his large and scrupulously regular handwriting, so was revealed a mind filled with things that stood to reason, or needed no other explanation. Ordinary common sense beckoned towards an open space, an *agora* where could be found sitting inescapable truths, much like landlords in their crisp white shirts. It filled her with an ache, a yearning, watching Yanni fire off these remonstrances. Life with him was so simple.

Then one day he surprised her. He had found a job as under-manager of a securities vault. They liked him there for the same reason she liked him – his exquisite manners and gentle strength. He was, moreover, lacking in that most dangerous of modern virtues: greed.

'What about his gambling?'

'Maybe I made too much of it. He was a social gambler.'

'You mean he was a good loser.'

'I suppose so.'

'Was he more careful after he got the job?'

She thought about this and wrinkled her nose in surprise.

'I hadn't thought of that. Yes, maybe he was.'

As time went on, he found out Nicholas's identity. He knew only that she had a more or less regular bloke who kept her on in the flat, but came seldom and sometimes not for weeks on end. He asked a few questions in the beginning, but then seemed not to worry about it.

'So how did he find out?'

'I told him,' Judith said.

'Oh yes? For what purpose?'

'He didn't pump me, if that's what you're thinking. I confided in him.'

'Yes, but why?'

'We just talked. We were always talking, chatting. I just told him.'

'And so they met.'

'Yes,' she said, much less certainly. 'Sort of.'

She had this vaguely pleasing fantasy that Nicholas would walk in one night after a Commons vote and find this grave and polite Greek with his shoes off, watching a World Cup qualifier, while Judith washed her hair in the bath. She very much wanted them to meet. She wanted to make Nicholas jealous.

They met, of course, not at the flat but at the security vaults. Once he had a name to fit to the face, Yanni realized that Judith's other lover, the mystery man so teasingly alluded to, had all along been a valued customer.

I was doodling a pig with a box body and a triangular head. It had ears and trotters and a nose like an apple balanced on the end of its snout. It was my anxiety doodle, an old friend.

'Okay. Now listen to me Judith. From now on, I want the absolute truth, or what passes for the absolute truth on this earth. I don't want any more monkey business, understand?'

'I haven't been lying to you before.'

'That doesn't matter now. If I'm going to help you, I want to know exactly what happened next. You may be in big trouble.'

'What sort of big trouble?' she asked, nervous.

'The sort where the sky falls down.'

Once he could identify Nicholas, Yanni came less frequently to the flat. This was disappointing to Judith. He had cut himself a set of keys but now he would never come before phoning first. She put it down to his old-fashioned sense of tact. It was distressing. It seemed to her she had succeeded only in making him afraid, by telling him about David. This had not been her intention at all. She found she missed the big lunk.

'Just keep to the facts. You say you thought Yanni might be afraid. Do you mean jealous?'

'Jealous, yes. Hurt, wounded.'

'No, Judith. Think. He is married to a whore and when he first meets you he knows you're not running a seamen's mission.'

'Does that mean he can't feel hurt?' she flashed.

'No,' I acknowledged, after a pause.

'He rang up one day and asked me to Brighton for the weekend. He was going gambling there in a big way. We wouldn't stay at a hotel – he had the use of a friend's flat on Montpellier. We drove down and I slept with him for the first time. The only time.'

She hesitated, staring at the carpet.

'He really wasn't that interested in women. This place we were in belonged to a gay friend, another Greek. I thought it was utterly naff, but he liked it. It had a corner bath, that sort of thing. Mirrors over the bed. I wanted him. He didn't understand.'

'You're not saying he's gay?'

'He's just neutral,' Judith said bleakly.

'Are the children his?'

'Yes, of course.'

'Did you really fancy him?'

'He was a holiday from David,' she said grimly.

'Did Sonia know about all this?'

'No! I hope not. I don't think so.'

'Take your time. The bloke asks you down to Brighton for the weekend. He has the use of a flat with a mirror over the bed and you fancy him. That should lead to one thing, normally.'

'You don't say,' Judith muttered.

'But nothing happens.'

'I didn't say nothing happened.'

'Tell me about it. But first: could Sonia have been in the frame as well? Could the two of them have been playing you along?'

'For what purpose?'

I stared at her in disbelief.

'What have you Oxford people got for brains?'

The significance of the Brighton trip was that Yanni saw her naked for the first time, both beside him and reflected on the ceiling. It was an indication of how much she trusted him, and wanted him. After the first shock, he understood that. Her most recent rope burns and bruises filled him with a genuine dismay: she had not told him what an unkind friend David really was. It was outside his experience that men could abuse women in this way. There he was, big enough to break her back, or simply crush her to death; and the extent of his own passion was to link little fingers with her and kiss away the hurts the other man in her life had inflicted. Hairy as a gorilla, huge as a Bulgarian weight-lifter, he rubbed cold cream into her bruised skin and told her – but respectfully – that she was a fool.

I sat back, shaking a little. Judith watched me, perplexed.

'Open another bottle of wine,' I commanded.

'What's the matter?'

He must have counted the bruises on her body like banknotes. Here he had a nodding acquaintance with a junior Cabinet minister whose secret life was divided into two: what Yanni could see in the mirror above the bed, and a strongbox in a security vault. Maybe, up until that moment, he had been a little bit in love with the amiable and romantic Judith. But suddenly, and quite accidentally, the picture had fallen off the wall. Now, if only his mind could get round the possibilities, he had a killing on his hands. He could clean up.

On Sunday, at an antique shop in the Lanes that was open for the tourists, he bought her a gold brooch with money he didn't have. The night before he had played the tables with a recklessness uncommon even for him: he had dropped seven grand in less than two hours. They drove back to London and he came to the flat for an hour. He asked her exactly what it was that David Nicholas did to her. She told him because she felt flattered by his solicitude. She told him, from a desire to be honest, about the photographs.

'Did he ask you where they were kept?'

Judith looked at me in complete misery. It was beginning to get through to her.

'I told him I didn't know.'

He held her hand and kissed the webs between her fingers. He told her a story of how, in his father's village in Epirus, a notorious wife-beater had been buried alive under the boulders of a stream by three brothers and a deserter from the army. The cairn was so constructed that only his head was free. For four days the villagers had waited for it to rain. On All Saints' Day there had come a cloudburst. When they came out of the church, the ravine where the man was buried boiled with water eight feet deep. Police discovered the body over a mile down the mountain, three weeks later.

'But you weren't in the market for retribution,' I pointed out. 'You liked what David did to you.'

'You have a great way with words.'

'All right. There was nothing you could find inside yourself to stop it.'

'He understood that. He didn't have any choice but to understand it. Before he left that night, he told me he was planning to rob the vaults.'

The hair rose along my forearms.

'He said what?'

'He sort of indicated why he was working at the place, why he had gone there.'

'Did he say he had partners?'

'No.'

'It was all his own idea.'

'He had thought of a way to do it. He worked out the details for himself.'

'Had he told anyone else?'

'Like who, for instance?'

'Like Sonia.'

She shook her head, bemused.

'Did he offer you a share of the loot, or say to you "now we can go away together"?'

'Don't be a jerk. I had told him a secret. Now he told me one. That was all. Why are you looking at me like that?'

'I was wondering whether in "Goldilocks and the Three Bears", you thought Goldilocks was right to eat their porridge. What are you, Judith, an idiot?'

I went out on the excuse of going for a bottle of Scotch. I walked in the park for a while, my hands plunged into my pockets, thinking about Yanni and trying to picture him as Judith saw him. He was a handyman at heart, a home-improver. He could fix the iron when it went on the blink, that sort of thing. For Judith, who knew all about Wordsworth and Tintern Abbey, that was but a step away from having the skills to turn over a vault protected by the latest electronic alarms. But maybe she was right. Maybe the hours were long and undemanding, and what the surveillance cameras saw as good old Yanni writing to Terry Venables yet again, was in fact the big guy dreaming the loner's dream, of a single almighty blagging. One thing was certain. If he had felt at all curious about having David Nicholas, MP, as a valued client of the business, after the Brighton weekend this curiosity was honed to an edge that could cut paper. If Yanni had been sitting there numbering the steps in the scheme, then sudden and dramatic revisions could be made once he knew the secrets of David's sexuality and the fact – or the strongest supposition – that the evidence lay inside a particular box. If I had been Yanni, David Nicholas would have been moved up to #1, with triple underlinings and a forest of exclamation marks.

The sun was low and red. It crashed down behind stupendously ugly buildings, lending their silhouettes a decent melancholy. Or maybe I was indulging in observer error. Inside my heart there beat tremendous feelings of sorrow and pity – not for him, but for her. One reason for calling a break was to see whether she stayed put or did a bunk. We were beginning to get to the pith.

She stayed put.

'Okay, you tell him a distinguished MP is beating you up. What happened next. What did he do?'

'There were silly scenes. He sent me flowers and presents – it made me feel as if I had an incurable disease. He offered to find me somewhere else to live. And let me tell you something. Until I met you, he was the only man who thought I was worth changing.'

'Did he get on your nerves the way I do?'

In spite of herself, she laughed. While I was out she had made minestrone. We ate and watched televison with the sound turned down low. Some worthy nonsense about stately homes was passing more or less dramatically before our eyes. Two men quarrelled in a wood. I took her hand and bounced her attention back to me.

'What happened next?'

The man with the moustache hit the man with white flannels and he flew back into the undergrowth. Judith tore herself away from this, sighing.

'It was all dying down. I hadn't seen him for weeks. You're the damn brainbox. You say what happened next.'

'Little David came round and said he might or might not have killed some black kid called Wilma.'

She blew smoke at the ceiling.

'He said nothing like that at all. He came round and told me about Wilma, yes.'

She looked at me, serious and unsmiling, a tear trembling on her lower eyelid.

'Don't rubbish me,' she said. 'I don't meet too many people like you. I've told you, I don't think he killed her. And I should know, for God's sake.'

The tear in her eye overran the wet lashes and tumbled down her cheek. We embraced like babes in the wood. It was terrible to see the gratitude with which she greeted any form of loyalty. It was worse to have to hurt her more.

'This is the meat in the sandwich, Judith. I have to know everything. It's too late to hide. There's at least a ton of bricks over your head. One wrong breath and they all come down.'

She broke away, nodding and wiping her cheeks on her sleeve.

'The night it was in the papers that Wilma's body had been found in the Thames, I rang David at home. It was something he asked me never to do. His wife answered. We fenced for a moment – it really was seconds – and then she suddenly said "Are you one of his punchbags? Well, you'll have to beat yourself up, he isn't in."'

I kissed her wrist.

'You were surprised that she knew.'

'I was terrified.'

'Okay. Next day or the day after, whatever, you tracked him down. What did he say?'

She stood and rubbed her shoulders. She walked to the window and drew down the paper blinds.

'He said he spent that particular night in Leeds. His wife could corroborate it. He said he had no idea what I was talking about. He had never heard of anyone called Wilma Curtess.'

She spoke this in a flat, emotionless voice, as though she

had grown familiar with the lie Nicholas was prepared to live. There was a long silence between us. I could hear the breath whistle down my nose.

'Look at me, Judith,' I said gently.

But she couldn't. She switched a table lamp off and on, off and on.

'Just by chance, Yanni rang a few minutes later. I was crying. I got him to take me to a club. I told him what had happened. It was my idea that we blackmail David. That's what you want to hear, isn't it? I drank until I was sick in his car and then I suggested we do David.'

'For how much?'

'Left to me, it would have been his life, everything.'

'But in the meantime?'

'Anything. Anything that would hurt him.'

'And Yanni said he would think about it.'

She laughed shrilly.

'Yanni was all for having him snuffed. He was for burying him under the rocks and waiting for it to rain. He knew people in London and in West Germany who would do it.'

'That's what he told you.'

'That's how it was.'

She was still signalling off–on with the table lamp. I dragged her hand away and left her slumped on the couch while I went to look for the Scotch waiting on the draining board of the sink, still in its tissue wrapping. I picked it up with a heavy heart. Glancing back, I could see her with her head buried in her hands. I looked out of the kitchen window. Across the roofs, a girl of about twenty came into a room looking for the evening paper. She opened it to study the television page and then walked out again. The light stayed on, the room stayed empty. I broke the cap on the Scotch and poured a single glass.

'No,' I said slowly. 'Yanni was already planning to sleep in monogrammed pyjamas for the rest of his life. He'd found a way of doing the vaults, or he was close. He must have been very close. David was no use to him dead. He needed David, and you delivered him into his hands. You had given the noble Greek a trigger. All he had to do was pull it, David could get him out of the country, and then you could go screw yourself.'

'No,' she wailed.

'Yes.'

Screaming, bellowing like an animal, she threw herself on to the carpet and began rolling this way and that, the spit flying from her mouth. When I ran in and snatched her up, she beat on me with whitened knuckles, the breath heaving up out of her.

'Let it out,' I gasped. 'Let it all out.'

She flailed until she was too tired to lift her arms. We stood in the centre of the room, upright but shipwrecked, dismasted. I rocked her like the baby I had never fathered and she sobbed like the child she had never been allowed to be. My jaw ached, I was deaf in one ear and my heart leaped like a deer in flight.

'I've got you,' I said. 'I won't let you go.'

She slipped through my arms and fell on to the carpet. I fetched a cushion from the sofa.

'What have I done?' she whispered.

You have frightened me into loving you, I thought. I knelt beside her, stroking the hair away from her burning cheeks.

10

It was making sense at last. A pattern was forming. I stood in the shower, letting the water bounce off my head, thinking about Yanni's present whereabouts. Somewhere he would be eating, or watching the dancers on the disco floor, a grave and imperturbable presence, friend to the waiters and beloved of cab drivers. How much of his English wardrobe did he take with him, or had he stood in his pants and shirt while some voluble tailor had measured him up for the best there was locally, while outside the traffic screamed down narrow streets, and in the square with the broken fountain the girls sauntered about in their hotpants, looking for trade? A certain fondness I felt towards him placed him in some Mediterranean setting where he was not too far from Greece.

When I came into the bedroom she was under the duvet, reading a paperback edition of Nora Joyce's biography. Like an old married couple, we had decided that sufficient unto the day were the evils thereof. She hadn't asked me to stay the night and I had no intention of getting into the dog-smelling Renault.

I was surprised to find she wore glasses to read. They were the kind of glasses with which Jeanne Moreau saw to do her knitting while Oskar Werner was being driven round the twist, après la guerre. 'Your starter for ten: who played Jim?'

'What are you talking about?'

'Jules was a stranger to Paris. Then he met Jim. Djim. Who played Djim?'

'Henri Serre,' Judith said, without looking up from the page. She gave a grimace of irritation as I bounced the mattress getting in beside her. I lay on my back, staring at the several cracks in the ceiling. They flew my mind back nearly forty years to a house a couple of miles away – but what miles! I was thinking of my grandmother's house in Lambeth. There the cracks in the ceiling ran like cranky Amazonian rivers to a huge ocean, represented by a greeny-brown stain by the door. Beside these rivers might live anybody, I reasoned as a child. But no one, I had yet to realize, quite like our Judith.

She rolled on to an ample hip, and turned out the light. It was just a matter of waiting. After a couple of minutes she flounced all the way round to face me. Our knees knocked together painfully. The irradiated warmth from her body was like a furnace.

'You may as well know everything. You're going to get it out of me anyway. David got him away. So you were quite right. He drove David and the family across on the ferry.'

She was annoyed when I started to laugh. I was feeling mildly hysterical and fonder than ever of the big chump.

'He drove them to Tuscany? I don't believe it.'

'There was some fix with the passport, of course.'

'I bet there was. It's beautiful. Don't spoil it for me by saying David thought it up. I want to believe it was Yanni. The man is a prince. He's a genius.'

'So now you know everything,' Judith said in the dark. Her hand touched my belly. I kissed her shoulder.

'*You* put the stuff by the reservoir,' I said. 'Yanni sent you the negs and the rands before he left. He did a deal with David and then he gave you a chance to nail the bastard if you felt like it. And you did feel like it. But then you changed your mind.'

There was a long, long silence. I pushed back the covers and kissed the slope of her breast.

'I love you,' I said.

*

Love, making love, being in love, loving: did it mean this –
plunging haplessly between her packed thighs, lifting her by
her buttocks from the bed in some sobbing torment of never
being able to keep her? Or on my back, holding her upright by
pushing with the palms of my hands against her breasts, her
wild hair apparently touching the ceiling? Were these words to
be prospected, mined for, dredged up and panned, all on two
bodies not in the slightest way sentient themselves, but given
their shape by two buzzing minds that could not otherwise
agree whether to eat pizza or steak, let alone share a single
description of the greater world?

Judith crouched over me. The sweat from her hair and face
dropped into my mouth. Slowly, she retreated down the bed,
the tips of her breasts brushing my body. As she went, her hair
painted my skin. I reached my arms for her.

'No,' she said, muffled. 'This.'

Afterwards, we lay entwined. My mind was exhausted, but I
could not rid it of the image of poor abused Judith, walking
by the reservoir, sowing the ground with poison. When he
came back, there would have to be a confrontation. He would
have spent three weeks in some farmhouse trying to work out
whether he'd got away with it.

'Got away with what?' Judith asked drowsily.

I kissed her eyelids.

'Nothing. I was talking in my sleep.'

Her hand moved. I kissed her again, half drunk with weariness and (couldn't she see it, couldn't she sense it?) despair.
The one thing she had omitted to do was to reply to what I
had said so impulsively to her. I love her, we make love. She
stays silent. But that wasn't the cause of the despair.

David Nicholas MP would have spent the holidays trying to
work out whether he had got away with murder.

11

He came home from the Tuscan hills two days later. Kiddies bored, wife with a dreamy tan, Pops still with that little element of strain about the eyes. At the top of the road where they lived in St John's Wood – and we were fibbing there a little, too – was a right-on greengrocer's and, on the opposite corner, the kind of pub where the senior citizens wear blazers and speak about the raddled hags who eventually come to join them as the bride.

'The bride's taken it into her head to go to Wales this weekend, Barry,' the principal blazer informed a simpering Australian lad behind the bar.

'Is that where they have the surf?' this idiot asked.

'She isn't going there to surf,' Blazer said. I sensed him staring at me and turned back from my observation post at the window. I inclined my head politely.

'Don't mind me,' I said. 'I always drink standing up.'

'Why's that, then, squire?'

'I'm a sword swallower.'

But then, you could have said anything to him, he was so impenetrably stupid. We were soon hearing how you could give a rifle to an African and there was something in him, some want of essential sugars in the brain, or maybe the very size of the brain itself, that prevented that African from firing that rifle anywhere near straight.

Somebody's bride came out of the greengrocer's and crossed the road. Her frock was backlit by strong sunshine and revealed the silhouette of very good legs. Her hair was cut like a child's and she walked with a child's bounce. Not bad for a mother of three. She had four or five leeks in her hand, carried as carelessly as a bouquet picked from the floor of an ice rink.

'It's Mrs Nicholas home from Italy,' the brain expert exclaimed.

Mrs Nicholas ordered a large gin and tonic from the threshold of the pub and then spraunced her way in. She blew a kiss to Blazer, who raised a toast to her across the rim of his pewter tankard.

'Good hols then, milady?'

'Deadly boring, Bill. Really quite awful. Poor David was working practically the whole time.'

She was looking at me the while and I too raised a glass in cheerful fashion. One little mystery was solved, at least: David Nicholas had a drunk for a wife. She was still very good to look at, but drank with an unadorned ferocity and wiped her lips with the back of a brown hand. Every ten seconds or so she touched the leeks to remind herself she had come in with something.

'I'm not at all up on Tuscany,' Bill Blazer said to a chorus of silent disbelief. 'Florence bored me to tears, quite frankly. All right at dusk and dawn when the light is low. Makes a pretty picture then. But otherwise a bit, well, dull.'

She was still looking at me. I smiled.

'How are you?' I asked in my most winsome manner.

'You're Ralph Codicote,' she cried.

'Gordon,' I corrected, with what Edgar's drama group would have called dancing eyes. 'Ralph's my twin.'

Mrs Nicholas held out her hands to me.

'I am most fearfully sorry. How lovely to meet you here by chance. May we sit down?'

'Fellow who likes to stand,' Bill Blazer said, with a little of the dancing eyes stuff himself. She was obviously used to wowing them in the damn pub on her lightning visits between shopping for vegetables.

'Bill, I really must find out exactly what happened at the Wallensteins. Do excuse us a moment.'

'Be my guest, fair lady,' he said, with a generous sweep of the arm. Mrs Nicholas led me to a corner table. We sat, she with her back to the bar.

'All right,' she said. 'Who are you really, you creep, and what do you want?'

'How's old David? I hope he's had *some* relaxation and pleasure. They work so hard, don't they?'

'Who are you, what's your real name?'

'I need to talk to your husband. Where is he, hiding behind the sofa again?'

'I could ring the police,' she threatened.

'Do. That might not be a bad idea. Is there a pay phone in here?'

'Oh Christ,' Mrs Nicholas said. 'I bet you're from one of his girls. How disgusting. What do you want, money?'

Bill Blazer tottered over with a second large gin.

'Here we are, my dear,' he said. 'I'm just waiting for Brenda to come in. We're off to Wales at the weekend, you know.'

'Oh lucky, lucky you. Bill, be an angel and fetch Gordon a whisky and water.'

'That's Famous Grouse,' I advised.

He went off back to the bar, a little huffed, I would say, in the back and shoulders department. I watched him fiddling with her leeks, standing, as he might have put it, upon his dignity. He showed no signs of ordering anything.

'I can't do anything until you tell me your name,' she repeated.

'Nonsense. And you can cut out all this snooty-nosed stuff. In my family, we didn't think Winnie was wonderful. We thought he was a warmongering old butcher.'

When she laughed it was full-throated and easy.

'We did in ours too, actually.'

Her Christian name was Lydia. When I rang the house

earlier, she answered not with the number but with her own name. And she was quick-witted. She agreed to come to the pub after only a second's hesitation. Now she studied me thoughtfully and came up with a good idea.

'You look like a policeman. Are you one?'

'I'm a rock gospel record producer.'

She was no great believer in underwear. Apart from the knickers showing through the muslin frock and a pair of shoes, she was naked. That included the ring finger of her left hand. As if to draw attention to this she rubbed lightly at the space beneath her collar bone. Her nails were unvarnished. The corners of her mouth were wet and she looked a little cock-eyed. I guessed she had been drinking since ten.

'What's he done?'

'You tell me. Look, I don't want to spoil your day. I need you to convince your husband that he better see me.'

She snapped her eyes away from mine and cuffed at her lips.

'He's gone down to Wiltshire. We have a house there. Is he in real trouble?'

'I haven't said he's in any trouble at all.'

She smiled.

'I'm not simple,' she said. 'Would you like some lunch? I generally make a salad. We could sit out in the garden.'

'That would be great.'

She took a slug of her gin and nodded absently.

'Where did you get that sweater? In a sale, at a guess. You look like an out-of-work actor.'

'Just now you said I looked like a policeman.'

'I was looking at your eyes then,' Lydia Nicholas said.

Dawn and Edgar would have loved the house. In fact, I think Edgar would have killed for it. We ate outside in designer sunshine, sitting on mirrored Gujarati cushions. The salad had been tossed into dinky Chinese rice bowls. From time to time she cut me a chunk of sausage and fed it to me on the point of the knife. The blade winked mischievously. As my

114

mother would have said, we were getting on like a house on fire.

At our backs a conservatory had been jammed cleverly between the two bays of the house. All over the ground floor interesting things were scattered, piled and shelved. It had the indolence of real riches, the Nicholas place. You could be sure that not a single effect came from an interior-design magazine. Things were that way because Lydia, principally, liked them that way. While she made the chicory salad I glanced at some of their books and rummaged along a shelf of fossils and watch faces. Half a dozen jokey clocks from American and Japanese novelty stores showed quite different times. Her indoor plants looked great. The pine table she stood at had the mellowed honey colour of age. Even the light had been tamed. It did circus tricks at her bidding from copper, brass and crystal. She cut up the chicory to a rollicking Bach sinfonia.

'Where are the kids?'

'My parents' house. What business is it of yours?'

'Damn right.'

In the garden, Lydia sat with her frock up to her hips, topping up on sunshine. Out there in Tuscany she had tanned easily and swiftly. She poured me another glass of wine.

'It's all to do with sex, of course,' she said in her loud, flat, inflectionless voice. 'Life I mean.'

'Ah.'

'Power is sex for stupid people. He isn't stupid, whatever else he is. Well, he is, but not in that way.'

'A bit too deep for me,' I objected. And a lot too loud. Were the neighbours deaf, or simply away in Kenya for a month or two?

'You can grasp simple ideas, if they're in your own interest surely? Perhaps not all life is screwed up by sex, but his is. And so is mine. Although I dare say you and I could get by without making too much of a mess.'

'Of course, then we wouldn't be doing it the right way.'

'Be an angel, try not to amuse me. I'm trying to explain, I don't share his fathomless desire to find the answer to all existence up somebody else's orifice.'

'Do you share his desire to get away with murder, perhaps?'

She took me to be speaking metaphorically.

'Are you the girl's ponce?'

'Which girl is that?'

'No idea. He's scared, I know. He's probably expecting you. It was pure torture on holiday. But then it always is. What has he done?'

'How did you come to meet him?'

'Oh dear,' she scoffed. 'What's this, polite conversation?'

But it came out all the same, by indirection. She pulled her frock over her head and lay back in the sun. If she intended to intimidate me by this wanton gesture, she half succeeded. I lay on my stomach and pretended to be interested in her face.

Before she got on to the booze, Lydia explained, and while she should have been out looking for a husband, she was ruining her nose with coke. Her father, Lord Perslade, was beginning to despair. Here he was with a gammy leg from Korea (the extreme cold had saved him from a battlefield amputation); a bloody great house in South Lincolnshire with prize deer roaming in the gloaming; and a daughter who could hardly count past five. All she ever brought home were fellows the Chinese would hardly have wasted bullets on. What's more, she seemed not to have inherited the Perslade penchant for bed. His wife, the Countess, was a little more shrewd. She had divined a possible explanation for this parade of wimps and hairdressers. Lydia was afraid of failing. Consequently, as happens in such cases, she was failing in rather a big way with every day that passed. The Countess had some slight sympathy with her daughter. Not everybody gets a catch in the throat from owning a lot of bloody silly deer.

She met Nicholas in Delhi. Even after an extended period of insanity with the god-bothering companion of her travels,

Rory Blake, she found her future husband striking and peculiar. He was doing legwork on the upcoming Indian election for an indolent back-bench MP and pestering the life out of the good-natured BBC correspondent. He strode about Delhi in a safari suit and a floppy white cricket hat, taking tea at the hotel each day with bemused American retirees on their way to Jaipur. He felt free to advise them on any and every aspect of geopolitics. Lydia, washed out and penniless, a stone and a half underweight, watched from a safe distance. Her body was burned a cinnamon brown and offset by bleached and ragged hair. Rory Blake had taken his leg ulcers and his penile ring down to Poona, where enlightenment was being cranked up daily by the Maharishi. Sometimes the guru spoke in English, but the real buzz was to be got from his three-hour addresses in Hindi. You don't have to understand a language to know something beautiful is being said.

Lydia may have under-achieved at school, but she knew how to put the bite on a fellow countryman abroad. She bummed the return air fare from the strutting little nincompoop, the fledgling man of affairs. She assumed there was a price – but when she lay on his bed with the bones of her hips protruding like hatchets, Nicholas gently demurred. He told her he was a devotee of a certain kind of pleasure he did not feel it right to confess, not just at that moment. She assumed he was gay. They flew home together – David, Lydia, and her intestinal worms. Once the worms were safely bottled and out of the way, she took him home to meet Dad. Lord Perslade was entranced. Here he was, almost having given up hope of finding someone stupid enough to take on his daughter, and fate and India had supplied the answer.

Nicholas confessed his sexual preferences to Lydia, saying he had at last met someone who could see them clearly and see them whole. They would in no wise interfere with his affection for her: they were something he had learned to keep separate from real emotion. It was best to be honest about things.

Didn't she think so? She thought it was utter madness to be honest about things, but she bit her tongue. She explained how she was a bit of a feckless cow with a complete disdain for the niceties of life. But Nicholas, though young, was no mug. Only the very rich or very poor can talk such tripe. Lydia was loaded. He proposed in the Perslade drawing-room during a concert of harpsichord music. She accepted.

'What happened to Rory Blake?' I asked.

She laughed.

'You're quite a collector's item, do you know that?'

Rory died of pneumonia in a beach hut on the beautiful coast of Goa, two years after Lydia and David were married at St George's, Hanover Square.

'It's a great story,' I said.

'What would you know about it?'

'Ah now, no regrets. It's something to pass down to the children – how Daddy liked to beat up loose women and Mums thought it was all such a terrific hoot. You hadn't actually made too much of that, but it's there, in the background. Naturally, I bear in mind that you are a distinguished children's author. So maybe you were just trying out a new angle for my benefit.'

She suddenly seemed to remember she was only wearing knickers and a gold watch and reached for her frock.

'What on earth was I doing, letting you into the house? I must be mad.'

'No, not mad. Desperate, Mrs Nicholas. Something's happened that's never happened before, isn't that right? Little David's got the wind up about something. He's not sleeping too well and he's coming out in hives. That's new.'

She jumped up and pulled the frock over her head.

'Right, I'm going to phone the police,' she said.

'Good. I'll wait.'

She stared at me with real fear.

'How much do you want? I can give you about two thousand by tomorrow. We are not rich.'

'You are loaded, sweetheart.'

'Then how much?'

'I need to talk to him. That's all. Give me the address in Wiltshire, tell him I'm coming, leave the rest to me. But thanks for asking me back. You've been very entertaining.'

'And you,' she said, with a tardy flash of common sense, 'can fuck off out of this garden.'

I drove down to Wiltshire feeling another little piece of the jigsaw had come to hand. Lydia Nicholas must sometimes seem to her husband like the penance he owed: I could not myself imagine a more daunting experience than to come home from a Division late at night to find Lydia in full flow, stoked by a bottle or two of gin. Leaving the house, I had seen an astonishing thing. In a little Victorian walnut frame was a photograph of Lydia as a child of about eleven, naked save for daisy chains round her neck and waist. In the background were the walls and gables of what I took to be Perslade. It was an amazing thing to exhibit in a position where even the most reticent of picture browsers could be sure to see it. The child Lydia sat on a stone toadstool, legs crossed at the ankle, her tummy-tum-tum as fuzzless as the cue ball in snooker, and with a look of ineffable smugness on her face. Was it her idea to show it off now, thirty years on; or his? What were we supposed to think?

The Nicholas second home was a mile or so from Tidsbury, over a hogback ridge. I drove past the house a hundred yards or so and parked the Renault on a broad verge under a stand of beeches. The roadway was filled with wisps of straw and a harvest moon was pasted up in the sky. It was all wonderfully quiet and fragrant. A reliable witness could have sat up there in those woods for ever, musing on the tramp of legionary feet and the things that really matter. I switched off the ignition and with it the Shostakovich Second Piano Concerto and got out of the car. The lights to Nicholas's cottage glistened in a faint mist that rose from the valley. Things were just about perfect. The funny thing was, now that I had him in my sights at last, I didn't know exactly what I wanted to do.

I shouldn't have worried. He was already dead.

12

Mischief and confusion. From that moment a whole new spin was put on the ball. Everything began to run faster; jagged edges came sawing out of the ground. While I waited for the police, a deep, deep rage replaced the original panic I had felt on discovering him. I wanted to shake him awake, bang his head on the quarry tiles until he came round. I wanted to kick him into consciousness, shout in his face to pull himself together and answer a few simple questions. As, for example, who had killed him.

All very well but not so easy. He lay on his back on the bathroom floor. He was naked, and had risen from the bath, which was still full of warm, grey water. The hair on his chest and arms and the black tuft at the base of his belly was wet. Little apologetic pools of water gathered at his hips and between his legs. There was even a tiny pond filling his navel. The Italian sun had done little for him: he was very white skinned and almost womanishly plump. I had always made him into a lean and hungry man. Nicholas was only average height, with poorly defined musculature. Far from looking a monster, he seemed, soft, flaccid.

But what shrieked out at you was the small and regular entry wound above one eye, and the colossal amount of blood that had been blown from his brain a nanosecond later, as the bullet crashed out through the back of his skull. A great mist of bright pink oxygenated blood had blown against the wall of the bath, the wash-basin pedestal and the loo. The myriad threads of it, no thicker than cotton, were still in motion. That end of the bathroom was crawling with him.

It was that more than anything else that shook me up. I had arrived within minutes of his dying. Standing in the bathroom with my own blood roaring in my ears, it seemed impossible I had not heard the shot or seen his attacker. I walked through the rest of the ground floor. His CD was still pumping out Mahler. In the oven was a casserole on a low temperature. Even his word processor screen was lit. There was nothing on it save the reminder he was typing in the line format (+ LSpace 1½). The cursor blinked with more or less the same interval as a blue light on a squad car. I peeped into his sitting-room. The french windows were open to moths and the scent of stocks. The lights of the house lit a large, rolling lawn that dipped to a stone wall. Beyond was a paddock strewn with dock and nettles; and beyond that, woods.

I picked up the phone again to call Judith. My hand was shaking. I looked at the receiver for what seemed like hours. I could hear people – a couple – shouting. Dogs barked. Maybe I shouldn't phone Judith after all. Maybe she was running about in the woods down there. What point of the compass was that? Was it north or east? And what *was* this Mahler?

There was a sound of light footsteps running down the brick path and a middle-aged woman appeared, breathless. She caught me still with the phone in my hand, my mind ajar.

'Isn't it awful?' she said. 'The poor man. I've rung for the police, I went back to my own house to do it, I must be mad. My husband saw you arrive we're neighbours I should have rung from here that was the rational thing to do my God I just bolted Andrew rang them it is all quite awful.'

'I think we should wait outside,' I said, replacing the phone on its cradle as if we were both underwater. My legs felt like Chinese noodles.

She was called Mrs Sharpe and lived in the cottage across the gardens. She had come round to wish her distinguished neighbour a happy return from Italy. As she shut her back door she heard the shot. She had been running distractedly this way and that for three or four minutes. Although she did not seem to know it, she still had a welcoming pint of milk in her hands.

'You must be a friend or colleague or something. My husband saw you arrive. He was spraying in the greenhouse.'

'What greenhouse?' I asked foolishly, like an obstinate drunk.

'The greenhouse. Our greenhouse.'

'Do you smoke, Mrs Sharpe?'

'Not now, but you do, please.'

'I mean do you have a cigarette?'

The husband Andrew lumbered down the path, nodded to me and took the milk from his wife. He placed it carefully on the window-sill.

'I was telling this gentleman you were spraying in the greenhouse.'

'I was fumigating the greenhouse,' he said, and I realized with a flood of gratitude near to actual tears that he was going to make a good witness.

'You don't happen to have a cigarette, Mr Sharpe?'

He shook his head in disapproval and touched his wife on her plump arm.

'You haven't moved anything in there have you, Joyce?'

She shook her head vehemently, discovered she no longer held the milk bottle and snatched it back from the sill.

'We're not close you can't be with people like that but you do what you can. And I'm very fond of the children. But what they'd think, to see their daddy with no clothes on and –'

The milk slipped from her hand and shattered on the path. Mrs Sharpe wailed. Her husband turned to me. He was embarrassed for her.

'It's been a shock,' he said.

'You saw me arrive. I parked up there – you saw that, apparently.'

He looked at me for a long and unfriendly second.

'Oh, *you* didn't do it,' he said.

First one squad car tore to a halt in the dusty road, then another two. There was a considerable confusion for ten minutes. An incident room was created in a tiny scout hut, not far from where I had parked my car. The Sharpes and I began our account of things there and then were whisked to the Salisbury HQ building. We sat at separate ends of a room turned over to the murder enquiry, drinking coffee in styrofoam cups and watching young policewomen doing their work in among all the bustle. A hugely fat girl called Erica was leaving the following day. As well as conducting the investigation, a well-wishers' card was being circulated behind her back. It was my first visit to a police station since working in one myself. Although I knew what everyone was about, their rank and their likely responsibilities, I might as well, from the emotional independence I showed, have been Mrs Sharpe's slightly simple brother. I watched one man after another come up and say something jocular to Erica of the bursting blouse and the Nana Mouskouri glasses. After an hour of waiting about, playing with pencils and paper clips within my reach, a shrewd young Detective Sergeant took my statement in an adjoining interview room. I tried to cadge a cigarette.

'This is a no-smoking building now, you know.'

'A nick, and you can't smoke?'

'All for the best, they say. Had an appointment to see him, did you? What sort of an appointment?'

'I haven't said it was an appointment. His wife was going to phone to say I was coming.'

'That's right,' he said calmly. 'She did.'

When I looked baffled he smiled, but without too much warmth.

'Ansaphone message,' he said.

I felt my skin crawl. What had Lydia said about me? That this nice man was popping down from town for a chat or what? I cursed myself for not having been more observant. I had been standing with the phone in my hand and hadn't even seen the answering machine. The DS was watching me just that fraction too casually.

'She rang to say you were coming,' he reassured me.

'Well then, he was expecting me. There was a casserole in the oven.'

'Planning to give you a meal, perhaps.'

'That may have been on his mind.'

'Thoughtful chap.'

'No idea,' I said, beginning to feel very uneasy.

'Oh really? Why's that?'

'I've told you. I'd never met him before.'

I was being drawn into details that did not matter; and he knew it. He would have gone on, but we were interrupted by the arrival of a heavy-set pipe-smoker with shoulders like bags of cement. The Detective Sergeant stood up. Ted Gerson stared at me for what seemed like all eternity before coming in and closing the door behind him. He sat down in the Sergeant's place with a grunt and began reading the longhand statement, clouds of smoke blowing over his shoulder. The uniformed constable who was also in the room winced.

'Go and fetch us some coffee,' he muttered to the DS when he had read through the material twice. 'And get him some cigarettes.'

'The Chief Super has a no-smoking –'

Gerson looked up, as if pained. When the young DS had gone he plucked his nostril a few times with a blunt thumb and then pushed the statement away from him in disgust.

'You were on to the bugger,' he suggested, with a crudity that rocked the uniformed copper back on to his heels.

'He was being blackmailed.'

'So it says here.'

'What else do you want me to say? I saw his wife this lunch-time. She gave me a meal. I asked for the address, she gave it. I suggested she phone ahead.'

Gerson stared me down. He was, I knew, quite as sorry as I that Nicholas was dead.

'Come on, Ted. What is all this? I'm gobsmacked to see you here. You of all people.'

Which I most definitely was. He poked about in his pipe with his car keys, snuffling and apparently deaf. I threw up my hands.

'He and this girl Judith Firestone were being blackmailed by someone who had a neg of them doing it. He wanted a grand. I was the go-between. That's the story.'

'Who was the someone?'

I hesitated.

'It's in the statement.'

'I want to hear you say it.'

'Edgar,' I said, glancing at the young kid in uniform.

'Edgar who?'

'Detective Inspector Edgar Martindale, Hampshire CID.'

Gerson found a button loose on his jacket. He grew absorbed in winding the loose thread up and knotting it. You could hear the dust falling. The sweat was running down behind my ankle bones into my socks.

'Funny old summer you've had of it, one way and another.'

'You can say that again.'

He began to fill his pipe with tobacco from a blue plastic pouch.

'A senior police officer tries to blackmail some friends of yours. You are a former officer in the same force. You would know exactly what to do in such circumstances. Even this kid here leaning against the wall would know what to do.'

The young constable straightened up, flushing from his neck to his hair-line, where the pale blond spikes flopped.

'I've signed a full and voluntary statement. The neighbours

saw me arrive after he'd been shot. As far as I know there are no charges being prepared against me. Nicholas was not my friend. The girl is. I was thinking of her.'

'I see,' Ted said, with a flick of sarcasm.

'It's not a crime.'

He ran his tongue over his front teeth with a juicy noise and spelled it out all over again.

'A serving police officer known to you is seriously out of order in a matter concerning a junior Cabinet minister and you decide to busk it for a while in order to accommodate a girl you've been humping. And then this junior Cabinet minister has his head blown off.'

'You'd have seen that coming, of course.'

'Don't get smart with me. What got you involved? What got you into it?'

'I got involved.'

'Answer my question. For love, was it?'

His pale blue eyes were unwavering in their animosity. I began to hate him back.

'Yes, for love.'

'Don't piss me about, you cretin.'

He upended a Metropolitan Police internal post envelope and out came some familiar snaps. Gerson waved the kid to the far side of the room.

'This the lass?'

There were a few new ones. She hung from the banisters of the murder house in Wiltshire and was chained to the table where Nicholas had his word processor. Most horribly, she was spread-eagled across the stone toadstool where Lydia once played fairies. I put my head in my hands.

'Listen you pillock,' Ted snapped. 'You are in dead trouble. This bloke was bent, as far as women are concerned. He was a well-hard bastard. You know a lot more than you are telling. There's a big file on him up in town – a *big* file. You say it was the little twerp Edgar who was pulling something. But what about you and this evil cow? That could be just as likely. What's your game, the pair of you?'

'We didn't kill him.'

'*You* didn't. She might have done.'

'A head shot? And then a complete disappearing act? She's not Annie Oakley. She didn't kill him, otherwise you wouldn't be here talking to me.'

He scooped the prints up off the table and stuffed them back in the envelope.

'The trouble with you is, you don't know when to be serious. You never did. But you're up shit creek now. I wouldn't touch a slag like that with the toe end of my shoe.'

'Leave it out,' I said, sharp. He raised his eyebrows.

'What did you say?'

'She doesn't have to suit your taste in women. That's not a crime, either, that she doesn't. Up yours with the toe end of your shoe routine. Don't try to intimidate me, see? I won't buy it. You're talking out of your arse.'

He suddenly leaned forward and pulled me half-way across the interview table by the front of my sweater. My chair clattered over behind me. He was close enough for me to smell the tobacco on his teeth and lips.

'You listen to me, you prick. We were friends once, but you like to walk alone. You don't need friends. Have it your way. But be careful the friends you had once don't bury you.'

He threw me backwards and I fell to the red vinyl floor with a sickening jolt. When I got up, I could see the shame in his eyes. For him the worst thing in the world had happened. I had made him lose his temper. Finding a pen under his foot, he sent it skittering to the skirting board. He dragged the metal table straight with a screech of its metal legs. I had made him madder than I could ever remember.

'If you want to make a complaint against me, get on with it now. The constable here will be your witness.'

'Get stuffed,' I said shakily.

The door opened and a tall, bespectacled Chief Super looked in at us as if we were dogs on the loose. He smelt the tobacco smoke and saw the mess on the floor where Ted had cleaned out the bowl of his pipe. For a moment that seemed to upset him more than anything else. It certainly added to the curtness of his nod.

'Out,' he said to the big man. 'I don't know what game you're playing, sonny, but you had better have some explanations handy. I've a line through to the Met and I'm going to chop your legs off. See me in my office. But right away now.'

Ted picked up his pipe and pouch and walked out without a backward glance. The Chief Super studied me some more to see if I had fouled the floor or dropped hair on his vinyl, and then he left too.

'Christ,' the young constable said piously. Outside the windows we could hear a helicopter setting down on the lawns. The boy fumbled in his pockets and came up with a packet of Tunes. He passed me one. By making this man with the smell of the big city want to whack me, I had impressed the kid. When he gave me the Tune, his hand was shaking. Perhaps he thought Gerson was being reported to his superiors at Scotland Yard for smoking in an interview room. Or maybe he wasn't as green as all that.

More than an hour later, a tall good-looking bloke in his thirties came in and asked if he might ask some questions.

'Yes, if I can see your identity.'

'This is a police station,' he laughed. 'What do you think I am, the *Daily Express*?'

'I don't know. Are you?'

'You will simply be assisting the police in their enquiries.'

'I have made a voluntary statement.'

The good-looker ran an experimental hand over the table, as if looking for dust.

'What's worrying you?'

'You are.'

He smiled thinly.

'We mustn't get paranoid, old chum.'

'We mustn't get chummy, either.'

'Would you like me to fetch the officer in charge of the enquiry?'

'Yes please.'

He shrugged and left. I didn't see him again. Or anyone else.

I was released at five the following morning. An elderly sergeant gave me the location of a breakfast joint in Salisbury that opened at six, it being market day. But a night in an interview room can dull the appetite. What I needed much more was a toothbrush. The car-park area of the building was fenced with incident tapes and a boy copper was acting as gateman. In the trees, tucked away, was an Army RT truck. The squaddies were quietly brewing up at the back of it. A police helicopter dripped morning dew from its rotor arms. At the entrance to the HQ complex was a gaggle of press, including a TV crew. It was all heavy-duty. The nation had lost a favourite son.

The Renault coughed like a pensioner before it would start. I drove slowly up the A303, shivering from delayed reaction. Glorious sunshine streamed over the plain, chasing out the last shadows from bumps and hollows, refreshing even the littlest things. A yellow fertilizer bag caught in the hedge burned with the intensity of a Van Gogh. I rang Judith from outside an Army barracks. There was no reply. Either she too was talking to the police, or she had engineered one of her famous disappearing acts. Or she was sitting under a gorse bush somewhere, wondering whether to keep the gun or throw it away.

On the wall of the phone box was scratched a message about the sexual inclinations of a Major Roberts. Someone more loyal to the CO – or maybe his friend – had tried to obliterate his name. To a child the inscription read 'Major Scribble Sucks Scratch'. I stood staring at this for quite a long time. While I was thinking about the lucky (or luckless) Major

Scribble, the mystery man who had come to see me in the interview room drove past in his Audi Quattro, heading for London. Sitting with him was an animated and gesticulating Lydia Nicholas.

Hilary was waiting for me. Like an anxious mother he stood in the lane at the entrance to his little domain. He was wearing a threadbare cotton robe from the bottom of which poked very thin, very white shins. When he recognized the Renault, he waved his arms over his head in fury.

'Now you might like to tell me what the bloody hell is going on,' he shouted. 'I have had the police here all night. They have only just left.'

'Did they have a warrant to search?'

'They had a warrant and they had dogs. They've more or less taken the railway carriage apart.'

'How about your place? Did they take anything away with them?'

'They intend to return here at their leisure. Later this morning. I take it you've done something stupid.'

'David Nicholas was shot last night,' I said.

Hilary's reply was instant.

'Which one of you killed him?'

'Have you seen Judith?'

'Would I, under these circumstances? Do you know what they were looking for? Semtex. Explosives. No doubt you have a ready explanation.'

I fell back against the car in amazement.

'They were looking for what?'

'Exactly,' Hilary spat.

The spots of colour on his cheeks were burning like plague sores. He actually wrang his hands in despair.

'I am obviously not getting my point across to you. Whatever you have done, I would like you to pack your traps now and go. It is quite one thing for the police to roust *you*. You may deserve it for all I know. But I am a very different kettle of fish, I can assure you. I have no intention of being dragged into this.'

'Have you anything in the house they might find interesting?'

'What do you think?' he asked bitterly. 'Not if they are looking for explosives, no. But that won't stop them looking. I detest you for having brought all this down on me. You've ruined my life.'

Judith arrived, driving at sixty down the rutted farm lane. It was too much for Hilary. He went into the house and slammed the door. Surrealistically, a pane of glass fell out of his sitting-room window and shattered on the rockery beneath. His howl was like a vampire's. Wallace, the loyal Wallace, shot across the grass to evade Judith's car and disappeared round the side of the house. I glanced at my watch. There was forty minutes to go before a newsbreak on television. I had the strong feeling we were in for a surprise.

13

One thing was certain: at least *she* had not killed Nicholas. At the time he had stared with a final tardy glimmer of realism at the round O of a pistol barrel aimed at his head, Judith was once again with her accountant. The famous Waxman was actually in the flat when the police arrived. They had not been talking tax matters – the police discovered them listening to Waxman's Mel Tormé records, including a bootleg tape of Mel singing at a private party in Las Vegas. I listened to all these homely details with the feeling she was passing me an armful of blacksmith's anvils.

'Forget Mel Tormé, you dope. An MP is shot in deepest Wiltshire and the first person they want to interview is you. Doesn't that do anything for you?'

'But I was there, at home. They knew I couldn't have done it.'

'Yes,' I said wearily. 'I know. But the point is they thought you were capable of having done it. You were a principal suspect.'

She had been taken to West End Central, leaving Gerald Waxman to gather up his Mel Tormé in wonder and astonishment. Not the first, not the second, but the third detective she spoke to was a large man with pale blue eyes and rose scratches on the back of his hands. He was in a hurry. He seemed excited, but almost in an absent-minded way. He sped through his questions, took no notes, seemed indifferent to how she answered. She had the feeling she stood accused of breathing the same air as him.

'Did he have some of the photographs with him?'

'Yes,' Judith admitted in her smallest voice.

'You explained it was just a bit of fun between old friends, did you?'

Her eyes flashed. I could picture Gerson looking at her with his burly dispassion, picking at his teeth with a split match. It was hard, hurting her, but she seemed incapable of realizing for herself what had happened. I held her by the arms.

'Look at me. Two months ago, how Nicholas got it up was a matter between you and him. It was a secret. He put the secret in a safe place. Now everybody in London seems to have the clue. There are pictures of you and your ha'penny blowing about in the wind like confetti. Doesn't that give you a buzz of anxiety?'

Our stories corresponded, roughly. She had come to me to help deflect a case of blackmail. She had no idea of the source. As to the content of the photographs, she had known and respected David Nicholas since their days together at Oxford. The pictures showed something that happened between consenting adults. I smiled. Even Gerson must have got a laugh out of that one.

'Did he ask you about Yanni?'

'What the hell has Yanni got to do with it?' Judith asked, exasperated.

'Maybe that was the question he asked you.'

I had told him I loved her; and I did. But there was a price. I was beginning to realize she had a bottomless capacity for lies and evasions. She tore a wand of alder from the ground and began peeling the bark. Her face was dark and sulky.

'He told me for a fact that Yanni and I had been lovers.'

'Did he mention specific places – the casinos, or the flat in Brighton? It's no use sulking, Judith. Snap out of that right now. I have to know.'

'He knew all about us,' she shouted. 'What difference does it make?'

'It means they have had you under observation. The police –

you know, the busy and overworked police – or if you prefer, the nosey, interfering pigs – have been spending the public's money on you. Why? Because they've also had your boyfriend Mr Nicholas under observation. Can't you grasp what a mess you're in?'

I snatched the slimy wand of alder from her and threw it away. She had tears of vexation glittering in her eyes.

'It isn't me that's done anything wrong. I haven't done anything. The other detectives were okay. It was this bastard who was making the trouble. Everybody wants to blame me. You too. But I didn't kill David.'

'He knows that. It isn't about David's death. It can't be.'

'What then?'

We walked slowly back towards the house. Across the valley, the harvesters had been out since dawn. Rooks marched sentry in the stubble. You could smell the shaved fields on the breeze. I wondered how long it would take to forget this place; whether it would ever come about that I could drive past and not remember how I had met her and how the spirit of the fields and woods seemed sometimes to flow through her. I took her hand up to my lips and kissed it. She was crying.

'It'll work out somehow,' I said.

'When he left, the big detective, he turned round at the door and said when it all came out I would be flushed away like a piece of shit. His words for it.'

'Don't get bitter. He's a rose grower. His wife is a little sparrow of a woman with arthritic hands.'

'You *know* them?' Judith asked, incredulous. A plume of white smoke was rising from the location of Hilary's house. He was burning something in the grate. When Judith took my hand again I held it far too hard. I was more scared than I had ever been in my life.

The BBC news at one o'clock – for all that I had been expecting the worst – came like a bombshell. It was like staring at an intricate and sinister mechanism you knew was going to blow up in your face. The lead story showed the senior detective in charge of the murder enquiry standing on the steps of the Salisbury HQ building, looking like a blond and aggravated farmer with a grievance against somebody inside. He asserted for a fact that the killing had been accomplished by a professional gunman, and used the word assassination, artlessly corrected to brutal murder. But running alongside this story was the arrest in Swindon of three people on charges made under the Prevention of Terrorism Act. Armed police had raided the house at dawn. A cache of arms and explosives had been discovered. The arrests were linked to the Selfridges outrage earlier in the summer. The implication was that somehow the murder of a Home Office minister was part of this same hand of cards. The BBC newsroom, conscious of a scoop over their colleagues in print journalism because of the timing of the events, had decided to go with the two stories in tandem.

The Prime Minister's regret and commiseration employed the coded phrase 'this callous and cold-blooded murder'. You would have had to be an Eskimo not to be able to recognize and identify the expression as an old friend of Prime Ministerial press statements. The short interview, given on the steps of Number Ten, was followed by a background piece on the recent incidence of mainland terror, and the steps being taken to safeguard other public figures. Lydia Nicholas was shown being driven away from the house in St John's Wood under police protection.

Somebody somewhere was laying it on with a trowel. It was only three and a bit months since the Oxford Street outrage and feelings were still running very high. Nine people had been blown to hell then and another sixty injured. The link between the death of Nicholas and the discovery of the house in Swindon was just too irresistible not to forge. If you looked at the thing closely you might see a scrupulous separation of the two events as to the letter of the thing. But the spirit was unmistakable. In the sort of pubs where most people drank, where the short answer to any question surrounding foreign radicals was to nuke the bastards, David Nicholas had been shot by the IRA.

I switched the set off. Judith glanced across.

'Does it mean they did it?'

'Wouldn't that be grand?' I said, and was rewarded by seeing her flinch as from a blow. Hilary came into the room. He waded in without ceremony.

'Much as I have enjoyed your company, etcetera, I would now like you to clear off, both of you. And let's make that for good.'

'They've just been saying, on television –'

He held up his hand.

'I'm not deaf, Judith. I'm very glad he's dead and I have some moderate sympathy for both of you. But I want no more part of it. You must go, and go now.'

'Don't you want me to wait until the police come back?'

'I can't think of anything more awkward or damaging. You want to solve things. It's in your nature. I do not believe things can be solved, any more than grass can be commanded to stop growing, or to change colour. So pack your bags and clear off.'

'Hilary . . .' Judith began. But he waved her words away.

'You have got what you wanted,' he said. 'The poor bloody man is dead. You have had your revenge. And you have saved your own skin into the bargain. Go, Judith. And take him with you.'

'What does it mean when you say she's saved her own skin?'

'Just go!' Hilary screamed.

We drove back to London in separate cars. When I came in, she was making tea and Wheelchair Waxman was sitting on the couch. He was about forty and rather dramatically solid above the waist. A dangerous, argumentative intelligence shone out of his eyes. Although he wore a suit, he had yet to shave. His chin was the blue of gun metal.

'Shot by the IRA!' he declared cheerfully. 'Oy, these madmen. Who could believe it possible, except it happens every day? A wife loses a husband, three children lose a father. I hardly know the man, I am weeping when I hear it, you understand what I'm saying?'

I wondered why his language lived far, far away in another country, but he was ready with the explanation. Leah Waxman's brother Harry was a stage designer for all the big shows in Vegas. They went out there each year and stayed at the Dunes, on Harry's tab. Harry was like that.

'Not a pushy man, still very English, but liked and loved, you know what I'm saying?'

Judith passed him his tea.

'This one I love,' he said fondly. 'This lady is very special. I know the man treated her badly, but to be shot by the IRA!'

'He wasn't,' I said. 'That's so much bullshit.'

'This is the big expert talking,' Judith scoffed.

'He wasn't shot by the IRA? Then who killed him?'

'Who killed Wardell Gray?'

Wardell Gray was a sax player to be set alongside Charlie Parker for melodic invention and purity of tone. One day he was found out in the desert, not far from Vegas, his hands tied and the back of his head blown off. Nobody was ever charged with the murder. Some say the Organization did it, some that it was a little problem of drugs or money. One way or another, the world lost a great jazz genius. Waxman was blinking furiously. He was on the case, as he might have put it. He nodded at last.

'I hadn't realized,' he said softly.

But Judith was in a combative mood.

'Don't listen to him,' she said to her accountant. 'He's looking for difficulties where there aren't any. One of these Irishmen they've arrested has two counts of murder against him already.'

'And one of them is a woman.'

'What's that got to do with it?'

'It's just too neat.'

'You think the authorities framed up three innocent people – are you crazy?' Waxman asked. 'I watched the news at three o'clock, man. They showed pictures of the house in Swindon. Guns, everything. It was an active service unit. The classic kind.'

'Have the IRA claimed responsibility?'

'Not yet,' Waxman admitted. 'But who can say how their minds work?'

'You and Judith, apparently.'

'You make me sick,' Judith said suddenly. 'Every time you get to a point where things could be left alone, you want to go on. Why are you like that? D'you think you're always in the right?'

'I think I'm always a couple of steps behind the truth.'

'The truth! The truth!'

'I don't like being cheated.'

She gave me the hard look. Waxman coughed delicately behind his hand. I went into the bathroom, showered, cleaned my teeth and drank four handfuls of water from the tap. Then I went to bed, crawling under the duvet that smelled of the oil she rubbed into herself to keep her skin supple. Though I was asleep in what seemed seconds, my mind flitted like a house-martin. Yanni was pedalling for dear life down a poplar-lined road in France. I was following on a motor bike I had found in the canal. Every so often, it sneezed to a halt and I had to begin repairs. When this happened, Yanni's toiling back would dwindle to a dot on the horizon. I knew I had to catch him. Judith took no part in this dream. Judith was hoovering the flat. I could hear her, even from sunny France.

Gerson saw me, after an hour and a half's wait, in a pub near Olympia. He lumbered in looking truculent and refused a

139

drink, saying that as soon as he had done with me he was driving home. It was nearly eight at night, and I was a bit light-headed, myself. The room gave an occasional spin. He accepted an orange juice and watched me fumble a cigarette.

'I want to know what to do,' I said.

'You want to know what to do about what?'

'About what I know.'

He tore a beer-mat in two for the pleasure of watching his hands at work. He tore one half in two again, and so on.

'I should do whatever you feel like doing. Just don't do the wrong thing.'

'Look, Ted, I'm not making trouble for you.'

'That's very nice of you,' he said, with a thin smile. 'Go and get me a vodka and two tonics.'

'Who's the lady?' the landlord asked.

'He is,' I said, pointing to Ted.

'Stroll on.'

When I came back, the barmaid was clearing away my empties and his bits of beer-mat. He swept the crumbs of it on to the floor with a careless gesture. His pipe smoke smelt like a bonfire of sprout stalks.

'What's on your mind?'

'What I want to know is, am I in the clear?'

'You tell me.'

'Is she in the clear?'

He studied his hands for a moment, then looked up at me.

'I don't claim to understand a thing about life with a capital L, so I can't say why you want to screw yourself up with a whore like that. I don't go looking for problems, either. What you really want to find out is whether I got warned today. So I'll tell you. Yes. The world has been given a political martyr, just when the Government needed one. What a bit of luck, eh?'

'She's in the clear?'

'Do you vote?' he asked. 'Do you read anything deeper than

the back of sauce bottles or cornflake packets? This Government is dead in the water. Not even the political assassination of a Cabinet minister can save it. But if the Government isn't everything to you or me, it is to a back-bench MP, maybe. You have to keep your seat if you want to get your snout in the trough. But the Party is a greater thing still. Without the Party you'd lose all sense of direction. The Party gives you a horizon.'

'You've thought about all this, have you?' I sneered.

A look of ice-cold pity came across his face, such as he might otherwise reserve for a shrew chopped in half by a spade, or a starling savaged on his lawn by a neighbour's cat.

'I agreed to see you because you're a lightweight. You know enough about the business to know that I could break you, would break you, if it suited my purpose. You're enough of a lightweight to see that. In books, the hero goes right on to the end. I would stop right here, this moment, if I were you.'

'He wasn't killed by the IRA.'

'No, this is shit creek you're wading up now, boy. The three Irish have killed and maimed thirty-seven between them. They moved to Swindon from Blackburn a fortnight ago. Before that they were in Waltham Cross. One of them is a shooter with three counts of murder against him. There was enough explosive in that house to start a quarry business.'

'They didn't do it, though.'

He stared at me with his pale blue watery eyes, a ghost of a smile on his expression.

'You dick. If I thought you were telling me this for a fact, I would finish you. I know more about her than you can begin to guess at. And she's sculpted from dog-shit. You don't know anything.'

'I know that somehow a fix is going in.'

'And what's your theory?'

'He killed the black girl called Wilma Curtess,' I said. 'Someone offed him by way of revenge.'

Gerson smiled broadly at last. He leaned over and ruffled my hair.

'You ought to be in the pictures. You set up this meet, you put your balls in my hand and you challenge me to squeeze them. Get it through your head. You're nobody, nothing. I'd cut your cods out without a second thought if it suited me.'

'You're saying he didn't kill Wilma?'

'I'm not saying anything. You're doing all the saying. You got me a warning today: exceeding the strict duties assigned to me by a superior officer. On a complaint by a Chief Constable. A bollocking by a DAC with a degree in Russian, see, from Oxford. A politician's policeman. Who set me right on the facts of the Wiltshire enquiry. The official story is that the Irish boys shot him. You think that's a fix. Well, you do something about it. What are you going to do?'

'This isn't you, Ted.'

'What, you think I should be more idealistic?'

I rubbed the stubble that was beginning to make my neck itch. All round us the punters were talking up an evening's drinking. There was about as much intellectual content as a phone-in. At the table nearest us they were going over the Corfu holiday snaps with screams of laughter. Ted indicated them with a nod.

'This is the world, kid. This is the lucky side of the fence. It's so bloody simple out here. And it's where *you* live now, or where you could live if you used your brains. Football, tit, dosh. It won't last, but it's good for a few years yet. Nobody's got the guts to say otherwise. And you want to risk all that for a girl who would see you dead before she uttered a single honest word.'

'Or for the truth.'

He waved the smoke away from his face and gave me his most dangerous smile.

'That's what I like: the principled civilian. You think the truth matters to anyone in here, do you? The whole fucking thing is held together by lies and deceit. Even these morons can understand that much. You've seen birds' nests held together by spit, haven't you?'

'Who killed him, Ted?'

He shrugged.

'Who cares? They did us all a favour.'

He poured the second tonic on the dregs of the vodka. But I knew he couldn't drive home with it all hanging in the air like this.

'How d'you know about Wilma – your poxy tart tell you?'

'Don't be stupid, Ted.'

'That's right. She wouldn't tell you where her other tit was.'

He was watching me closely.

'She's human, she's real,' I said. 'She breathes just like you and me. She reads books, cooks meals, pays taxes. And she's clean.'

'Good. How's Mr Waxman?'

It was like a needle jolting into my heart from nowhere.

'What about him?'

'He's her accountant, right?'

'He lives downstairs.'

'That's nice. How much money has she got in the bank?'

'How the hell would I know?'

'Ask Waxman. He keeps the books, doesn't he?'

And then, like a man who has abandoned a conversation about football as pointless, he was gone, wading from the bar like a giant with better things to do with his strength.

We made love on the floor of the sitting-room with the windows wide open and a breeze billowing the net curtains. I was angry with her, and she with me. The sex was violent. On both sides it was violent and ill-tempered. True, we had drunk two bottles of wine and exchanged insults for over an hour: the meal she had prepared was floating in the sink. Judith knew how to provoke violence and, once provoked, orchestrate it. We had not undressed. The furniture seemed to crowd round of its own accord, the better to watch us. The hi-fi system thundered: she had this infuriating habit of remixing crudely with the graphic equalizers so that almost all the top was annihilated. The CD was Albert King. We battled and swore. When it was done, I lay with my head on her breast and heard her heart pounding. She began to cry, and so did I. If there was a way forward from this, I could not imagine it.

'Don't you cry, you self-centred bloody wimp,' she shouted. 'Don't you dare feel sorry for yourself.'

I raised myself to my elbows. To my horror, in the course of this little dish of horrors, she had bitten her lips until the blood ran. It gathered in the corners of her mouth and her teeth were stained with it. Her eyes were as green and cold as grapes.

'Yes!' she said. 'See what you've landed yourself with, choir-boy.'

Her breasts had spilled out of the torn blouse. Before I could stop her, she reached inside my arms with a shuddering moan and tore at her own flesh with her finger-nails. I threw myself down on top of her.

'Stop it, Judith. Stop it now!'

Her breath roared in my ear like a furnace.

'I want to die,' she wailed. 'I don't want to live like this.'

'I love you, I love you.'

'Don't be so fucking *wet*.'

I rolled away. Drunk or not, we were going mad. We lay on the carpet, separate and exhausted, as the darkness slipped into the room. It finally grew so quiet I could hear the clock burying us. I was as heavy as a mountain. And twice as desolate.

14

There used to be a wonderful old Detective Sergeant called George Austin when I was a probationer. I was teamed with him on three murder enquiries.

'What you have to realize, son, is that for some people the world is not a very crowded place. It's just a few dozen people, topside. Remove this one little obstacle – a wife, a husband, a boss – and the rest will just close up, front and back, and on we go again.'

I woke at four from a wrack of cushions on the carpet, and now I stood at the bedroom door, looking at Judith naked and sleeping, arms forward, hands joined together as if bound, one thigh advanced. In the half light, her skin looked almost umber. The deeply shadowed parts of her were not quite blue, not quite mauve. And though I looked at her a long time with compassion flooding every chamber of my heart, something terrible happened: like a steel shutter winding down, I regretted saying that I loved her. More than that, I stood in fear of ever having spoken the words.

'Just cop a glance here,' George would say, sitting on the blood-stained bed in some council flat and smoking a panatella to sweeten the air of its excremental odours. 'You've got the plant pots standing on Royal Doulton saucers. Nothing in the fridge but eggs and tins of cat food, the whole place painted out in primrose yellow – and three nice little saucers like that. Now where did they come from?'

Watching Judith sleep, her mouth slightly open, her hair

wild, put me in mind of George and his imperturbable common sense. It was as though he stood at my shoulder.

'With murder,' he always said, 'you've got your two possibilities. The axe is already there, so to speak, leaning against the wall and more or less inviting you to pick it up and have a swing. Or, you're going to have to go out and buy one. You know – go to a shop, tell 'em about the big old plum tree you've got in the garden and then walk home with the blade wrapped in a bit of brown paper, all shiny and new.'

'Trying to follow you, George.'

'The first lot could be me or you. They know that life is complicated and that killing people is no real answer, but in the heat of the moment – wham! – they forget: as soon as it's over, they realize the consequences. But I sometimes wonder if the other lot have any idea.'

'Maybe they do. Maybe they just don't care.'

'Aye,' the ghost of George warned, as he melted away from my side. 'Those are the awkward bastards. You never want to meet one of them, straight up you don't.'

I had said I loved her because I felt sorry for her, and I felt more sorry still, now. At the top of her thighs and below her buttocks, was a delicate but wide-mouthed funnel of flesh which led, as it does in all women, to the origin of the species and the future of the world. These curves, which described a disposition of fat and muscle she shared with all her sisters, were, for as long as she lay like that, so obvious, so naturally beautiful and apt. But then she rolled on to her back, still asleep, and the long scratches she had inflicted on herself were revealed. My eyes prickled painfully. Maybe it wasn't that I didn't love her, but that to do so would be pointless.

I tiptoed back into the living-room, my skin goose-fleshed. After messing about dressing and then opening the fridge with exaggerated care to fish out some orange juice, after searching her handbag for Anadins and splashing water on my face from the taps above the filthy sink, I'd had enough of being inaudible and careworn. I collected her car keys and drove across the river with no more purpose in my mind than taking my misery to the only Tom Tiddler's ground I'd ever truly known. Life is not all action: I needed to think. As my grandfather would say, watching me with a saw in my hand and a pencil mark on a bit of two by two, 'hang on a minute, this needs a coat of thought, china.'

It happens that of all the houses of my childhood, only Uncle Arthur's is left standing in the neighbourhood. My gran's, Lil's, Knavvie Walters, Sid and Minnie Rosen and a dozen other addresses, have gone. To drive down Biddulph Street is to ponder the Asda depot where once lived what seemed like everybody I ever knew. The Feathers is still there on the corner, but unavailable for comment at half past five in the morning. The cinema is a mosque, the church a recording studio. On the site of what used to be charity almshouses is a concrete cornflake packet housing the social security personnel, whose hand-outs keep the citizens alive. Just over a mile away is Westminster where men in the mould of David Nicholas exclaim daily, to anyone still childish enough to listen, that the standard of living has never been higher. The people who watch these assertions on television and who live locally might as well be witnessing life on Mars.

Check her bank accounts, Gerson had said. Check them for what? Discover another little dishonesty to add to the tea-chest I had already filled? And maybe not just a little one – maybe she was fooling the world in a big way. And if she was, when did I get off the merry-go-round? I parked the car in Lime Tree Walk, bang outside the sooty terrace where Uncle Arthur once had a couple of draughty rooms. Gervase and Julia live there now, with, yah, a fax machine and the odd Stan Getz recording to console them when the mark and the yen do, you know, funny things. I could easily picture them, asleep in the room where Arthur kept his budgie and his sheet music. They would be dreaming of money flowing like water over the weir, some

147

of it wetting their shoes, if only they stuck with the non-penetrative sex and the Perrier. Was Judith sister under the skin to all this, too – the greed, the passion for money that is closest to gluttony in its operation?

Calling my grandfather's pal Arthur 'uncle' was an honorific. There was no blood relationship. The old fella met him in the Blitz and took a shine to him. Uncle Arthur suited him well as a title of honour. He was very correct and held his head high in life. He was a considerable talent on the piano accordion, and once worked the West End hotels with the La Paloma Tango Dance Orchestra. There was a photograph of him in band costume that used to fascinate me – he looked like a tall and tubercular gringo dressed in Mexican duds, just waiting to be shot through the bellows by Zapata's boys. The tasselled brim of his hat flopped to his shoulders. The feature that made him look most like a Yanqui impostor was a moustache as cruel as a pencil slash: it and the faintly crossed eyes were the genuine article. One hand rested on the accordion. From the other poked a cigarette. His shoe lace was undone. This unhappy detail was often remarked upon: he blamed the poncey photographer for making him look doolali-tap. However, since he habitually looked out at the world with a maddened expression, the photographer might have found the untied shoelace a thing not worth putting to rights. Uncle Arthur was a life member of the awkward squad – and proud of it. He spent his last years effing and blinding at the course of popular music.

At six the newsagent's opened. I bought all the morning papers. As far as the tragic loss of David Nicholas was concerned, Judith and I were still zeros, noughts. They were coming forward in droves to remember a hard-working member of the Cabinet, whose life had been all sun-filled innocence. In two of the tabloids there was a photograph of Lydia and David smiling at some Party Conference ball. They looked a couple of good eggs, not so stuffy that they couldn't front up for an evening-dress bash with the loyal nobodies, but not the sort to stay late either. The news interest in them was shifting. Two of the editorials in the quality press wondered whether the Prime Minister would use the outrage to call a general election, rather than issue a writ for a by-election in David's constituency. The *Guardian* considered with rue the possibility that Nicholas's murder may have saved the Government at the eleventh hour. The Chairman of the Party was assembling the inner Cabinet to meet over the weekend.

I dumped the papers and walked half a mile to find a café. I rang Judith from a wall phone by the counter, watched by three plasterers eating bacon and eggs. Huge molecules of fat floated about, while Radio One went about its tireless work of stewing brains. The chef, a Cypriot, picked his nose and read the *Sun* with a faint frown on his face.

'My car's been stolen,' Judith said.

'I have it.'

'Where are you?'

'Round at Uncle Arthur's.'

'I'm glad you can still joke.'

'I can laugh like Burt Lancaster this morning. The *Guardian* thinks David might have saved the Government. That's got to be good for investment.'

The plasterers exchanged glances. As for Judith, I might not have uttered for all the reaction she made.

'There's been a phone call for you. Gerson rang.'

'Where from?'

'How do I know? What is this Uncle Arthur shit?'

'He played the accordion and had a budgie called Peter.'

It took me nearly an hour to cross the river and get up into Knightsbridge. I inched along, thinking about all the people in their cars, and the idea that would grow on them, almost as if they had thought it for themselves, that poor bloody Nicholas and his hole in the head was worth a general election.

I found Judith in the shower, sitting in the tray, her head in her hands. I pulled her upright and hugged her. She waited until I was drenched and then switched off the water. I had this flash image of Dawn. Dawn, of course, would have had Judith on the Cambridge Diet within hours of meeting her. With Dawn as a chum, Judith would be too busy taking up squash to sit around in any shower moping. Fifty-quid haircut, air tickets to Miami, new bikini and sod the police.

'I'm scared,' Judith said, instead.

'Me too.'

'What have you got to be scared about?'

'You.'

Sometimes her expression was unequivocally baleful. She pushed past me and snatched up a towel.

'If you don't like it, go.'

'I'm thinking about that. Just working out the angles.'

She paused, the towel at her hair.

'What are you talking about?'

'The angles, Judith. Maybe you're home and dry. Maybe not.'

Her expression changed to something a bit more hesitant and uncertain.

'Rubbish,' she said.

But at breakfast she asked me again what I meant. I dunked a croissant in my coffee and managed to get it to my lips before it collapsed.

'The Government is sitting in a leaky boat. They're out on the lake, darkness is coming down and they are having to bail. They can see all the pretty lights there on the shore, but the boat is leaking.'

'What a load of crap.'

'You think so? At the moment, your pal David was shot by the IRA. They haven't said that, and I don't think they can ever bring charges, but that's what the public wants to think. Good. The whole thing could even be worth a snap election. But then, suppose Sonia has a sudden rush of honesty about

Wilma Curtess? Suppose Yanni is caught and starts talking? It all starts to come out – sex, conspiracy, murder. Who do you suppose would be a star witness?'

A thought occurred to me: how did Sonia know about Wilma? Maybe it was all round the kind of clubs she went to. Maybe that's how Ted Gerson knew. Maybe the very papers that were this morning sloshing whitewash over David Nicholas also knew. It was my day for flash images – I saw some smart-arse young freelance with gold wire specs sitting in front of a word processor in, say, Ladbroke Grove, saying to himself *yes, and I know too.*

'Now what's bugging you?' she asked.

'Somebody – more than one person – thinks David killed the black girl. I can't be certain, but I think he was under investigation on a possible charge of murder. Got it? Not rumour, not gossip. A criminal investigation. Two nights ago, he is shot dead. Think of it this way: in his hand is a string that leads back to you.'

'So what?'

'In his other hand,' I went on, 'is a second string that also leads back to you, via Yanni. Somehow or other, this bloke they're interested in also has a connection with the Greek of the Year. How about that?'

'But the police have questioned me and nothing has happened.'

'Isn't that great? And last night that's what I wanted to believe about it, too. But now – maybe, just maybe – the Prime Minister, who hasn't had a good press for a year or more, wishes to make more than a political martyr out of the pile of shit you once told me was your whole life. The plan is for his death and funeral to trigger an election. I won't trouble you with the concerns of the little people in this matter – let's just say that a lot of money is riding on the outcome.'

'I can't help that.'

'You ignorant, self-centred cow. The question is, whether you can hinder it. Getting a picture?'

She stared at me a long time.

'They'd shut me up?'

'How do I know what they have in store for you? But if it were me, I'd bury you a mile deep.'

I pushed away my coffee. She might not be too scared, but I had succeeded in terrifying myself. I needed a change of scenery. Judith sat chomping stolidly on a croissant, much as if I had already gone. The simplicity of her expression appalled me. It was as if she was sitting there thinking maybe I should buy the white dress, but then if I bought the white dress I would need the blue shoes, too, and not the red.

All Saints Church was little, green and mossy. It had a Norman doorway but was largely rebuilt in 1840 by one of Lydia's forebears. Here find interred, along with most of the folk from the big house, Abraham Ruckle, the blacksmith–poet who once drove Dr Johnson and his cronies to tears of despairing laughter. He lies close to Amy Liddle, Benefactress. Amy's father had been an Oakham brewer and left her possessed of a considerable fortune. She gave the whole lot away in the cause of reconciliation between Christian and Jew. She died, as her plaque testifies, regretted by all her friends. I passed on to more recent parish news. Mrs Hilda Shutt ran the Bible Study classes. Andy and Jenny Moat were at home on the first Thursday in every month to the One World Fellowship. Next meeting: Father Ignatius of Nicaragua by Mike Fenner of Grantham. Sukie Brownhill owned an italic fountain pen filled with green ink and would welcome a little help with the Tots' Club. The Vicar hoped that well-intentioned youngsters would not feed the goat, as its appetite for banana sandwiches, ha ha, was spoiling the purpose in keeping it, which was to control the churchyard grass.

The goat and I waited for Lydia in a pleasant mist of rain. Most of the wood pigeons in the East Midlands seemed to have gathered for a coo-in. The whole place was lovely. It led to a real hunger in me to live next door to the Fox and Hounds in a little two-room cottage, with perhaps an occasional invitation to the Moats' once in a while for quiche and plonk.

A green Volvo swept up in a fine hiss of tyres. The door opened. I walked down the tiled churchyard path and got in. We were moving before I could shut the door.

'I'm just going to drive anywhere, if that's all right,' Lydia Nicholas said. 'I need to drive. I need something to do. We can talk in the car. The bloody Press are hounding me to death. How are you?'

'I'm glad you're not too distraught to see me.'

She glanced at me. We drove slowly and with what must have been a habitual care, down empty roads now and then turned into dazzling rivers of silver when the fitful sun came out. Flat fields gave way every so often to fine stands of trees. Lydia obligingly pointed out the ownership of the bigger houses.

'The Mortons live there. It's really the lodge to Clive Seton-Flinders' house. He's a complete shit.'

We passed garages with gently flapping bunting and huge barns with wisps of straw in their walls. We passed through silent and empty villages, their church towers adorned with blue clock faces. She smoked as she drove, brushing away the smoke from her face with a brown arm decorated by a massive ivory bracelet. The first four buttons to her shirt were open.

'I suppose I ought to make it clear –'

'Oh, I know all about you,' Lydia said. 'I mean I know you had nothing to do with David being shot. The police really are intensely stupid people, don't you think? Do you know an officer called Gerson?'

'We used to play football together.'

'Really?' Lydia asked. 'I don't think he'd pick you for his team now. I can't tell you what he said about you.'

'I could never really cross a ball from the byline.'

She laughed.

'Are you screwing one of these girls David had? Not a lot of fun, I should think.'

We came upon a tractor ambling along, and it seemed the most natural thing in the world for Lydia to fall in behind it, despite the furious waving on she got from the cab.

'I hated David. I expect you know what that's like. It was as though there was nothing or nowhere he could not poison by his presence. We took contagion with us wherever we went. I used to watch him at dinner parties, or on television even. He always reminded me of those disguise kits we used to have as children – beards and false noses, silly plastic spectacles. The bug we carried about with us was insincerity. Do you understand what I'm saying?'

'He was dressing up.'

'He was trying to be someone else. He was altogether a very stupid man. You can have that as the wife's conviction or as something the daughter of an earl *would* say – take your pick. He was second rate. It explains so much about him.'

The tractor turned in at a farm gate and Lydia waved absent-mindedly as she passed. We resumed a thirty-mile-an-hour meander.

'So, as you see, I am hardly in mourning. You were clever to telephone. If I had known your number I would have done the same. You can tell me what all the fuss is about.'

'I think the principal fuss is that he's dead.'

'I should have thought you found favour with that.'

'The IRA killed him, apparently.'

'Pull the other one,' Lydia said.

'How much do you know about him – his predilections?'

'What a lovely word. Sex, you mean? It was his best disguise. He was really quite useless at it. There isn't that much to know. I got very ratty with his tarts from time to time. After the children were born we slept separately. He had problems. He was very frightened of women. I expect you realize.'

'Have you found time in your intense grief to speculate as to who might have killed him if it wasn't the IRA?'

'Oh, don't be dreary,' the widow said. 'What he was doing was incredibly dangerous. I did think at first it might have been you.'

'And the man who drove you back to London from Salisbury – what does he think?'

She glanced over again.

'He felt sure it was the Irish.'

We were coming to a village on a little lump of a hill. Lydia drew up outside the village shop. When she turned to me, her shirt gaped and I saw again her girlish breast. She tugged on the cotton with a faint smile on her face.

'Don't be a beast. I saw you today because I really can't bear to be hunted up hill and down dale by you. He was a complete bastard and I'm sorry if it affected your girlfriend. But it's all over now and that's that. There's nothing you can do. Be an angel, therefore, and call it quits.'

'Let sleeping dogs lie.'

'*I* always do. I'm going to get some cigarettes. Want anything?'

'No,' I said.

It occurred to me to check the route we had taken. I opened the glove compartment in search of a map or a gazetteer – and there, right under my nose, was a foolscap envelope. It was crisp and clean and straight from the writing desk at Perslade. By weight, I calculated there were inside three sheets of the sort of paper on which Napoleon signed peace treaties. The address was G. A. Theodopolous, c/o Minerva Island Tours, Athens. I got out of the car with the letter and waved it at her as she came out of the shop.

'Poor old Yanni's going to have to pay excess on this.'

She gave a short smile, snatched the envelope and posted it into a wall box.

'I don't know what you're talking about.'

'Yanni. The big guy who drove you across the Channel when you went to Florence. Great manners, fun for the kids and with those lovely liquid eyes. You remember Yanni.'

'The letter was to Giorgiou Theodopolous, or hadn't you noticed?'

'Pull the other one.'

She suddenly made a dash for it. It was a race for how quickly she could get into the driver's seat and I into the passenger's. Very startling to the old pensioner who came out of the shop and saw us. He stood there leaning on his stick in perfect English indecision as Lydia batted me about the face while the village clock struck the quarter hour. Her little finger poked me in the eye. I rocked forward and cracked my head on the angle of the door jamb and dashboard. She drove off, and the whiplash nearly broke my neck. It had all ended in tears after all. Mine were twice as real as hers. For a mile or so I thought I had been blinded.

The Salt Box was one of those pubs that seems to have strayed to the roadside from somewhere else. We sat in a drowsy room smelling of chips and vinegar. The landlord was sawing up chipboard in the yard outside. He was making a Wendy house for his grandchild. Sunlight struck through the grimy windows. She loaned me a handkerchief from her bag for my eye.

'Did he go all the way to Tuscany with you?'

'No.'

'But it was more than a brief shipboard romance on the ferry.'

'Why on earth should I answer? I mean, really! – you're nobody.'

'Indulge me.'

She was shaky. I was drinking pints to her vodkas. At the rate she drank I could be left for dead in the snug within the hour. The beer tasted of flooded graveyards. It was advertised on the pump by a picture of a merry fellow who could have been a child molester or indeed a grave robber. Lydia prised my puffed eye with strong little fingers. I felt her breath on my lips.

'All right,' she said. 'To begin with, I had no idea who he was. David told me – and I believed him – that he was a bodyguard, someone to do with the Anti-Terrorist Unit. We met him at Dover. He was very polite.'

'And when did you dump him?'

She flashed me a dirty look.

'I was intrigued by him. We put the car on the train in France. I was feeling fed up and flirty. We talked. He told me about his children. David was elated, high. Yanni ignored him completely. At Paris, when he left, I did too.'

'A whirlwind affair.'

'Whatever you say. I have friends there. I told David and the children I was staying with them. They're architects – we did actually go there for the first night. Yanni was doubly polite and attentive – they found him enchanting.'

'He speaks French?'

'And German.'

She stirred the ashtray with the stub of her cigarette.

'He had enormous self-possession. By now I knew he wasn't any damn policeman – so who was he? Next afternoon we took a hotel room and sat up drinking until four the next morning. I made a dead pass at him, but he wasn't interested. To my amazement, when I asked him who he was, he told me.'

'That he had robbed the security vaults. That he had blackmailed David into getting him out of the country.'

Lydia shrugged.

'What did he have to lose? Who could I tell?'

'Did he tell you how he had blackmailed David?'

I was thinking of Wilma, but she merely wrinkled her nose.

'I didn't ask. He just said he was in big trouble. That made sense. David *was* trouble.'

157

'So you sat up drinking.'

'We sat up drinking. Want to know the name of the hotel?'

'I want to know what you talked about.'

'Everything.'

'Give me an example.'

'Everything,' Lydia repeated. 'You're just dying to tell me he isn't the man I'm describing. Well you can go to hell. I liked him. I even liked him for being a robber. I wanted him to screw me. I wanted to swallow some of his strength and his ordinariness. I wanted to kneel on that damn carpet and eat him, like a religious meal. That give you a thrill?'

'You wanted to start the holiday with a bang.'

'Very funny.'

'You silly cow,' I found myself saying.

She was confused for a few moments and then the penny dropped.

'Oh God, not her,' she said. 'Of course. Oh God, how stupid!'

So, in some hotel room with peach stones behind the wardrobe and oily patches on the wallpaper above the pillows, Yanni talked to Lydia about Judith. Some triangle. David has a mistress with the beginnings of creases in her back and a pronounced belly and he has a wife who is slim and pert. Yanni knows them both. In his baggage is the three million he has lifted from the security vaults, plus a few snaps of the kids. Self-possession was a mild way of describing his state of mind.

'I should have realized,' Lydia said, with tears in her eyes. 'I should have guessed.'

'I don't see how you could. Come on, stop crying. It has its funny side, I suppose. What happened? Did he fly to Athens, promise to keep in touch?'

She put her head down and bellowed. It brought the landlord back in. He carried a sheet of marine ply with two square holes cut in it for windows. He wanted our opinion. He was for roofing the Wendy house with maybe a little chimney stack, but his son-in-law was anxious that Kylie would drag the whole bloody lot down and brain herself. Just as he didn't want proper windows for fear little K would trap her fingers.

'Salesman, see,' the landlord said obscurely, with half an eye to Lydia sobbing her heart out. 'Drives round with a bloody cellphone, thinks he's lord of all creation. Tells me he spends twenty quid just to get his hair cut.'

I drove the Volvo back to Perslade, Lydia slumped against the door, feeling the hit from mixing strong emotions and three double vodkas.

'God, how you must hate us,' she said.

'What was in the letter you posted?'

'I told him David had been shot of course, and asked him to write to me. That was all. I have to talk to someone about it. You can see that, surely?'

'Your parents?'

She put her face in her hands. I was trying to think. I could not be sure, but I was pretty certain she knew nothing about the Wilma Curtess angle. That would have been Gerson's first delicate enquiry. Had she known, I would not have got anywhere near her. At the very least, we would have been followed. They were not treating her as an accomplice to murder.

'Come on, Lydia, stop crying. I didn't come here to make you miserable.'

I slid the Volvo into a sandy lay-by. A huge grey wall marked what I suddenly realized was the park boundary of Perslade. I unbuckled my seat belt and hers. She fell forward into my arms like a dummy. I patted her on the back, waiting for someone to pass who could recognize the Volvo, and with the acumen to phone the papers.

'I know what's going to happen. You'll go away thinking that somehow Yanni and I fit together. That there's some plan, or conspiracy. It isn't true. I was lonely and unhappy and I showed him that. But he turned me down. He doesn't need women. Apparently.'

'Has he written to you at all?'

'Not once.'

'But you have written to him.'

'Care of this Minerva Tours place. It's called acting out. I wrote pages and pages every day we were in Tuscany. But I know I'll never see him again. I was snatching at straws.'

'Have you checked the address to see if it's real?'

Her throat reddened. What did that mean – that she was too much in love with the great chump to question his honesty; or that she was deflecting a question from a vexatious stranger? Three million of untaxable loot is a lot of money. Did Yanni blow her a kiss before leaving and set out with his new passport for other climes? Or did the sentimental fool actually set off for Athens, via the undemanding airport of Thessaloniki; and out of the kindness of his heart suggest she write to him begging for what he could not offer? Was he sitting in some café staring distractedly at the letters? A gloomy thought occurred to me. As a man who knew security vaults, he might have taken a box in the commercial quarter and be quietly relishing the reinsurance David's wife had provided him with.

On the other side of the road to the car was a conifer plantation. We climbed a gate festooned with brooms of hazel twigs and jumped down into a fire lane. On either side the trees stood packed and sombre behind shallow ditches. We walked down a carpet of spindly wild daisies for a few hundred yards. Lydia snuffled and snorted, wiping her tears away with the back of her hand.

'I realize in all this that I don't know a damn thing about men.'

'Be grateful, therefore.'

'Well who are you, for example? Where do you come from?'

Trying to explain about Uncle Arthur would take too long. And in any case, the question really meant how dangerous are you? To that, I had no clear idea. I felt about as dangerous as a raspberry cane on an Oldham allotment. In a curious gesture, she had stooped to pick a posy of the daisies. The rain of recent days had battered them. Few had their full complement of petals. She held them to her face. They were scentless.

'Are you doing this for money?' she asked.

'I haven't seen any yet. In my part of the woods there isn't any. All we have is our gratitude to the greatest Prime Minister of the century.'

'I hate that sort of talk.'

'I bet.'

It was wet underfoot, and tiny pearls of rain-water clung to her legs, as high as the knee. The trail we had made through the daisies was a meandering double line of green. Lydia shrugged.

'We have pots of money. My father takes a perverse pleasure in selling off the best pictures and plate. You should see our place sometime. Most of the principal rooms are empty. The children skateboard in the dining-room. It used to drive David crazy, of course. It was the only real wickedness he understood – the rich abandoning their own privilege. I think he saw us living at Perslade, after my father died, and re-establishing the aristocratic virtues.'

'Not much of an economist, was he?'

'You mean it will all come crashing down round our heads long before that? Yes, maybe. But he wasn't a dreamer. He was a butcher. The world was there to be slaughtered and eaten. I don't know what your Judith got from him, but that was the sole attraction to me.'

'She was meat,' I said, bleak. 'Remember?'

She threw away her posy of flowers and wiped her hands on her jeans. We had reached the gate. In turning to speak to me her breast brushed softly against my arm. She was standing, as if by accident, inside my own arrested stride.

'Then are you doing this for love?'

A car passed on the road outside. I tried to answer the question without letting my face betray what was there in my

161

heart. Lydia stood on tiptoe suddenly and brushed her lips against my cheek.

'You don't have to tell me. I was scared of you before. And now I'm sorry to have hurt you. You probably understand more about love than I ever will. Thank you for coming.'

Which was our signal for parting. She walked to the Volvo and I set off down the road in what I hoped was the direction of the church, where the Renault was parked. I walked with my hands in my pockets, wondering whether to get drunk or buy petrol. The Volvo slowed as it passed me.

'At least let me have your telephone number,' Lydia called, and took it, before driving off again at a sedate pace. The car disappeared round a bend in the road. When I reached the same point, I expected to see the outlying buildings of Perslade village, but there stretched instead over a mile of grey stone wall. To please the restless shade of Uncle Arthur, I whistled 'Tipperary' as I tramped along the country road.

15

The phone was ringing when I got back to the flat.

'Can you talk?' Gerson asked.

'She isn't here. I've just got in. I was supposed to ring you back this morning.'

'Yeah,' he said. There was a long pause. I could hear a typewriter clacking in the background. He wasn't calling from his own office. I tried to imagine the location. The typewriter stopped and started up again. I waited.

'So. What do you make of things?'

'Me? You're asking *me*?'

'Have you talked to the accountant?'

'We've met, but not today, no. What is this, Ted?'

'I think you should get out.'

'Where are you speaking from?' I asked cautiously.

'From work, of course. Look, you think I've come down on you too hard. I talked to the missus about it last night – the whole story. She sends her love by the way. She says it's nothing to do with us.'

'What isn't?' I asked stupidly. I heard him say, 'Yeah, I'll be right there, Gerry, tell 'em I'm on my way,' to someone passing through the office.

'Sandra says we should leave it be. You know how it is with the two of us – I trust her judgement. You remember that much about us.'

My hands were shaking. The last time I saw Sandra, the bones in her wrists and ankles were barely functioning and she

163

weighed less than eight stone. That he should seek his wife's advice and then ring me to pass it on was scary.

'Look,' Ted said, 'I won't beat about the bush. There is more to this than either of us have cottoned on to. Christ knows why you're still in. But do yourself a favour –'

He broke off suddenly for a few seconds. When he came back his voice had resumed its official rasp.

'Get back to you,' he said.

Her kettle was cold. She had the habit of piling the dishes into a washing-up bowl and leaving them to soak. I did the plates slowly and thoughtfully, wondering where she was, and what she was doing. The flat seemed exceptionally dead and airless. Ted Gerson's call had done nothing to restore a sense of ease – not that I'd experienced one for a while. I thought of Sandra and her arthritic joints, listening to her husband's rumbling account and monitoring his face with those bright, intelligent eyes. Whatever she had said at the end of his recital had made a deep impression on him. There was an obvious reason: I could not imagine two women more poles apart than Sandra Gerson and Judith.

I looked in the fridge for something to cook and then gave up, too troubled to concentrate on the task. If Ted had rung to say he was thinking of coming out and wearing the skirt and blouse he had always secretly coveted, he could not have surprised me more. Sandra: Judith. The rose garden: this stuffy flat with its overelaborated calm. Just about now Sandra would be watching the clock, wondering whether her Ted was coming home for a meal or not. And here was I, looking down the street from an upstairs window, waiting for Judith.

Waxman was surprised to see me. He sat at his dining-room table with a stack of files and papers, headphones crammed over his ears, hammering furiously on an old-fashioned calculator with one spidery hand. Leah admitted me with friendly curiosity, but excused herself immediately. She was watching a television programme about things that creep and crawl in the Mojave Desert. Waxman shook his head. He switched off his Walkman.

'A woman from Finchley with an aversion to grass, even. Lawns, she's afraid of. But show her somebody else's wildlife, it's like opera to her. Snakes, the funnel-web spider, jellyfish that can kill just by brushing against your skin. Leah's your expert.'

He put down his pen and scooted to the drinks. His wheel-chair made an unpleasant squelching noise on the carpet. He looked tired and uneasy. The flat smelled strongly of cooking.

'You two are serious, you and Judith?'

'Accomplices.'

'Tell me something I can understand.'

'Pals.'

'That's nice to know,' he said, managing to suggest the exact opposite. 'Have you heard any more about David Nicholas?'

'Have *I* heard?'

'Don't you have contacts? You were a detective weren't you? What, it's a secret? I'm her pal too, you know.'

We drank in silence for a while. Leah Waxman came back in, deliciously shaken by pictures of the sidewinder in action. She told me about the order of venom in snakes. The gist of it was that all snakes are bastards. Only in Ireland and New Zealand were there none to worry about.

'Two great places to live,' Waxman scoffed.

'I never want to go anywhere where there are snakes.'

'You go to Nevada,' I pointed out.

She glanced quickly at her husband. There was something odd in her reaction, but his was extreme. Waxman waved his hands about in front of his face, as if swatting flies. A vein in his temple throbbed.

165

'What are you looking at me for?' he shouted. 'You *do*. You go to Nevada. Las Vegas is in Nevada. Nevada has snakes. Talk to the man. Be natural.'

Leah winced. He poured two more whiskies. She hesitated by the drinks cabinet and decided not to join in. She excused herself a second time.

'I'm living in Nutwood Common,' Waxman wailed. 'I married Rupert Bear's mother. She's like this all the time. A dreamer, I married!'

'How did you meet?'

'What, this is your polite? You want to show me manners now? If you really want to know, I was at school with her brother.'

'The one who lives in Nevada,' I said, trying to be helpful.

Waxman ground his teeth.

I managed to steal a peek at the accounts spread out on the table. He was doing the books for Plantation Records, registered address Effra Parade, Brixton. If they were a stall on the market, they were doing a bomb. If they were recording, they had Whitney Houston under secret contract. Waxman watched me carefully.

'Plantation have their own label?'

'A label! What's a label? Anybody can have their own label. It's just another bugsmeat outfit.'

'But doing great.'

'What are you, Fraud Squad? My end of it is the books. It's just a way of paying the rent. Understand what I'm saying?'

'Do you specialize in showbiz accounts?'

Waxman squinted at me with a mixture of blind rage and acutely visioned caution, as might someone who has opened a biscuit barrel and discovered a newly awakened sidewinder where before there were innocent ginger-nuts.

'You're a funny man.'

'How about Judith? How much is she worth?'

'*Big* gags!' he exclaimed. 'I thought you and the lady were partners.'

166

'But not financial partners.'

'I don't know what you're trying to say, but it smells like something on your heel. I keep her tax straight. It's a neighbourly thing to do. I would do it for you, theoretically anyway. I like her. We get along.'

'How long have you lived here, Gedder?'

'My name is Gerald,' he snapped.

'Five years, ten years?'

'Fourteen years. Happy about that?'

'So you saw the new tenant move in. Nodded to her for a year, then found out her first name. Struck up a friendship.'

He affected to be perplexed by the question.

'So?'

So, indeed! How the hell did I know what it meant?

On the nine o'clock news, the BBC's political correspondent was asked directly by the anchorman of the show whether the Prime Minister was considering a snap election. He hesitated with his usual scruple for honesty before saying that certainly some back-bench MPs were floating such an idea. But the Prime Minister was a very tough customer, etcetera, with the declared aim of seeing the life of this Parliament out to the very end. I learned that David Nicholas's funeral would be held in the church at Perslade. For security reasons, as much as to honour the wishes of the family, the Prime Minister was unlikely to attend. There was a short clip of Lydia receiving flowers and telegrams at the door to Perslade itself. There was nothing in her demeanour to suggest to even the most lubricious viewer that she had recently or indeed ever rolled around in a Paris hotel with a Greek security guard. In fact, Lydia looked what my mother would have called a well set-up woman.

The older I've got, the more I've realized that the rubbish my parents spoke on most public issues and which pained me so much as a child was not incoherent venom, but a reflection of common opinion. Thus – on politicians and governments –

167

they're all in it for what they can get. The rise and fall of political fortune was a song without words for them, or more accurately, television with the sound turned down. But they lived long enough to see their dearest and most incoherent dream come true – a British government declaring blitzkrieg not just on the poor, the black, the people who live in council houses and keep Alsatians, but also on the stuck-up toffee-nose gits of teachers, the smarmy-arse doctors and nurses, middle-class know-all leftie twats with beards and anoraks moaning on about the bloody whale, hooligan young people, poofs, car workers, mine workers . . . and on a broader canvas the krauts, yanks, wops, wogs, chinks and darkies that infest the world and steal our oxygen and ozone and all that. If the murder of David Nicholas could save the Government, it would save it for the likes of my parents and their habitual lowering stare of suspicion; who did not in the least mind being thought of as the salt of the earth, and repaid the Government now rolling to a halt with the loyalty they had previously reserved exclusively for Royalty.

Interesting, but not worth writing to BBC Television News about. I sat with a bottle of Sauvignon, trying to work out a simpler issue of the hour – whether my relationship with Judith had deteriorated to the point where I could search the flat without feeling guilty. In fact I felt jumpy. Nothing in the news was reassuring. I tried to calculate the number of people known to me who would have to be shut up if the Prime Minister were to hold an election on the law and order issue.

The damn flat was just waiting to be turned over. Ted would have done it. I lit a floor lamp and read for a while from a book of essays by the son of Kingsley Amis. He had discovered the possibility of the imminent end of the world, something which had lain shrouded in religious dust and scientific obscurantism until he put his mind to it.

I could search the flat and, if I found anything, shop her. That way – and the thought petered out. I drank the rest of the bottle. All this drinking and pondering had given me a sledgehammer headache. What's more, I had killed the desire to eat. I cleaned my teeth a little unsteadily, thought about a shower and then collapsed on the bed, a defeated man of action.

She wasn't coming home tonight. Why didn't I turn the place over? It was quiet enough to hear dust fall. Gerson would have had the entire contents of Judith's gaff bagged and labelled by now. For a while I had stood in the kitchen and watched the young girl in the window opposite. This was a sure sign of something, surely? As Judith had pointed out, what seemed like weeks and not days ago, I was a spectator. When Miss in the softly lit room opposite trod her jeans to the ground and pulled her sweater over her head, I turned away in shame.

At one the phone beside the bed rang and I snatched it up, trailing wisps of a dream about sea spray and daisies.

'Judith?'

It was Sonia Kyriakides.

'Who is this?' she asked cautiously.

'The man who fixed your kitchen tap.'

'You! What the hell are you doing there?'

'Every job is different.'

'Such a comedian,' Sonia laughed doubtfully.

'What's that music in the background?'

'I'm phoning from a club. Come over and have a drink. Ricardo's, just off Cambridge Circus.'

'Judith isn't here,' I said. 'Can I take a message?'

She said something to another person and then put the phone down on the bar. The music was very Sonia. Tina Turner was giving it the works. Voices were raised. There was a scrabbling sound as she picked up the phone again.

'I'm going to be here until about two. Why don't you –'

The phone was taken from her.

'Where is she?' a Caribbean voice asked. 'Come on, white

169

trash, don't mess with me. This is the biz. You tell her she get her arse over here. That mean now.'

'The biz?' I asked, bemused. 'People are still saying the biz?'

There was a pause while he cupped his hand over the receiver and (presumably) asked Sonia who the hell he had on the line here. Her reply must have been far too tentative.

'I'm sending a car for you,' the voice promised. 'You're special.'

'And up yours.'

The line went dead.

I jumped up and, after some deliberation, decided against a kitchen knife and in favour of the bathroom towel-rail. I sprang it out of its plastic fittings. It was metal, all right, but too long, too light and too shiny. But it was something. I lit the lamps in the sitting-room and then crept downstairs. The air in the street was quite chill. The parked cars glistened with dew. I ran my hand over the roof of one and wetted my face. My hand trembled. When they said they were coming, I believed them. I found a pitch next to an industrial size refuse bin and stood in its shadow. I felt a bit foolish with the chrome towel-rail and laid it gingerly between my feet.

A quarter of an hour later, the car arrived, a quiet and unassuming Merc not much larger than a badminton court. The driver stayed put, but his passenger came out with lazy arrogance. He was black, he was in a dinner-jacket, and one glance told me his occupation was bouncing. The whole point of my standing there with the absurd protection of a two-foot length of towel-rail was to see how he made a lunge for someone who he must suppose to be three locked doors away.

He took a key-ring from the pocket of his trousers and let himself in.

I watched, feeling sick. After a minute or two, chummy twitched the curtains to Judith's flat and looked out. Another three minutes, and Waxman's lights went on. I put the foolish chrome bar into the dustbin. After five minutes, the black bouncer came out. He lit a cigarette, looking up and down the street. The Merc rolled gently up. Bouncer got in and they drove away. I fished around in the cartons and sheafed paper for her damn towel-rail, gave up, and went back to the flat. I was shaking so hard I could not think what to do first. Even when I had calmed down, I could not think what to do next. For pleasure, if pleasure were needed, I would have trashed the whole damn place.

She kept her telephone directories crammed in a shelf of junk mail below the phone itself. There were details of French properties, up-market mail order catalogues, time-share offers. And, nestling between the British Telecom volumes, a small Silvine notebook with a selection of personally important numbers. I read them over carefully. There were a couple of Americans – I recognized the New York area code. In different inks and pencils, scribbled down higgledy-piggledy, were a mass of London numbers, together with box doodles, artichoke doodles, palm trees, flagstaffs, drop shadow letters and forgotten reminders like 'Tax' or 'D/Glazing'. A few of the London numbers had names to them – Derek, Paul, Elliot, Salamon. I rang Salamon and got reception at the Grosvenor House Hotel. I glanced at my watch. It was coming up to two in the morning. I looked up the second American dial-code and bingo. Vegas! Someone answered after only five trills.

'Harry?'

'This is Ralph.'

'Okay. I'm phoning from England. Put me on to Harry. It's important.'

There were a few seconds of unpromising silence.

'Harry who?'

Harry. Leah's Harry. How was I supposed to know Harry's second name?

'You gonna answer my question?'

'Harry the stage designer.'

It upset Ralph.

'What is this? You got shit for brains? You're some kind of faggot, or what?'

'Don't run me around, Ralph.'

'You,' Ralph said, signing off with wince-making severity, 'can go fuck yourself, buddy.'

I was pouring a large Grouse when the doorbell rang. I opened cautiously. Standing in the hall was Leah Waxman.

She was wearing a wool dressing-gown over a light blue nightie and had been torn from sleep. Her feet were stuffed into joke slippers, showing Mickey in black and white felt. He peeped out from under the hem of her gown, looking not less apologetic and uncertain than she.

'Gerald wants you to come down.'

'No kidding.'

She reached out and touched my sleeve.

'Be careful. You're probably much cleverer than I am and understand it all, but be careful.'

'Know anyone called Ralph in Las Vegas, Leah?'

She looked at me in complete innocence.

'Ralph?'

'Never mind. What's your brother's surname?'

'His professional name? Hartsilver. But he's nothing to do with it.'

'With what?'

She flapped her hands about, the loyal little sister.

'Whatever it is. I don't know what it is.'

Waxman was also in his night attire – dark blue pyjamas with white piping. The vein in his temple throbbed painfully. Like me, he had steadied himself up with a huge belt of Scotch.

'You are the dumbest man I ever met,' he said at once. Leah actually made a little whimper, like a scolded dog.

'Keep your voice down, for goodness' sake.'

He pointed a finger at her.

'This man is trouble for you and me. Don't tell me to keep my voice down. Go into the bedroom. Put the pillow over your head.'

When she had done this, or some part of it, he squeaked his wheelchair to the mock fireplace and indicated I should sit. He swigged greedily at his tumbler of Scotch. The fear of God must look much the same as Waxman's expression.

'Have you any idea what you are doing?'

'I don't move in accountancy circles the way you do. So tell me.'

'Believe me, if I thought that was funny, I would laugh. My hand to God.'

'Who cut the keys for them? Come on, the guy got in as if he lives here. How did he get the keys?'

'Okay,' Waxman said. 'I give you a name. Frank Givens.'

'Another brother-in-law.'

He came close to gnashing his teeth.

'Givens! Frank *Givens*. Don't joke. Do you want to get yourself killed?'

'He's not your brother-in-law?'

'You dumb bastard. He is well-wicked Frank Givens. He runs things, understand what I'm saying? He is the real thing.'

'And you do his books. Two bigshots. Now I get it.'

Waxman stared at me with a fully fashioned loathing and contempt.

'You should talk to someone. You have a real attitude problem. See those accounts on the table? Plantation Records? Givens owns it. He has two clubs, houses, a hotel in Marbella – not a guesthouse, a *hotel* – he has thirty per cent of the WBC Middleweight Champion, for Christ's sake. He owns a damn island in the Florida Keys. This is police racism you're giving me. Should he be standing in Ladbroke's, betting in coins?'

'How did he get the keys to Judith's flat?'

'How do you think?' Waxman asked bitterly. 'Get it through your head. The man is somebody. I can't think of anyone he couldn't reach.'

'How about reaching Nicholas two nights ago?'

He goggled. He made frantic patting motions in the air, as if he were trying to quell me in a crowded restaurant.

173

'For God's sake! I don't want to hear this! I live under a stone and keep my mouth shut. I don't have ambitions. I have a wife and a wheelchair. I have eyes I want to keep.'

'How did he get the keys?'

'What difference does it make?'

'A little, Gerald. Some black nobody you met in Notting Hill sends his bouncer round here, who lets himself in, comes to you and puts the wind of heaven up your arse. You call me down because the boy has something to tell me the boss has told him to say. So go ahead, tell me.'

'You poor bastard,' Waxman said, close to ecstasy. 'You haven't understood a word I've been saying. She told you about Wilma Curtess, or you found out? I hope you found out. Otherwise you're going to get snuffed for nothing, for being funny. Givens did not like what happened to Wilma, to Billie. They have witnesses who will swear to it being Nicholas. You got that? They can prove Nicholas killed the black kid. Can the police do that?'

'The message,' I demanded. He wiped his lips with the back of his hand.

'You ignorant know-nothing bastard. They are going to do you. Both of you.'

'For what?'

'Her for being Nicholas's whore. You for poking your nose in.'

'Bullshit. Nicholas is dead. Unless they did it, the story's over.'

I was watching him carefully. There were bright rinds of tears in his eyes.

'Maybe they did do it.'

'You don't really believe that. Now listen to me. You wouldn't figure in any of this if someone Givens knew, or Givens himself – damn it, *listen* to me, Gerald – if it were just a case of murder. You know what I'm saying. It's something else. You'd better say what.'

He put his head in his hands and appeared to be washing his face.

'I can't.'

'Yes, you can.'

'I'm a bookkeeper,' he sobbed. 'I don't want to die. These people are serious.'

'What people? You give me some name, the name of some nonce, who may or may not own a club off Cambridge Circus, and the bits: suddenly we're talking a syndicate.'

He lifted his head.

'They walked into her flat with their own keys. Doesn't that tell you something?'

'What? That you and Judith may have seen the word truth written down but have no idea what it means? Yes.'

He scooted his wheelchair to a locked drawer in the writing bureau and withdrew a couple of unmarked video cassettes.

'Enjoy,' he said.

Her hair was longer and in an outmoded style. Her breasts were firmer and higher and she looked younger, but not by much. There were other girls and three black men, none of them conceivably Givens himself. The videos had no plot and though they were shot professionally, looked uncertain; or perhaps uneasy was a better word. Maybe the cameraman had scruples. Judith was quite clearly out of her brains on something and hardly able to keep her eyes open. Like the film itself, she dived in and out of focus. Like real life, she got the worst that was going. When the camera lingered on her, sprawled, bloodied and choking, I switched off.

It was a possible but unlikely explanation of how she came to be at home to Mr Rude whenever he felt like calling. But I had the certain feeling that Waxman was trying to run me around. I prised open the cassettes with a pair of kitchen scissors and tore out the half-inch tape. I cut it up randomly and rolled it in a *Guardian* before dumping it in her swing-bin.

If I was crying, it was not all from sorrow. Some of it was rage, vexation. Her deceit, her amorality, was bottomless.

If Givens had these tapes, and if he knew of the connection one of the girls had to Nicholas, his capacity to blackmail the smarmy-haired bastard until his sweat was blood predated Yanni's by several years. But he hadn't, or there was no sign that he had. So something else was going down. I wondered whether I had it in me to strike and terrorize a man in a wheel-chair.

I went into her bedroom with a cup of black coffee and took the drawers from the chest. They contained nothing but her clothes – knickers, bras, sweaters, shirts. A white bikini. Pink and grey check shorts. The fitted wardrobe held only one surprise – a tennis racket. The grip was still sheathed: she had never swung it. Her shoes smelled faintly of sweat. Half a dozen bags and satchels were empty save for the odd coin and discarded lipstick.

Searching premises is an art. It can be done with persever-ance, the way Sunday painters more or less depict what they see. But to look for something in someone else's possessions is a matter of intuition. Lovers do it least well of all. I found a few things I would rather not have discovered – a blood-stained belt, a magazine of men ejaculating over the hapless faces of stupid-looking girls who an hour earlier had been sitting next to someone like you on the Tube. A jocular letter from her father, written on lined paper, dated 1987, to say here he was again in sunny Bournemouth and the old place was just as frisky as ever if you knew where to look. The Lady with the Dog was on for it as per usual. He had signed himself Your Everloving Dad with a casual slash of an exclamation mark, followed by a coy question mark.

She had nine hundred in her current account, and a further eighteen thousand in saver accounts and building societies. The flat was hers, not David's, secured by mortgage repay-ments of two hundred and eighty a month. She made covenanted gifts to War on Want and Save the Children. There were neat files for her doctor, dentist, garage, rates, gas and electricity.

What there wasn't was her passport.

The doorphone rang. I snatched up the kitchen scissors and answered it far too loudly.

'Get your cigs and get your arse down here,' an unmistakable voice said. 'And don't hang about, kid. This is serious.'

16

The most terrible thing about it was that I knew the hospital. It wasn't the one to which I'd been admitted after my kicking: I knew it from long before that as a place to sit in, bored and weary to the bone, helmet on knee, waiting to take statements from drunks and their victims. By knife, by fist, by boot and car, the innocent and wicked alike came through here, some to go home after stitches, some to lie for weeks in coma. Some never to go home again.

'She's off the thirty-minute obs,' Ted murmured. 'The X-rays are all good. Her skull's okay, there are no lesions. She's going to pull through. No permanent damage.'

We were in a side ward of women's surgical, filled with unwanted medical equipment – trolleys, drip stands, folded wheelchairs, gas cylinders. Ted perched his massive weight and presence, his calm and authority, against the wash-basin. I could hear the fixtures creaking. His arms were folded against his chest – he seemed carved from Easter Island rock. I was the one who felt light as a feather, helpless as a mote of dust. Judith lay in the centre of the room, grunting through hugely swollen lips. She was placed on a traction bed with steel side-pieces to prevent her turning her head. Her naked arms were outside the single sheet covering her; a drip ran into the crook of her left elbow, secured by a little tab of plaster. Above it were the dark blue marks of someone's fingers, someone not so loving and caring as had been the nurse in placing the drip. The light that streamed in on us from the fourth floor window was refracted by the tucks and folds of the bag above her head and its chrome stand. This light suggested crisp purity, collusion with the hospital authorities, as if it were itself an adjunct of treatment. But though it danced and winked, snicked this way and that, it could not ameliorate the presence there on the bed of bruised and tortured flesh. Judith – unconscious, away, gone, out to lunch – whistled softly through the spit that ran from the corners of her mouth. There was a faint foetid smell in the room, a horrible sweetness that came from her. Not caring what Gerson thought, I knelt on the floor and put my lips to her splinted fingers, sobbing. At long last, someone had beaten her up for real.

He took me across the road from the hospital to a pub hidden in the shrubs and lawns of a neighbouring estate. It was one of those pubs built not as a rest for travellers, but merely to keep the residents pacified. It was as if even at the drawing-board stage, back in the sixties, some prescient bastard knew that the poor devils doomed to live there would one day go mad without a place to lose themselves. And that's all it was now – a dour and dingy Oblivion Arms, serving a community with its full share of new cars and satellite dishes, but otherwise representative of the undead. Nicholas and his Cabinet cronies affected to serve and cherish such people. They returned the solid vote on which everything depended. Its strength and solidity sprang from an uncritical, sleep-walking naïvety. Their role on earth was to treat life as a restaurant, consume as much as they could and leave without paying the bill. For that, the Government called them heroes. Political philosophy had been remodelled to accord with their unshakeable view that someone else, somewhere else, was to blame for the rotten things in life. That was the political triumph of the age. The enemy within was anybody the people of this estate, and hundreds more like it, had reason to fear. The trick of it was giving voice to the voiceless.

179

Meanwhile, here and now, the lawns were ripped up and scabbed, the borders filled with cans and crisp packets, you could smell the beer and chip fat wafting from the bars and lounges. A promotional banner for an Australian lager hung forlorn from the mockery of a Tudor gable. Ted took my elbow and steered me to a broken plastic seat. The back had been ripped clean off, leaving a jagged white edge.

'Sit down,' he said. 'She isn't going to die. Just sit and smoke a cigarette and get a hold of yourself. I'll fetch some drinks.'

And if this sounds fanciful it is all the same true: the only other occupants of the garden at that moment were a boy with the sleeves torn out of his tee-shirt and his girl. They were flat out in the dirt, screwing through their clothes. His ghetto-blaster was doing the max, with the max distortion. His backside rose and fell to the beat of the moog. And I wanted to get out of my ruined chair and use its rusting legs to beat these two kids, smash the whole place to bits. In that five minutes or so of rage after coming away from Judith, if there had been a destruct button to hand I would have sent the whole world up. I had many times arrested people with the same manic intent in their eyes, reeling about in the forecourt to railway stations, or wading up the busy shoppers' arcades. They had been shouting aloud what I felt inside me now: that reality was a sudden bony finger poked through this whole tissue of lies and deceits, dreams and nightmares. In my time I had floored such soothsayers with a joyous hatred of their arrogance. I had arm-locked them until the joints squeaked.

Ted ambled out of the pub, glasses pinched up in his rose-grower's fingers. I tried to think of a way of hating him, too: but he was the antidote. My scowl simply bounced off him. He glanced at the figures writhing on the lawn and putting the glasses down on the table, walked up to them. He picked the boy up by the belt of his jeans and the collar of his shirt. The lad thrashed about, howling thickly.

'You looking for trouble, pal?'

'Yes,' Ted said. 'How about you?'

The girl lay with her blouse wide open, staring at me with a hatred I had just a moment ago reserved for her. She pulled her dusty black skirt down as far as it would reach and dragged the wings of her blouse together.

'I'm gonna deck you,' the boy promised Ted. 'You're gonna hurt right now, fatso.'

But instead, he flew back, as if on elastic ropes, and fell into a raggy bush. The girl scrabbled to her feet, looking for her shoes. Ted picked up the ghetto-blaster and switched it off. He held it out politely.

'I want you to go somewhere else,' he said. 'That's not too much trouble to ask of you, is it? Just to please me?'

'He's *fifty*, Gaz,' the girl said. But then she wasn't the one who was going to have to do the business. Gaz picked himself out of the border. He cursed and spat. The girl snatched the radio-cassette. There seemed a moment's ray of hope for them both when a man my age came out of the pub and stared. Ted lifted his eyebrows in enquiry. The man went back inside.

'Moron,' the kid shouted. 'Animal. You better not be here in five minutes.'

'Bye-bye,' Ted said gently. 'Mind how you go.'

They left. Ted shrugged and sat down.

'What a dump. What a shit-heap.'

I had to get a grip on myself. I had to fight back the sense of having been blinded and deafened. He was a god, a colossus. I was just the shit on someone's shoe. He passed me the Scotch.

'Remember the Wellington? I took you there once – big yellow-brick place near us. No pool table, no quiz machines, no music. And of course, no customers. The landlord's a sweetpea man. Prizes and so forth. I drink there, most nights. You don't get any of this.'

'What happened to her, Ted?'

'We don't know.'

'Where did it happen?'

'She had a key to the house in her bag.'

'What house?'

He stared.

'Didn't I say? She was found outside your mate Hilary's. The door was open and so it's likely she had gone inside. She got a good hiding from someone who knew what he was doing.'

'Where was Hilary?'

'You tell me.'

'He wasn't there?'

I tried to understand, but I could not get my mind into gear at all. He was watching me with sympathy, but there was also in his expression a reserve of something else. I licked my lips and tried to concentrate.

'She was surprised by someone in the house?'

He hesitated.

'Maybe. Maybe not.'

'Come on, Ted. You don't like her – but I have to know if she was ambushed. Or followed there. I have to know if it was planned.'

'All you're doing now is telling me that you're going it alone again. That's bad policy. In fact it's crazy. I can't help you if you won't help me. Who would ambush her? Who would follow her? And where from? From Knightsbridge? Tell me something that makes sense.'

I avoided his glance and sat staring at the huge pink funnels of a mallow near by. The mower whined on indefatigably in the neighbouring gardens. I was mentally drained.

'I'm not going it alone to be a hero,' I havered. 'Nobody else can be bothered with her. She's over there in that hospital and nobody in the world gives a toss. Except me.'

'And whoever put her there,' he suggested.

I was trying to calculate: did he know of Ricardo's and the Givens connection? Was he just playing me on a loose line, waiting for me to say something (what for God's sake?) that would add another pebble to the cairn he had already built?

'All right, then. Say she was knocked about by someone in her line of business. As a punishment, I mean.'

'Like a pimp.'

'A pimp, maybe, yes.'

'Does she have a pimp? And what's she being punished for?'

If he had cards, he was not showing them. He pulled out his pipe and tobacco.

'She was well alibied for the time of Nicholas's death. So were you. It would be very nice, very neat, if you just dropped out of it, the two of you. But you keep popping up.'

'Was she surprised by someone in the house, someone she didn't expect to meet?'

'Maybe,' he said, with elaborate care. 'How do you read it?'

I knew what he was thinking. She was naked when she was found, except for the brassiere round her neck and a shoe. When people are surprised by someone else in the act of burgling a house, they either run for it, or deliver one wild swipe and *then* go. They don't fight you to the ground, tear the clothes off your back and beat the living shit out of you. I saw him waiting for my question.

'Was she sexually assaulted?' I asked.

'I'm afraid so.'

'One person? More than one?'

'Come on,' Ted said, with a faint sign of disgust.

'And how do you come into it?'

'She was found this morning at half-past five. Some bright young coppers in a patrol car.'

'Who just happened along. I lived there for two months, remember. I never saw a patrol in all that time.'

'Your old mob down here wanted to talk to Hilary,' Ted murmured.

'At half-past five in the morning?'

There were wasps in the garden and one landed on his shirt.

He let it crawl without attempting to bat it. His smile was non-committal.

'They'd been looking for him. I think they hoped to find him in. They found the girl instead. She wasn't there at eight last night. She was at five-thirty this morning.'

The wasp crawled round the collar of his shirt. He lit his pipe and tossed the match away.

'What was she doing there?' he asked.

'I don't know.'

'She had the key to the place. The door was open. Say she let herself in. Did she know Hilary had flitted?'

'I don't know. Has he flitted?'

'I just hope you're as innocent as you seem,' he said. 'I don't like this end of it. I don't like it at all.'

'Well that's great to know.'

'I talked to the doctors,' he said to his shoes. 'She had semen in her mouth and hair. She's been badly torn, down below. She wasn't set on by someone in a funk. I think she was followed there. I don't have to tell you all this, remember. It isn't my enquiry. But somebody with a sick mind did her over. It's best you understand that. Somebody got a thrill out of what they did to her. It was more than a beating.'

The whisky rose up to scorch my throat. I left him to walk into the pub. Half a dozen baleful glances followed me to the gents. I was a stranger, not any more welcome to them than a passing Hottentot or Eskimo. They drank in the worst pub in Christendom and I had discovered them in their misery. The barmaid sat on a stool, her head in her hands, waiting for last orders. Inside the gents, I leaned over the filthy sink and threw up Leah Waxman's breakfast. The hot-air dryer hung off the wall. I pulled it all the way clear and kicked it into the urinals. Shaken by sobs, I wiped my mouth on a sheet of toilet paper. When I got back to the garden, Ted was smoking peaceably.

'Why should anyone want to do it to her?'

'What is that, a rhetorical question?' he asked. 'I don't know her as well as you do, remember.'

'But you've a file an inch thick on her, you bastard. So don't get smart.'

'Nobody I know,' he admitted, after a pause.

He stood, hitching his pants.

'Back to town?'

'I can catch a train. I need to think.'

'To *think*?' His voice had a sudden edge of incredulity. 'How much more has to happen to you? You need to talk.'

'What can I talk about? I don't know who did it. If I did, I wouldn't tell you. When I find him, I'll cripple him.'

'You're not seeing straight, friend.'

'I asked you last time we met if she was out of the woods.'

'Did I answer then?' he asked simply. 'Would I be daft enough to say yes now?'

I had this sudden perception of what I had lost by falling out of the system. For Gerson, for everyone in work that day, life was more or less replicated on sheets of more or less important paper – and filed. The system was indeed a filing system; and not much else. It ran in parallel to the world of real events and was the necessary abstraction of it. For the first time I could understand the disdain of someone like Hilary for such a crude and cruel arrangement. Nobody on the outside of the system could temper or alter a thing that lay within it. Nor could anyone exist for long without being added or – when the necessity arose – subtracted.

'Look,' I said. 'Nothing would please me more than to quit. But it's too late. Isn't it?'

The simplified version. Ted shrugged.

'Answer me,' I demanded.

'The woman is garbage,' he said bleakly.

'Fine. Great.'

'You don't know, kid.'

'Who pays you, Ted? Where do you find your loyalties? I mean what is so bloody special about you?'

'I know what's in store for her.'

'Does it include this – her rape and beating?'

It wasn't worth answering. Whoever did it to her was free-lance, opportunist, outside the system. The system destroys by entanglement in nets, by the infliction of a thousand tiny wounds. Or, in the last resort, by shredding. What had happened to Judith up to now had been done on my side of the fence. The system had yet to play its hand.

The line ran into Victoria through sooty canyons that once had risen from their foundations like dragons' teeth. In such places as this my parents had been born, and before them, their parents. My grandmother had gone to work across Vaux-hall Bridge at the age of twelve to empty chamber-pots for one of the railway hotels. The man she was eventually to marry lived two streets away and worked a goods hoist in a factory that made ink. And this he did for thirty-seven years until a compassionate V1 glided down on to the roof. Twenty-eight girls and older women were blotted out in an instant. Dick, my grandfather, was buried under the rubble a day and a night with another two men. They were all Londoners. They blamed the Jews for putting the factory there in the first place, and Jerry for finding it and knocking it down. Before the events of that morning at the hospital, Dick and his fractured hip, lying in a lake of ink at the bottom of his place of work, was the most outrageous event any of us in our family had ever had to endure.

I walked up from Victoria to Kensington, with just enough money left to nurse a pint in one of those pretty, sought-after pubs where many of the clientele arrive and leave by cab. I sat just inside the door, watching the yuppies come jaunting in.

Opposite me sat a skinny New Zealand redhead who was waiting to be interviewed for a bar job. She smiled faintly and I asked what she did. She said she came from New Zealand and was a student of drama.

'You're a drama student,' I corrected. 'I'm the student of drama.'

And that ended that. Come fourteen thousand miles and get a smart-arse with yellow teeth and uncombed hair giving you the wise words. She turned her long narrow back on me. Where her shirt had jumped out of her jeans there was revealed a little golden crescent of skin.

I was still searching for a simile when Sonia Kyriakides walked in, her head of honey hair on fire from the afternoon sun.

She drove me back to Judith's place where, of course, the rooms looked as though they had been ransacked, and made me a cup of coffee while I showered. We did what I was too stupid or too male to have thought of doing myself. We phoned flowers to the hospital and rang her father's flat in Bracknell. Judith's real name was not Firestone, but Smight. Sonia knew that casual detail: was I always going to be the last to find out the obvious, ordinary things about her? A dull, slow woman answered the Bracknell number we got from the operator. She took it all down on a piece of paper with maddening precision and promised to tell Stan when he came in. He was up at the Church Centre, attending a class on God and the Community. The woman added that it was a shock to her. She had not realized Stan had any kids. He had never mentioned any.

'Well, aren't there any pictures of her, snapshots?' I shouted. 'I know you're stupid, but are you blind?'

Sonia took the phone from me and replaced it on the cradle.

'Go and shower. Find a clean shirt. Don't drink any more.'

While I was in the shower, sitting on the floor, crying, she found me a shirt and a clean towel and put the drawers to the chest back. She even made the bed. When I came into the sitting-room she held out her arms.

'Come here,' she said simply.

I hung on to her, this faintly overripe, faintly preposterous tart with two hundred quids' worth of clothes on her back. That lunch-time she had been working at the Grosvenor, entertaining some old crazy who was over from Denver for an auction at Phillips. He had paid her handsomely to eat with him in his rooms, not dressed as she was now, but in a costume he had brought with him, folded carefully in tissue-paper wrappings. It was a drum majorette's tunic, buttoned to the neck with maroon frogs. She told me the story as if I were a child. She took my hand.

'All right, okay. Listen to me. I love the woman, I've told you that. Whoever hurts her, hurts me. I wouldn't talk this way if you were an ordinary mark, you know that. I want you to leave it to me. I can fix it.'

'Fix it?' I repeated foggily, thinking of Judith in her traction bed.

'I know people who know about this sort of thing. We can find the bastard who did this to her.'

'It may be someone you know.'

'Don't be stupid, darling. Don't show your ignorance.'

'How about Frankie Givens?'

She bounced my hand up and down in her warm lap.

'Don't say things like that. You're talking about a friend, someone who knows her from way back, long before you came along. Frank wouldn't harm a hair on her head.'

'I'll tell you that after I've seen him.'

'No,' Sonia said. She meant no, you're not going to see him, stand him against a wall and tear out his eyes. She lit a cigarette and passed me the packet.

'I can see you got it bad. It don't make sense, but I see what I see.'

She opened her bag and withdrew a folded wad of twenty-pound notes.

'Get yourself some clothes, maybe hire a car for a few days. Go and see her in hospital, tell her you love her, tell her the flat's waiting for her when she comes out. Tell her nothing that's happened in the past matters now. It's all in the past. She won't believe you and it won't be true anyway. But get out of it now, while you can. Both of you.'

'On your money.'

'The girl worked for me. It's the least I can do. You're going to refuse the money, is that it? Boy, she's found a dilly in you.'

She glanced at the thin gold watch on her wrist.

'Tell her I love her.'

'Can I tell her you'll visit?'

She studied me with her fine grey eyes.

'All this stuff – let it be. If you must have her, no matter what, then go away, find somewhere you can live and try to trust each other. You're very welcome,' she added, with a sudden tinge of contempt.

Her farewell kiss was dry and perfunctory. She brushed her hair, dragged the waist of her skirt straight, examined her nails, her bracelets, checked her ear-rings – and left. In the pile of banknotes spilled so carelessly on the table there was £400. The money smelled faintly of scent.

17

I went to Ricardo's round midnight. The bouncer was filling in time by blocking a hallway done up in flock wallpaper. He was young and sullen now that we had him in the light. His mind was struggling with how to add a further key to a key-ring. Behind a desk there sat a large girl with luscious arms and a sunbed tan, who took twenty pounds off me before operating a door lock with the toe of her sandal. Nigel, the bouncer, nodded his head towards some stairs down to the basement. For twenty pounds, when the house was first built, you might have staggered down these steps with a year's supply of coal on your back. Now, on a tiny stage, a girl fresh from her GCSEs was dancing energetically to a tape of Wilson Pickett: we were in a bit of a time warp down here. Topless waitresses buzzed about with trays of lager and the clientele were comprised chiefly of a party of Welsh, who had lost Barry sometime after the pub with the transvestite, see? Only, we've got to find Barry, 'cos his wife'll play hell if we don't bring him home, isn't it?

There were a few *habitués*. About half of them were black. Sitting with them were girls in silver dresses, girls in gold. They paid no attention to anyone else, these regulars. At one table they were even having the coffee dregs read for them by a Turkish girl in black. None of them, these faintly bored punters, could be Givens. I sat at the bar. The dancer had been replaced by a guitar–sax duo who looked like students making their first gig. The alto player wore Eighth Army shorts and a black tee-shirt from a New York pizza place. His hair was spiked with gel. His guitarist was dressed straight Oxfam. But the boys' book was fresh and intelligent and they played exceptionally well.

Givens walked straight to me when he came down from upstairs.

'You're going to think I did it,' he said, nodding to the barman for drinks.

'If I thought that, I would put a match to this crapper right now.'

Givens frowned. He had spent money on making the place look like a B movie set; but he wanted more satisfying dialogue. I was a little taken aback by the look of him: he shared with Kenneth Kaunda a penchant for half-sleeve safari suits and well-scrubbed features. His suit was cashmere, to be sure, and black; but he looked vaguely out of place. He looked amateur.

'I didn't hurt her,' he said. 'I'll find out who did.'

'I'll do that for myself.'

He stared at the duo with a certain amount of doubt, momentarily distracted by 'Song for my Father'. The barman put a St Clements in front of him.

'Are these kids any good?'

'In the film, it would be Pier Angeli in a sheath dress.'

'Pier who?'

'Exactly.'

Givens touched my arm.

'I talked to Sonia. You have a friend there. Okay, you came down here looking for me. You can see the boxing weight of this place. You're smart. It's nothing, all this. It's a little business venture. Make it any different, you fill it with screaming children, trouble, drugs. Sonia says you're harmless. That's how I like people to be. It's the way I am myself.'

'Harmless, maybe. But not stupid.'

'Now what does that mean?'

'I'm talking about me, not you. Your girl, Judith, is busted up. She's been given the works. I don't think it was you, but Waxman is hiding under the bed. He could bring himself to believe it of you. He could even bring himself to think you killed David Nicholas.'

Givens smiled at last.

'It's a joke, what that man thinks,' he said. 'Did he tell you his brother worked in Vegas?'

'Brother-in-law.'

'And you believed him? Look around you. Look at me. Do I look like the kind of man who could have someone killed? The man's a wanker.'

He signalled one of the girls, and told her to go to the boys playing jazz for him. He told her to say he had not recognized one tune. People listened to music for tunes. Tell them to get that through their skulls.

'What sort of thing do you want?' the girl asked nervously. She was covering her naked breasts with a folded arm. He knocked it away with a brisk chop.

'Who are you, what's your name?' Givens asked. She was called, in the spirit of the decor, Margie.

'When I hire people to play for me, I don't have to pick the music. If I want jazz, I also want tunes. If I hire topless, I see topless. Got that?'

Margie was really terrified of him, as her nod indicated. She walked over to the guitarist and whispered in his ear. The boy glowered. Givens stared him down.

'You are poking your nose in where it's not wanted,' he said absently, while still giving Wes Montgomery the hard eye. 'I don't know anything about Nicholas except what I read in the papers. This place is clean. I'm clean. I'm giving you the chance to mind your own business. I don't want trouble. You understand that?'

He was also passing me a fistful of three-pound notes. He knew it: I knew it. The Welsh had formed the same opinion as him in the matter of the music. They were singing 'Penny

Lane'. Givens looked even more darkly on life. His frown intensified. He didn't like the Beatles any more than he liked Horace Silver, apparently.

'I'll spell it out,' he said. 'You get on my tits any more, I'm going to do something about it.'

He turned to the barman.

'Give me twenty out of the till. Get those kids off the stage, and put Margie on. Tell her she better shake it if she wants to stay working here.'

He put two ten-pound notes in my hand.

'Piss off, while you have the chance.'

'What is this, a frightener?'

He rubbed the inside corner of his eye with a weary gesture. Nigel, summoned by telepathy, or perhaps by the strains of 'Penny Lane', was coming down the steps, his jaw jutting. He raised his eyebrows at the boss as a way of indicating he was ready for business. Givens waved him away.

'You make of it what you like.'

'What I make of it, Mr Givens, is that you couldn't afford to run a car on what you earn from this dump. The whole place should be in black and white and introduced by Edgar Lustgarten. For a friend of Yanni's, you're not fronting up too well.'

He ran his tongue round his back teeth.

'A friend of who?'

His tone was a shade too level, as if to say, do your worst, what do I care? Up on the stage, Margie was bouncing away to Lionel Richie, hair flying, arms flailing. It was painful to watch, but then only the Welsh were watching, and not all of them either. Givens was looking at me, and only at me.

'I'd like to see the rest of the house – what you've got upstairs. Plantation Records, Plantation Holdings, all the rest.'

He looked intent. I waved my hand in the direction of the club entrance.

'I can read name-plates, if they're written in big enough letters.'

'While you still have eyes you can.'

'Now this is much more the Mr Givens I was expecting to meet.'

He laughed, but without humour. It was more like a fox barking. He turned his meaty back on me and signalled for another drink.

'We'll talk about this another time,' he promised.

I thought about this on the way to the hospital next afternoon. As it stood, Ricardo's didn't parse. It didn't scan. A crabby little club with as much charisma as a tray of mince from meals on wheels? Owned by a tubby man with grey hair and a safari suit? And this was enough to have the spit bubbling in the corners of Waxman's mouth? For the resources Waxman considered him capable of mustering, Givens's business must be something much more profitable than a cellar club in which Margie boogied her breasts to Lionel Richie. Nor did I believe that the real money came pouring in from a couple of rap artists signed to Plantation Records. Givens's money, like the sewers, ran deeper. There was only one real possibility. In some plantation far from Cambridge Circus they were growing more than cotton. Givens was on the millionaires' end of the trade. Only drugs and the profits from drugs can buy you an island and a third share in a boxer.

In such circumstances, the fact that David Nicholas had also been intimate with bishops and television producers, journalists and merchant bankers paled for the time being into insignificance. The fool had been messing with a whore, a madam and a thief. And now here was revealed this other dimension – a dark wood and winding forest path if ever there was one. How had that happened – did Judith, wittingly or not, drag the politician down, lure him on? Did he follow her into the forest until, when at last he looked back, the horizon had vanished, and with it the sun? Or – and it was my day for questions – had Nicholas so come to believe in the invulnerability of the rich and successful that he thought he could manage quite well, come what may?

Yanni had been his downfall. That was clear enough. Givens might bluster that he had been ready to point the finger at the Minister for the death of Billie Curtess, but it did not ring true. The one solid fact in the whole case was that Yanni did the vaults. And so we came round full circle to exactly what was in David Nicholas's box. Letters, negatives – and what else? Only two people could say for sure. One was sitting in a bar somewhere lighting cigarettes for people with hundred-drachma notes. The other was dead.

I walked upstairs with the hospital chaplain, or one of them. The lift was unaccountably on the blink and it was his suggestion we use the stairs. He asked who I was visiting and, when I told him, asked me what illness she had.

'She is a chronic liar,' I said.

'Is there medicine for that?'

'It's more in your department, perhaps.'

'I don't think any of us are chronically given to the truth, are we?'

'I don't know. Are we?'

I found her awake and able to speak. I bent down and kissed her forehead. Her skull bandage was off, and a nurse had washed and brushed out her hair. She was propped up against immense pillows and seemed to be waiting for something with stoic patience, as might an actress in make-up. The bruises on her neck and cheeks had ripened to a glossy plum colour. Her eyes glistened wet behind their slits.

'How are you?'

'Terrific,' she muttered crookedly.

'You look great.'

I held flowers in my hand. Their heads were shaking. The drip was gone, along with the traction bed. She wore a blue, check cotton nightie, unbuttoned and untied. Grey sweat was

195

running off her. The window was closed. I shook the flowers into a glass vase.

'I want you to leave me alone,' she mumbled.

'We're partners, partner.'

I sat in a chair, the seat of which was lower than the mattress of the bed, and held her hand. There was a faintly returned pressure, so light and delicate that it might not have been intended for me at all. Maybe she was just hanging on to anything she could. The room was infernally hot: hot, still, and – somehow – menacing. She lay like a waxwork and made no sign when I laid my head despairingly against her wrist. Outside the door was the tempestuous clamour of the auxiliaries bringing round tea. The ward manager's phone rang every few minutes.

'I don't want any more.'

'Judith, please.'

'Don't want you in my life any more.'

'Now more than ever,' I suggested.

'Stupid.'

The sweat began to gather in my eyebrows and run stingingly into my eyes. We could hear each other breathe. I was trying not to transmit the shakes I was getting through to her.

'Leave me alone,' she said at last, as if phoning from a great distance.

'I can't do that. Listen to me. I can't just walk away and leave you in here. Look at me. Turn your head and look at me.'

When she did the tears were running down her face.

'You're so dumb. You know nothing.'

'That's getting through to me all right.'

'Different world.'

'That too.'

'Where is Hilary?' she suddenly asked, in as close to an ordinary tone as was possible. She tried to laugh when she saw my startled look and a web of silver ran out of her nose.

'Dumb bastard.'

'Is that what you were doing? Were you supposed to meet? Were you going to flit?'

'Mind your own business.'

I had a bright idea and opened her locker. Inside was the purple corduroy bag she travelled with. It could not contain more than a change of shirt and underwear. In the drawer to the locker was a receipt for £483, issued by the hospital secretariat. They had left her a five-pound note and the coins in her purse.

'Where were you going?'

'Nowhere.'

'You were just going to let me come home and find you gone?'

The door opened and the Australian nurse with the musical laugh came in. She carried a container of tea with a straw attachment.

'You look hot as hell,' she said.

'It is incredibly hot in here.'

'Did you think to open the window?'

She pushed me gently out of the way, her crisp blouse rattling. Her young girl's skin was a mass of brown freckles. She unlatched the window and opened it to a faint breeze.

'Silly man,' she said to Judith. 'See if you can get him to feed you a cup of tea. Got some great grub for you later. Big chewy chunks. You'll love it.'

I saw Judith's arm lift an inch or two above the bedspread. The staff nurse smiled and took her hand. She did what I had done earlier and kissed the wrist.

'Tough as old boots,' she decided.

'Make him go,' Judith whispered.

'Yeah, I'll sling him out in a minute. But be nice to him first. He looks all right, for a Pom.'

She waltzed out, and I fed Judith some tea.

'I was running out on you, yes,' she said, after a while.

'That doesn't matter. I'd have found you.'

'Oh yes. Forgot. Love.'

Her contempt was complete. She indicated for me to put the cup into her hand, and when I did, sucked on the bent plastic straw, her eyes averted. I sat watching her for minutes on end, too dispirited to speak. Pale brown tea ran down her chin and neck: when she had drunk her fill, she let the container fall from her hand and it rolled on to the floor between my shoes. I had to bend to catch what she said.

'Wait and see.'

'Don't you want me to come and see you again?'

'Don't need you.'

She was trying to smile in triumph. Or was I projecting triumph on to that slit-eyed grimace? I stood, feeling the room spin for a second. A fearful noise began coming out of her, as of laughter or sobbing tears, I could not tell. I picked up the pink drinking mug and put it beside her.

'I told you once, Judith –'

But she turned her head away from me.

And so I left, without asking a real question, and having nothing real volunteered to me, except that abrupt turn of the head. Nothing could be more conclusive. The game was over.

Gerson and I had once gone to Paris together, as young men. We wanted to see the incomparable Trésor play for the national side in a friendly against Austria. It was a bitterly cold February weekend. After the match we came back into the city and found a little bar with thirties' neon illuminating drab zinc tables and there we sat in our topcoats, drinking and talking. Ted steadily drank himself to the point where he could reach out and touch the truth, it was so tangible. It was an easy collar. He said so repeatedly.

'Go on then, what is the truth?'

'The truth is, we'll never know,' he said, with such complete drunken earnestness that when I laughed, he staggered to his feet and left without me. Twenty-five years had passed and, until that afternoon, I had forgotten I ever made the trip.

18

Waxman was crying. He stinted nothing. The tears rolled down his chin and his nose ran. He wiped his face from time to time with the sleeve of his cardigan. Leah had been banished to the bedroom once again, but stood at the threshold, horrified.

'You think they're going to come and thank me, pat me on the head? They pat people with iron pipes, you bastard.'

'You're safe. Stop whining.'

'I told you a thousand times, I know nothing. All I know is one set of books. When I found out whose they were, I nearly crapped my pants.'

'How long ago was this?'

'No!' he shouted. 'I'm saying nothing. Nothing, you hear? If they even find out you were ever in this room they'll finish me.'

His terror was real. They had been breakfasting on finnan haddie. Radio 4 was chuntering away. It was Sunday, and all the papers were sure that a general election would be called in the week ahead. The Prime Minister had a slight cold, and had cancelled a visit to Paris. The Party grandees were meeting at Linton Castle in Hampshire, where once the Cavaliers had withstood a siege by Roundheads for eighteen days. Waxman laid his head on the table and wept.

'Tell me,' I said. 'A trouble shared, and all that, Gerald. Don't tell me it all if you don't want. But tell me how he bought you.'

'How does anyone buy anything?' he wailed. 'I was cheap.'

'Who introduced you?'

'Leah,' he bellowed. 'Make some coffee. Give him a cup of coffee and get him out of here.'

'Judith got him the work,' Leah said calmly from her post at the bedroom door. My jaw gaped.

'Say again, Leah?'

'Your friend Judith. Before that he was doing personal taxation, bookkeeping. He advertised in the free paper. We even had a card in the tobacconist's.'

'Go ahead,' Waxman said. 'Kill me.'

'Then *she* moved in. Gerald did her tax returns. He thought it was exciting. She was exciting.' She hesitated, tugging at her hair. 'He thought it was glamorous, I suppose. Anyone could see she was a tart. Before her had been a civil servant, a man from Ordnance Survey. And then her. She bewitched him.'

'Now I am dead,' Waxman said, lifting his head from the table. 'Thank you, Leah. You make it all very simple. First they come for him, and then they get the cripple. So make some coffee.'

'What is it, Gerald? Crack? Coke?'

'Oh sure.' He laughed hysterically. 'I'm going to tell you. I'm going to pay my debt to society by telling you. I'm a wheelchair. I'm a nothing. I do the books for his record company and one or two bits. A launderette. A set of lock-ups in Ealing. What, you think I'm one of his barons or something? I do the books. For his bugsmeat. You think I'm his financial controller? There are dozens like me. I'm his nought.'

'You're part of his laundry.'

'Yes,' Waxman said. 'Of course.'

'And what about Vegas?'

Sheer holy terror widened his eyes.

'Vegas? Are you crazy? You think because Harry Hartsilver lives in Vegas and not in Bournemouth you've got a story? What *about* Vegas? You turn up here out of nowhere, hanging on to the tit of a neighbour who's brought me nothing but grief, and you want me to sign a full fucking confession? I go to Vegas for my holidays because her brother foots the bill. Because once when we were little jewboys in Southall we went to school together. Because when the polio came, he stuck by me. You creep! You nothing! You throw Vegas in my face. Let me tell you, I was more in love with him than I ever was with that woman in there, his sister.'

Leah had reappeared. She folded her arms and stared at me with a surprising degree of calm.

'What he says is right. About Harry. You couldn't understand.' She indicated the room and all its shabby furniture. 'We don't need someone like you getting in our hair. This isn't much, what you see, but it is mine as well as his. He doesn't have to say any more. We both would like you to go. So please. Go.'

Sandra Gerson stood on tiptoe to kiss me. She had been reading the Sunday papers in the scratch-built conservatory Ted had fashioned at the back of the house. Her hands were hardly more than bumpy and knuckled clubs when I took them – the arthritis had cruelly closed her grip for ever. She was dreadfully thin, also, and her hair was lank. She led me to the kitchen and pointed. Ted was sawing up wood in the shed at the bottom of the garden.

'He's making the lad next door a soap-box car – you know, a what-do-you-call-it? One of those things. For the Lions Gala. He's called Brendan, the boy. Their grandson. Ruth and Ken's grandson.'

She managed somehow to turn the tap and fill the kettle. When she caught me staring at her, she smiled faintly.

'I knew you'd come, sooner or later. I told him you would. You were such great mates in the old days. And he likes you. It's important you're here. Maybe you'll understand why – he's very lonely these days.'

She meant in a work context, I knew, but the spirited innocence of the remark pierced me.

'Sandra, chuck me straight back out again if you like, if you'd rather.'

'Lord, no, that wouldn't do at all. I know all about it, of course, why you're here. He tells me everything. How is she? Is she on the mend?'

'More or less,' I said. 'I'm on my way there now.'

'Have some coffee. Hand me those cups down if you want to help. Tell me what you've done, what you feel, and then I'll let you off. You can take him up the pub. He'd like that.'

'Where would you like me to start?' I asked helplessly.

'From the beginning. The day you first met her.'

He saw us, of course, but waved nonchalantly and wagged his finger to indicate no, he didn't want coffee. The boy for whom he was building the cart came round with a pair of buckled pram wheels and the two of them conferred before disappearing into the shed. Sandra held her cup in her knuckled hands and listened intently as I went over the whole summer, from the day that Judith had appeared out of the blue one breakfast.

'You've probably told her you love her, have you?' she asked at last.

'Yes.'

'But you don't.'

'It wouldn't be very sensible.'

'That's not the point,' she said sharply. 'You don't, because you don't. Don't try giving me a lesson in what's sensible. And now she wants you to buzz off, too.'

I laughed, feeling choked and shaky.

'You make it sound so very simple, Sandy.'

'It isn't exactly difficult. You meet this woman, you think you can make a relationship with her, and then you back out. It's mutual. She feels exactly the same. I can't see any difficulties.'

202

'There is a small case of murder in between.'

'But you didn't have anything to do with that, and neither did she. You want to back out because you made a mistake. Perhaps she wants to call it a day because she can't cope with someone like you. That would make sense, too. I don't see there's anything to cry about. It's a good thing you both have your heads screwed on.'

'Well, I'm not too sure about that, either.'

Sandra shrugged her shoulders.

'You might have picked someone more lovable. She might have found someone more able to help her. But there's enough cruelty in you both for you to save yourselves.'

'Cruelty?'

When he first met her, Ted's Sandra had been the pert miss in her final year of teacher training. She planned to specialize in English teaching and was a bemused reader of texts flung at her by the college lecturers. She would come to watch us play football in a white mini-length mac and sit on a bench with Beckett and half a dozen files and notebooks at her side, loyal and frozen. Ted had bought her a huge Russian hat. The wind would rip the pages of the essays she tried to write as the lads chased the ball up and down the park.

'You can be cruel,' she said now. 'But you're not stupid, you know the effect you can have. Perhaps you don't intend to be, but the outcome is the same. Too much flimflam is a form of cruelty. It's postponing and disguising something indefinitely. She seems brighter than that, from what you've told me.'

Ted came out of the work shed with a cart made from the two pram wheels and two other, smaller wheels at the front. He tossed it on to the lawn and I saw that the front end was independently suspended. Sandra pointed to this surprising bit of ingenuity.

'That's clever. He sat up all last night thinking how to do that. It's the wheels from my shopping trolley. The springs are out of the garden chair. I don't know why he had to do that –

Brendan would have been happy with just about anything. But Ted's a fool with children, always has been. He's been messing about getting the front wheels to float since six this morning.'

'I feel I've abandoned her, Sandra.'

She shot me a loaded glance.

'That would be in keeping with the rest of your love life, I suppose. But maybe she's tougher than you think. Maybe not every woman you meet needs you. Have you ever thought of that?'

'And so what will happen to her?' I asked, to deflect the question. Sandra rubbed the knobby back of one hand against the other.

'Who knows?' she said gently.

The delighted Brendan sat in the cart and bounced the suspension up and down. Ted studied his handiwork with a slight frown. Brendan's grandfather leaned over the fence with a pint glass of lager proffered at arm's length. Sandra laid her ruined hands in mine.

'What does happen to people?' she asked. 'They wake up, they work their way through the day; for good or bad, it doesn't matter. Sooner or later they sleep. People are animals, too, remember. What they can't take, they spit out. What they're afraid of, they run from. Ted doesn't understand me any better than you do: but I'm right. I know I am. Give it up. Forget it.'

He came up the garden path and washed his hands at the outside tap. Brendan ran off with his cart under his arm. Ted was whistling idly, his sleeves pushed back to the elbow. I walked out to join him.

'Got enough in your pocket to buy a couple of pints?' he asked.

'Not surprised to see me?'

'Nope.'

'Your missus said she knew I would come.'

'Never wrong. She's sharp as razors. Got a reason for coming?'

The water that played over his wrists was crystal clear and languid, like a lazy rope.

'I need to try something on you.'

'Not here,' Ted murmured. 'Go back in and say you'll stay to lunch. She'd like that. She's fond of you, always has been. We can talk up at the pub.'

We walked the four hundred yards to the Wellington along sandy lanes. It was muggy and overcast. In many of the gardens we passed, the menfolk were washing their cars. An ice-cream van drove slowly past to the strains of 'Für Elise'. Ted found a couple of inch-eights in his trouser pocket, examined them briefly and transferred them to the patch pocket of his blue check shirt.

'I don't want to hear any heart-searching,' he said, as the pub came into sight. 'This is business or it's nothing. And don't be shy. You're not very likely to shock and amaze.'

'Frank Givens,' I said.

He nodded non-committally.

'Is that it? Is that what you wanted to run by me?'

'I want to know what you think.'

When we got into the pub and had found a table under the window, Ted took out his pipe and pouch. He was unshaven, and his stubble was quite white. He sipped the beer with a faint grimace, and brushed his forehead with the back of his arm.

'Go ahead. But keep it down. They know what I do for a living in here. You sometimes get people trying to earhole.'

I hesitated for a second or two and then shrugged.

'Somehow or other, Judith knows Frank Givens. Maybe she's introduced to him by Sonia Kyriakides. Maybe Yanni. They meet down at Ricardo's, I suppose, or there to begin with. The place in Cambridge Circus?'

'It's your story,' Ted muttered. 'Tell it any way you want.'

'The club's a nothing little drinking den. It's Sleepy Hollow. I talked to the accountant, Waxman. From the things he's said, Givens is making serious money. According to Waxman, he sees just a little bit of it, a fraction. But even from the kind of money going through the pisspot accounts Waxman is controlling, it has to be big. Much bigger than his place in Cambridge Circus. The business has to be serious. Coke, or crack.'

Ted's face was expressionless.

'Keep going.'

'Well, isn't that new? It hit me like a ton of bricks.'

'So tell me what it means.'

'I saw Givens at the club last night. Those boys claim they could produce witnesses to say the boy David killed Billie Curtess. They planned to blow the whistle on him anyway, if he hadn't been shot. But then David is tied into them through Judith. He's not stupid, he knows the score. They shop David, he shops them. It's a stand-off. Not very satisfactory, bloody dangerous in fact, but it's the price David has to pay. He's handling it. Then, suddenly, he gets his head blown off.'

'And you don't think it was the IRA?'

'We both know it wasn't.'

'Couldn't be, under any circumstances?'

Pressed, I could not answer that; nor, I think, could he. I guessed he was quoting the DAC who had pulled him in for reprimand. They had prime suspects, they had the probability of an IRA claim, albeit a tardy one. They had a media tsunami, a tidal wave of wishfulness, on their side. Ted rocked his glass for a moment.

'What are you saying, that Givens shot him?'

'Had him shot, maybe.'

'So all of a sudden, when we've been going along thinking it was all about sex, it was actually all about drugs. That it?'

'I came here to try that on you, yes.'

'And it never was a political assassination. Nicholas was offed for strictly business reasons?'

He drummed the table with his fingertips. The disc that was the surface of his beer danced gently.

'Let me ask you a question. What's the one thing in all this that doesn't gel? Who's the one person that doesn't seem to fit in?'

'I don't get you.'

'It's all cosy up there in London. The boy David and his little ways with women bring a small select circle together. Soon, he's trapped, surrounded. Everybody owns a piece of him. One cross word from David, one favour left unpaid, one fit of the sulks, the whole lot comes down round his ears. Not just his own political career, but the Government and all its works. The whole splendid record and success at the next elections. Heavy shit, eh? He can just about keep it under control, though. It takes some enterprise, he'd be better off with something easier, like insider-trading, for which he is also well placed, but he was born with his brains in his dick, and he's happy with what he's got. Who's missing?'

'I still don't get you.'

'I think you do. We've agreed so far, right? Trapped as he might have been, David was still sailing along pretty serenely, right? He hasn't put a foot wrong with the chums that came along in the wake of Judith. He's given no cause for offence and he may even have done a few good turns along the way. In return, his secret is safe. In time, the girl comes to you with a cock and bull story about blackmail, for sure – but long before Yanni did the vaults they had enough to bleed him to death. Even without Billie Curtess. This is a randy and stupid little bastard who consorts with a raft of cheapskate low-lifers for dirty sex. Not the Cabinet house style at all. All that was purged by diktat from the Leader, years ago.'

'Who's the missing person, then?'

'Hilary,' Ted rumbled.

I stared at him incredulously.

'Hilary? What about him?'

'For starters, where is he?'

'He's just an old fart who lives in the woods.'

'Good. So where is he?'

'You're not serious, Ted?'

'Say it's a jigsaw. What is Hilary – an unimportant bit of sky? Or what? Do you know? Can you say, for certain?'

'He knows Judith and David from way back. That's the connection. When David is shot, he panics. He does a bunk.'

'Yermm,' Ted said thoughtfully.

'He's nothing,' I said.

'Let me tell you what you worked out and why you're sitting in my boozer now. Nicholas keeps his gear in a deposit box. Yanni busts the vaults. Those are the two people who know what was in the box, I mean the full contents. Nobody else. That's a problem straightaway for Givens. This guy Nicholas is a shithead, but maybe he isn't completely stupid. Maybe there's more in that box than a few poxy letters and some negs. That as far as you've got?'

'Yes, but the Hilary thing is ridiculous. It doesn't make sense.'

'Frankie Givens shooting Nicholas doesn't make too much sense.'

'Hilary even less so.'

'Yes,' Ted said. 'It doesn't seem his speed. But I would like to know where he is. I'd feel happier. I think your girl expected to find him there two nights ago. I think she planned to disappear in the same way. I don't think it's over. For either of them.'

We had two pints and a last half, and then walked back the way we had come. The kid Brendan was riding his cart up and down the kerb, admiring the suspension device Ted had fashioned. And it was cute. It was a little work of art.

19

Was she sleeping, or was she feigning sleep? That morning she had been taken down for further X-rays after complaining of pain in her cheek and jaw. The night had been stressful. She had haemorrhaged slightly and the Sudanese consultant had been called.

I sat on the chair watching the wind tussle the tallest branches of a row of poplars. There was a Sunday somnolence about the main ward. The cheerful Australian was on time off and the nurses' station was being managed by a pockmarked and unsmiling Burmese sister. The relatives of more tender accidents and disasters than Judith's were tiptoeing in with the chocolates and the Lucozade, their smiles faintly aghast, their voices a whisper. I sat in the side ward, keeping watch with a bee that grazed the flowers crowding her locker top. There was nothing to report, except from time to time a small groan, as of someone dreaming. But by now my suspicions were so poisonous I could not be sure she was actually asleep. I scribbled her a note and then tore it up. I read her case notes at the foot of the bed and a Sunday paper she must have ordered. I thought about Hilary. What Ted Gerson wanted to know was whether somebody nobbled him. If they did, Judith herself was on that somebody's list also.

The house in the woods was under police observation. I had driven there after leaving Ted and Sandra. On the lane leading to the house was a parked Escort. Two people, far too young to be blackberrying, far too conspicuous to be courting, were mooching about in the little stand of beeches. I drove to the door, got out and knocked. The woman watched me with binoculars. I walked round looking for Wallace. There was no sign of her. I walked to the railway carriage. The door was hanging ajar. Inside were my books and clothes, some tinned food and wine bottles, scattered about. It was as though I had flown to Mars and back since last I set eyes on the place.

Judith snorted. Her breathing stuttered a few beats and she seemed about to wake – but it was only the prelude to her sliding away again, deeper and deeper into unreachable dreams. At last, agitated by the calm and silence, I let myself out of the side ward and tiptoed away. My shadow made huge brown stains on the glistening waxed floor. By chance I met El Souem, the consultant. He smiled down at me from six foot four of Sudanese strength and dignity.

'You are the boyfriend?'

'I suppose so, yes.'

'She is sleeping?'

'Yes.'

'You must go for a walk and come back later. She is a healthy woman. Very strong, very positive. Soon, she will be like rain.'

'As right as rain,' I translated.

'Yes,' El Souem said gravely. 'She will need you then. Love, you know. It is the best medicine of all.'

He touched me on the chest as if to implant some love into my heart, and ambled away, hands in pockets. His footfall was silent. I toyed with the idea of buying a second-hand book from a Friends of the Hospital display and sitting out there in the foyer, waiting for the day she would accept and understand love as a form of affection, as well as some kind of purchase, a bill of sale.

Instead, I went down in the lift with a rabbity man and his wife. In the lift the awful seriousness of the wards had found its siphon. Thus we might learn, scratched into the grey paint, that Kath gives head, or Mandy is a slag. Spurs had been there, along with Arsenal FC. It was as though, in the few moments of descent, the healthy just had to celebrate their victory over illness and death. The rabbity man inspected all these graffiti in turn. He carried a Tesco bag containing a few folded clothes and a pair of brown slippers. If the meek were ever going to inherit the earth, he and his wife had their plot staked out. Without expression, he studied a felt-tip drawing of what might just have been a canoe tied up in the papyrus of El Souem's native Sudd. His wife meanwhile looked fixedly forwards. It was as though she wanted to cry and wail but was quite determined that respectable people did no such thing.

'Do you know how the buses run?' the man barked suddenly.

'Where is it you want to go? I have a car.'

'Miles out of *your* way,' the wife scoffed, with a grim smile.

'I'm doing nothing. Come on, I'll take you.'

'See all this?' the rabbit said, indicating the graffiti. 'I would like to shoot the bastards who did all this.'

'They're scum,' his wife said.

'And now they want an election to let the other lot in. If I had a gun, I would shoot the swine. That's the kind of government we want in this country.'

'Scum,' wife said.

We were the lucky ones, the healthy, who had not been run over, burned, struck by a lightning bolt in the chest while painting the wardrobe, raped, mugged, or knocked sideways by an indifferent and unspeakable force.

'Shoot first, ask questions afterwards,' rabbit said vaguely.

I drove them all the way home – after a suitable stiffness, to many protestations of gratitude and surprise. In fact, they opened their hearts to me. People these days had no heart. The old sense of community had gone for ever. You could be ashamed of being English, which, when you considered the war and all that, was a bloody disgrace. They had noticed me speaking to the darkie doctor. The bloody hospital was full of them. People had no idea these days. A piece of steak in the supermarket was like gold-dust. Some of these rich people up in London who drank champagne for breakfast ought to try living on a pension for a change. The Government was only out for itself. Same as the Arabs who would one day own all the bloodlines in the country and then you'd see something (he was a keen punter). The Irish, who used to have good horses of their own, were now no more than a set of murdering bastards. As witness this bloke that was shot by them only last week. This Nickelby bloke.

I endured all this for two reasons. The first, as anyone knows, is the extraordinary difficulty of gainsaying a couple like this when they are on song. The second was sentimental. They lived, the rabbit and his wife, in a little hutch just two leafy suburban streets away from Dawn and Edgar. They asked me in for a cup of tea. Bonny, their Jack Russell, flew about the room like a wounded bird. While his wife boiled the kettle and shouted endearments at Bonny, the rabbit showed me a portrait photograph of a Chief Petty Officer dressed in white drills. It was their son, killed on the *Sheffield* by a French rocket fired from an Argentinian plane.

'That's Colin,' his father said.

Walking past the windows of their bungalow was someone I knew. The rabbit followed my gaze.

'A policeman, a high-up. The wife heard down at the post office yesterday. He's been put on suspension, see? Another stuck-up know-all bastard. They're all on the take, of course. He's been caught with his hand in the till somehow, you wait and see. And what do you do, by the way?'

'Print. Little print works. Nothing special. Just me and my brother.'

The rabbit nodded.

'Just hanging on, are you, so to speak?'

'The way it is now, you have to, don't you?'

It was what he wanted to hear, code for the sharing of belief. We were pals. After glancing back at the hullabaloo in the kitchen, he suddenly touched my sleeve in the unconscious habit of the pensioner. His voice lowered to a whisper.

'His wife? The copper's wife?'

His lips parted in a yellow, toothy smile. Say no more. For a moment I had become Colin, the son he taught to fish and ride a bike and then, in time, to drink a pint. It was as it might have been, had not a woman sent the *Sheffield* down the steep Atlantic stream. This Dawn-watcher, this student of life, walking down to the Sun with big Col, bursting with pride as the lad fished his wad from a bulging back pocket, standing the old fella another stout and mild.

Dawn answered the door to me fifteen minutes later. She stepped back a pace, her hand at her throat, the way they used to do it in silent movies. She had her hair cut in a schoolboy bob and I thought the set of her mouth was harder than when we last said goodbye. After Judith, she seemed tiny; a little curvy blonde from a Sindy catalogue.

'My God,' she croaked. 'It's a joke. You've got to be joking.'

'I was in the neighbourhood. I saw big Eddie out walking the dog a few minutes ago.'

She seemed confused. She darted back out under the porch to look at the drive.

'You've just missed him.'

'How're you doing, Dawn?'

'I've heard a hundred bad things about you. Eddie said the police were after you.'

'Really? I heard Eddie had been suspended.'

'He's tapped,' Dawn said bluntly. 'He's off his trolley.'

'The strain of contemporary living, eh?'

We stood uncertainly in the hall, under the case clock. Huge tears formed in her eyes.

'I was crazy about you,' she said, with a sort of hysterical finality. 'You were right about a lot of things. Things you said.'

'Come on, I bet you're having more fun now.'

She looked at me with a curious expression.

'I miss you. God knows why, you were never anything but bad news from the moment I got up in the morning. But you meant something to me. What do you want?'

'Where was hubby the day before yesterday?'

She pushed me in the chest with both hands, exasperated.

'See? I say I miss you, but then I always forget. You just have to know everything. You can't leave things alone.'

'It's important, Dawn.'

'I don't know where he was. And I care even less. Ask him.'

'Doesn't he talk to you?'

'Did he ever? I'm just a pair of tits. Not even that any longer. He's having it off with a neighbour, a girl-friend of mine.'

'Babs.'

She shook her head wonderingly.

'Yes, Babs. So you know all about that, too? Well then, why don't you go round and ask her? You can have a cup of tea here if you like but if he catches you, he'll kill you. You're right off his Christmas card list.'

We called a truce and sat in the spotless kitchen, drinking Earl Grey. There was not a thing out of place. One of the things that Dawn collected was pottery cats. They were displayed in a glass-fronted pine cabinet. I thought vaguely of Lydia and her kitchen. Dawn followed my gaze.

'It's all stupid,' she said. 'Everything is so incredibly stupid.'

She talked about the children after a while, things about them we had never before discussed. Peter was being tested for deafness. It wasn't serious, not yet, but there was definitely something wrong there, something not quite normal. Melanie had come home saying she wanted to learn the cello. Babs's Martin was head teacher to both children. He had advised against starting up the cello for another year, until Melons had more theory. The child had found that hard to understand and took it personally, as though Martin didn't like her. But it wasn't that at all.

'How about you?' I asked. 'Where are you in all this?'

'I need my own space,' she said lamely. She was almost certainly quoting someone else, maybe the tutor at the assertiveness training class Edgar had told me about. She threw me a lopsided and wobbly smile.

'I need something that isn't there. You're supposed never to think like that, it's bad for you. But you know what I'm talking about.'

'Maybe you need to get away.'

'You did,' she retorted sadly. 'And look what happened to you.'

Kissing her goodbye was almost like saying hello again. I felt her sag against me, the way she had always done. She hung round my neck with two bronzed arms, her soft breasts warm against my faithless heart.

'Edgar's in big trouble, isn't he?'

'Who says?'

'Babs. He's done something terrible.'

'That's why he was suspended maybe,' I said, the blood roaring in my ears.

'Since then. Something else.'

We disengaged, and she looked me firmly in the eye.

'That's why you're here.'

'I don't know why I'm here,' I said truthfully enough, but shaking like an aspen.

'It was in the papers. You know what I'm talking about.'

We stared at each other. Always before we had spoken to each other in whispers downstairs, as if Edgar might be hiding in the cupboard under the stairs. Now her voice was distressingly calm.

'If it's what I think it is,' Dawn said, 'fix him. Fix the bastard.'

'If you know something, tell me.'

She walked ahead of me into the utility room and reached for something wedged behind the deep-freeze cabinet. It was a pale blue golf shirt, caked with blood that had already oxidized to a black crust. She threw it on the thermoplastic tiles of the floor. Somehow her expression managed to suggest I shared in this horror.

'Kill him,' she said.

The ringing in my ears was of the phone. She walked back into the kitchen to answer it, and I left through the front door, my eyes smarting from the beautiful, harmless, harm-free sunshine that fell all around with what seemed the noise of a piano pushed over a cliff. They were mowing their lawns and twiddling their borders and nobody but me seemed to hear the piano's agony.

20

There is a little grass mound in the centre of town where on market days in the eighteenth century the reviled William Lidgett stood and preached. He was a publican gone mad with gospel, who eventually gathered enough followers in the south and south west to charter a ship and sail to America. They entered the Delaware River in 1764. Lidgett had left his wife and children behind in England and was being served by the handmaiden Jessica Lough, or Luff. She was seventeen. The community Lidgett founded for her and the others was set upon by the Conestoga Indians and later, the Paxton Boys. Lidgett died of flux after eating tainted meat and those he had sought to save were dispersed throughout Lancaster County. Jessica lived another seventy years. And how do I know all this? From sitting in the reference room of the Central Library until it closed, reading a pamphlet on the subject and planning how to cut Edgar from Strathclyde into a thousand smoking pieces.

But first, I drove round to Eric and Steve's. Only Eric was in. He looked a bit tearful and it came out in the kitchen while waiting for the kettle to boil that Steve was in Tangiers with someone called Vince. I hugged him and told him not to be such an old queen. He had been given the opportunity to go with them, but the invitation had not been presented quite as whole-heartedly as he might have wished. Now he felt as if his own heart had been ripped out. I poured his sherry and orange juice down the sink and made him a cup of tea.

'Vince is a squaddie,' Eric wept. 'Of course, he's not really a squaddie, that's just what he wants you to believe. Oh, I knew he was trouble the first night we met him.'

'He's young,' I suggested.

'Oh yes. He's forty going on nineteen. The Falklands, football and ear-rings. Très chic, I don't think.'

'But your Steve seemed to have his head screwed on the right way.'

Eric blew his nose loudly into a lilac tissue.

'Please don't give us your gallant friend bit. Steve's head is just somewhere to store his ears,' he said. 'There's nothing inside.'

We watched the early evening news, to see whether earthquakes had beset luckless Morocco. They hadn't, but my guts were churned all the same. The IRA had at last claimed responsibility for the death of David Nicholas. There was a twist. The claim had been made indirectly at an Irish–American fund-raiser in Boston. The Swindon Three were innocent of that or any other crime: it had been carried out by a second active service unit, hitherto unacknowledged, still gloriously at large, and bent on raising hell. Up yours to the British police. That's a laugh, from the BBC newsroom. Hear hear from the Home Secretary. Eric was fretful.

'Turn it off,' he begged. 'I can't be bothered. They're always killing somebody.'

'Doesn't it matter that they're going to be charged with something they didn't commit?'

But Eric was nothing if not impartial.

'So tell me what else is new?' he sulked, maddeningly. 'They're Irish, aren't they? Any Irish will do. You can't go arresting some poor Nigerian if it's a terrorist thing. It has to be an Irishman. Otherwise they'd be arresting people like us for all the shitty things that happen.'

'Did you ever meet him – Nicholas?'

'Not at all my cup of tea, dear,' Eric said. 'Where would *I* meet him?'

'He was bent as a butcher's hook.'

'Not to my knowledge.'

'Eric, I want you to tell me about Hilary.'

'What about him?' he snuffled.

'Anything.'

'A nice man.'

'He had nice parties.'

'Are you asking me or telling me?'

'He's done a bunk,' I said. 'Run away from the house in the woods. Scarpered.'

Eric waved his hands about.

'What do I care? I've got troubles of my own.'

'But you went there a few times.'

'In the old days. Everybody went there.'

He named a radio actor who had introduced him to the Hilary crowd. I just about recognized the name. Eric began to weep again.

'You don't know what it's like to be old and poor. I'm even fat because I'm poor. That was on *Woman's Hour* the other day and you can imagine what a cheer-up I got there. I've stopped my knitting! The knitting has gone to the wall! It's a crime, what life is doing to me.'

'Where would Hilary go? Did he have any family?'

'He was *ancient*,' Eric shrieked. 'His mum and dad must have been dead for donkey's years. What are you talking about, family?'

'Brothers or sisters?'

'I never heard of any. It *is* still quite legal to leave your house and go somewhere else for a change, you know. I mean, I realize things are bad, but we do have some freedoms left.'

'You haven't heard anything?'

'Do me a favour. I've had other things on my mind.'

It was a pretty long shot to have called on him, but when I said I must be going, he had a panic attack of tears again, and said that everybody wanted to use him. He reminded himself of one of those boot scrapers they used to have outside posh houses.

I took him to a pub within walking distance called the Gardeners. He ordered a large Campari and soda. He was in a mood to sulk now. No avenue of general conversation tempted him out, any more than the surprising number of men and women who came to ruffle his thinning hair and ask him how he was going on, then? He sat studying his nails in lofty silence. I felt myself falling out of sympathy. I would have to press him.

'There was a girl, Judith Firestone. Roy knew her. She's been badly beaten up. Show some interest, Eric, or I'll never talk to you again.'

'Oh well, that does get my womb in a twist, I must say.'

'She was a friend of Hilary's. That's how I got to know her.'

'I'm not stupid, dear heart,' Eric said. 'Madam's little dust-up has been on the news. Of course we know who did it, don't we?'

'Who?'

'Oh, I think you *do* know. Everybody else in this dump of a town seems to think they know. And you had a hand in it, too. Who stitched the bloke up and got him suspended in the first place?'

'Not me.'

'Somebody did,' Eric said primly. 'They don't like that. Coppers, I mean.'

He broke off to point to a man at the bar, lonely and defeated.

'See her? What a wag. But I mean a total *femme* goddess of her time. She's been all over Europe and America in her time, dear, and you wouldn't think so now, would you?'

The man saw us looking at him and walked over to join us. He showed no irritation at all at being called Gloria by Eric.

'This young man was asking about Hilary,' Eric said.

'Greece,' Gloria said.

'There you are,' Eric said. 'Your question answered.'

I looked into Gloria's eyes. They were, as far as I could tell, guileless. The only problem lurking there was whether the information he had supplied merited a drink.

'What makes you say Greece?'

'A very cruel country, unless you know it,' Gloria fenced.

'And hot in summer, yes. But just answer the question.'

Gloria looked at Eric.

'Who is this person, please?'

He believed Hilary to have gone to Greece for a ready reason. They had met on the railway station two mornings ago. Gloria was going racing at Newbury. Hilary was toting a bag with a luggage tag indicating a Greek travel firm.

'You can't remember the name of the firm?'

Gloria put his hands together, the fingertips touching his nose.

'I don't believe I can, cherub,' he said comfortably. 'Funny that, isn't it?'

'A new tag. Not some old souvenir of a thing?'

'I'd say he was tucking into the *souvlaki* right about now. I wouldn't give you a thank you for those Greek gentlemen. There's not a lot of sin in Greece these days. And not a single jot of style.'

'Manners maketh Man,' Eric observed reflectively.

'Abso-bloody-lutely,' Gloria agreed.

Mr Shah pressed me to take the plastic covered clothesline. I knew better. He also stocked the much less durable hemp variety which, as he pointed out, ladies no longer desired. I bought the hemp and a grapefruit knife with which to cut it. He giggled politely. The little corner shop was empty. It was nine-thirty and I was easily identified by him as an early evening drunk trying to be sensible and resourceful.

'You are wishing something else?'

I bought a little tin of curry powder and two bottles of Bulls' Blood. Now I had his interest.

'This is for party?'

'This is for justice. I'll buy some rice. Twenty cigarettes, a bread knife and a cake icing thing. Something you use for cake icing.'

'A piping bag,' he said gravely.

'Good. And a large jar of mustard.'

'Only one size.'

'Two like that. Make it three.'

'You wish chutney?'

'Yes, mango chutney. And some cake candles.'

'All this is for justice?'

'Some of it is for curried vegetables.'

'You live locally?'

'I was born under a wandering star.'

'I also,' Mr Shah said.

'Maybe I need a spoon.'

'Spoon?'

'For the mustard.'

I put all this in the car and went for a walk to try to sober up. In the end I went into a hideous, green-tiled pub called the Wheatsheaf, where a quiz night was in progress. I drank a couple of pints, answering the questions in my head, and thinking about Hilary. I was getting into overload here. The questions were being mauled about by the landlord on an almost unintelligible PA system. Hilary, Judith, Gloria, Hilary. Had Gloria existed, or had I invented him? Nye Bevan, Jackie Milburn. The Formosa Straits. Palaeontology. Don't know. Madison. I ordered a large whispy and water.

'Large what, chief?'

'Scotch.'

Hilary, Edgar, Othello. The General Agreement on Tariffs and Trade, Vivaldi, Martha and the Vandellas. Judith. That was it! – Edgar!

'You're pissed,' an old crone at the bar told me.

'I am, sweetheart.'

'Well, buy me a drink then.'

At the judging, only one other punter believed the answer to question 37 was Martha and the Vandellas. He was a dangerously large and bearded man who was so convinced of the rightness of his case that he punched out the teacher at the next table whose derision was a little too raucous. He was in turn hit in the meat of the back by a chair. A general mêlée ensued.

'It's always like this,' the old crone observed. 'People like to be right, don't they?'

'Human nature,' I said.

'Barry?' she scoffed. 'He's not human. His mother was a Wilson.'

It was dark when I left the pub. The little short streets of terraced villas were filled with an almost tangible sense of repletion. Food, booze, sex, sleep. The only people about were drunks like me, and men walking their dogs. Exactly. I found the car and drove off with an exaggerated attention to the Highway Code.

Drunk as I was, I had only to hit him twice. Once was as I came out of the friendly cat-smelling mahonia of a corner house called Glenside like a bat out of hell. The punch to the kidneys I gave him would have felled a runaway ox, let alone an unsuspecting surburban dog-walker. He went flat on his face, leaving Barney to scamper off, all ears and dog-lead. As Edgar got to his hands and knees, I kicked him in the throat with all the force I could muster. This time he went down and stayed down, his white shirt fluttering in the balmy midnight air. I rolled him into the Glenside mahonia and went to fetch the Renault, hidden round the corner. Barney came with me, and as an impromptu I let him into the car, where he scampered this way and that, the daft thing. Then, very, very carefully, I reversed back round to pick up Edgar. Princess Anne Drive slumbered on. Glenside stayed unlit. Maybe Mikey and Helen were watching snooker in the back, or maybe they had gone to bed at ten with the Habitat catalogue. What the hell did I care? Everything was going like clockwork. Edgar was calm and peaceful, no more human for the time being than a roll of lino. A car passed. Some corporal of commerce was weaving his way home from the golf club. And that's where we were heading. I tucked Edgar in, slammed the tailgate, and fell into the car myself. Barney barked for joy.

A road runs up between the fairways, a lovers' lane of sorts. It was really quite exciting. I drove through a gap in the out of bounds and bumped along in the grassy dark with the lights extinguished. Bunkers loomed like tank traps. We rolled gently along swales that caught the sliced ball, and through screens of bushes that gathered up the hook. At the edge of the fifth green was a large oak tree that had in its day ruined many a medal card. It seemed just about perfect. I got out of the car and began cutting up the clothesline with the bread knife. Then I rolled Edgar out. He made a satisfying crump. I dragged him to the base of the tree and sat him up. I tied off one wrist and ran the rope round the tree. After some bother, I found his other wrist and completed the job. I sat down for a smoke, my head spinning. Owls tooted. Barney galloped this way and that. I passed the time making a rope gag. Edgar seemed to be on his way back to us.

'Who's there?' he asked stupidly, his arms out behind him. He tugged furiously. 'What is this?'

But I wasn't there to banter with him. I slipped the rope gag round his head and tied it off. It was a pleasant moment when he recognized me. His eyes widened nicely. I employed the rest of the clothesline to make his head secure to the oak, wandering and stumbling about, round and round, feeling faintly dizzy. All the knots came from the Scouts, however. I had been a Kingfisher in my time.

'How you doing, big Eddie?' I asked.

He made urgent noises.

'Don't bother to answer. You're doing great. That's nice to hear. Well, I'm pissed, old love. But with a full heart. My heart is full. I'm here on behalf of Judith. Smight by name, Firestone by nature. I think you know the lady.'

He lashed out with his feet and I tied his legs together at the ankle. Barney watched. I made a noose out of the dog-lead and tethered Barney's perplexed little frame to Master's feet.

'You put her in hospital, right? Well, you didn't know that until you saw it on the news – you actually left her for dead. You beat a woman up and then raped her. You bust her ribs – she could have punctured a lung. Or drowned in her own vomit. That's as good as leaving her for dead. See? Follow me, get my drift?'

He was trying to say no, it wasn't him; or more realistically, it was him, but he regretted it feelingly now. I waved his head-wagging away.

'Maybe it didn't really matter if she survived. Was that it? You probably felt she deserved it in some way.'

I went round checking on the ropes and knots. I could plainly see Edgar's eyes bulging in the little romantic dusting of moonlight that fell on us. The spaniel had sat down and was contentedly listening to the music of the spheres, the way dogs do.

'You did all this out of spite, or stress, or because you wanted your revenge on women. Or for some other codswallop reason. Liberal opinion would be outraged at the way I'm dealing with it. It's very immature and solves nothing. Etcetera. You need counselling perhaps. Or perhaps you need play therapy. But tonight, Edgar dear, you've got me. It's way over the top and I sincerely hope I shall feel dreadful in the morning. But just tonight, I'm all out of liberal decency. So instead, we are adapting and borrowing freely from the Conestoga Indians. As they used to make clear in word and gesture, you've got it coming to you.'

I walked back to the car for the jars of mustard, the curry powder and the piping bag.

There was a lay-by in the little road through the golf course, or perhaps more of a passing place. I sat finishing my third cigarette with the window wound down, waiting for Edgar to chew his way through the rope gag and begin screaming. When he did, the sound was unearthly. He was trying to bellow, but it came out bat-squeak thin. Well, it would, wouldn't it? Barney was earning his dog biscuits at last, barking and whining as Edgar's convulsions flipped him base over apex and Mr Shah's clothesline twanged like a banjo string. I waited until Edgar found his true voice, or at any rate a deeper note, and left him to his manly screams, and retching noises that could be heard in the next county.

21

I woke on the bed in Judith's flat, my tongue stuck to the roof of my mouth. I tottered into the shower and sat for a while, drowning the butterflies that seemed to have replaced my brains. They flew their erratic course inside my skull to Mendelssohn, who happened to be Composer of the Week. Now there was a gifted lad. He wrote the string octet when he was sixteen; at that age I was hard put to distinguish Brahms from Beethoven, and in any case I was much more interested in the tight trumpet playing of Bunny Berigan. Classical music, as it was still called by its adherents, belonged to the sort of people who lived in houses called Laburnum Lodge and the like, families with violins and pianos scattered about, whose kids came to school with fiddle cases under their arms. My mother was wont to point the bread knife at me after observations of this kind, and advise me that I was free to go and live with such people. In fact it was her dearest wish.

Judith steals away from her neat white shoebox of a flat, leaving the gas, electricity and water turned on. She goes to Hilary – not to rob him, but to see him, to talk to him. Consult, confer. About what? She goes – I contradicted myself – to harangue him, to harry, hector. Or again, to plead, to implore. What occurs in fact is a common lesson of experience. Something else happens that is none of these things. She is up-ended. She is hit from behind by what must have seemed to her to be something coming out of nowhere.

I was just putting three soluble Vitamin C tablets into a

227

glass of orange juice and licking away the hideous froth when the phone rang.

'Nice one,' Ted Gerson said.

'Has he said anything?'

'Not that you would call speech, no. He has a nasty sore throat. But enough's enough, right? No more games.'

'Sure.'

'I mean this. He's in a bad way.'

'*Will* he talk?'

'Shouldn't think so. Would you?'

'Okay, no more games,' I promised. 'But do me a favour, Ted.'

'Fire away.'

It had to sound dead casual, and there's no more difficult trick in the book.

'Do you happen to know if Judith had her passport with her when she was found?'

There was a silence while Ted kicked himself.

'Matter, does it?'

'Only to me, old mate. I thought I would take her away for a day or two when she gets out. Bit of a holiday. I can't find the passport in the flat.'

More silence.

'She has it with her,' he said at last.

'That's okay, then. Problem solved. Cheers.'

'Planned anywhere nice?' he asked.

'You know. Abroad.'

'Sounds great,' he said glumly.

I opened all the windows to the flat and hoovered to Radio 3. Mendelssohn is now twenty-one and knocks out the first twenty bars to Fingal's Cave on a damp and rain-soaked bit of paper after a visit. The boat hasn't even left Staffa for the mainland. This dilettante rich kid, this inspired amateur with the foppish clothes, has already been to Holyrood and decided to write a Scottish Symphony. Is there nae end to his talent, the boatman muses?

The kitchen was a bit of a mess and I spent a recuperative half hour wiping fur from the kettle and the tea caddy, arranging the contents of the cupboards and generally making a nuisance of myself. The steady trip-hammer thump I could hear was inside my head and not out there in the great wide world. I made tea and read a year-old *Listener* from cover to cover, after popping one of the indispensables of modern living, a red Sudafed. I thought about running away with Sonia's money, maybe to Albania, where for all the buzz of reform, a thing still either is or it is not. No half-truths, no part measures. If there's something not quite right about you, then it's down to the nick for you, my son.

The phone rang. It was Lydia Nicholas.

'Can I see you?'

'That would be nice. Where are you?'

Only ten minutes later, she was making us both filter coffee in Judith's spanking clean kitchen.

'You look terrible.'

'Thanks a mill.'

'I have just had audience with that revolting humbug, the Prime Minister. Have you ever been inside that place?'

'Number Ten? Not often, no. Bit swank, is it?'

'It's ghastly. I went to receive the commiserations of the Chief Hypocrite in person. And guess what?'

'It turned into a photo-opportunity.'

'We shook hands by the fireplace,' Lydia agreed. 'The Prime Minister said that it was quite the worst part of the job, having to make grief public. Then I was dragged to some godawful sofa and had my hands held in a grip of steel, as an expression of comfort. So now I need you to cheer me up properly. Whose place is this, by the way?'

I told her what had happened to Judith. She listened with her head in her hands. I liked her for it. She was a serious person. As I was talking, I had a sudden rush of intuition and interrupted myself in mid-sentence.

'I should have asked you this the first time we met – how well do you know Hilary?'

She looked up, not in the slightest bit startled.

'I know several Hilarys. Which one do you mean?'

'This one's the artist. He used to live in a little gingerbread house in the middle of an enchanted wood.'

'Then what happened?'

'What happens in all good fairy stories – he disappeared.'

Lydia sat up.

'Is he all right?' she asked sharply.

'He's on his hols. Guess where? And don't say the Land of Lollipops and Rainbows. Can we say you *do* know him, among other Hilarys of your acquaintance?'

'My cousin,' she said, with that clipped, upper-class delivery that bids you ask no further questions. 'If you had bothered to read one of my books, you would have seen that he illustrates them.'

'Aren't we all cosy? You and old Hils cousins.'

'Strictly speaking he is a second cousin. And please don't call him Hils. How do you know him?'

'Don't let's play silly buggers, Lydia. How do you think I know him – through his long and warm association with David and Judith, of course.'

She jumped up, kicking over her coffee mug.

'Well how in hell did *they* know him?'

'Because he lives in a charming little cottage, far from prying eyes. He's just too, too sweet for words and very accommodating to the right kind of people. Sex parties, Lydia. Amateur photography, dope, prankish goings-on. And I don't know what else besides. But enough to make him run for it once the heat was turned up. I think Judith went there for help – or maybe as part of a plan they had. But Hilary had already bolted.'

'Shit,' Lydia said. She went to fetch a cloth to mop the floor.

'Look,' she said. 'This is all news to me. I have seen him

once a year in London for the book thing and he came to Perslade a few times when I was a child. I didn't know where he lived and I certainly didn't know there was a connection to David. I'm absolutely amazed to hear all this. You don't believe me.'

'Either you're lying through your teeth or life really is easier for people with money. Your damn cousin does book illustrations for you and you never once have the need or desire to visit him, or ring him up?'

'He said he preferred it that way. It made no real difference to me.'

'Your cousin,' I reminded her.

'What difference does that make?'

'You needed an illustrator and you immediately think of your long lost cousin or second cousin, who isn't on the phone and whose address you don't have. An obvious choice. Or did you bump into him coming out of Harrods?'

'Good!' Lydia exclaimed. 'I like this in you! I like the cheap sarcasms. They make me spark. I am going to get you to see, against all the odds and much to your annoyance, that you've met an honest person for once. If that's what you want a fight about, that's what we'll have. You want to know how I found him? David suggested him.'

I laughed in spite of myself.

'You people are wonderful.'

'Try not to talk like a child.'

'David just happens to say I know a book illustrator if you're looking for one. And you say good-oh. And *I'm* being childish?'

'Yes,' Lydia said tartly.

'David was arranging tripes, hearts, lungs and liver over a member of your own sex in this gink's parlour. And then screwing the mess. And of course being photographed. Probably by your illustrator.'

'Did *I* know that?' she shouted. 'I've just told you, I didn't know that.'

She riffled through Judith's CDs with shaking hands. There was nothing to her taste. She lit a cigarette and threw herself down on the couch next to me. I found myself taking her hand and apologizing. She kissed me on the lips.

'All right. When I was about ten or eleven, he came to Perslade with his parents for a family conference. He was in his late twenties and had been caught importuning little boys at some school in Oxford where he taught. I thought he might equally like little girls with no bumps. He took some snapshots of me and we went up on to the roof to sunbathe – that sort of thing. We were playing a game of hiding from the grown-ups. He taught me to talk to cats properly but rejected my offer to marry him – that sort of thing. Are you getting a picture?'

'It was just schoolgirl fun.'

'That's exactly what it was. When David mentioned his name thirty years later I was very keen to meet him. I made some enquiries. He seemed quite well known as an illustrator. In the end we met in a pub – where I met you, in fact. It was very irritating and inconvenient, but I put it down to a particular life-style. Of course, David did not once say he knew him personally.'

'Well there's some reason to suppose he's gone to Greece.'

She wrinkled her nose.

'Perhaps I'm being a bit stupid. But so what?'

'The home of Zeus and all that stuff. Where the *Greeks* live. Where you sent your letters.'

Lydia's mouth fell ajar and she blinked a few times.

'Oh God. Please don't tell me he knows Yanni as well?'

'I did ask him that once and he said no. The word of a gentleman, possibly. Now listen to me, Lydia. I don't think I could love life with the same joyous intensity if I met just one more liar. So tell me you've been speaking the absolute truth.'

'Everything I know,' she promised. 'Does it matter that he's gone to Greece?'

'I think Judith may have been planning the same thing.'

'But what does it mean?'

'Hard to remember, the pace of life being what it is today, but quite recently somebody blew your husband's head off.'

'*Hilary?*' Lydia shouted, incredulous.

'Somebody. And not the IRA.'

'But Hilary, for God's sake?'

'There is an extremely honest and dogged policeman plodding along in the wake of all this called Gerson. You met him. He's being asked to cover up something nasty. I don't think he has it in him, but in any case I think the lid will blow off.'

She jumped up and took off the jacket to her silk suit. Underneath she wore a sleeveless white blouse. The points to her breasts tented it out appealingly.

'I think we should have a very large drink,' she said. 'And then, since you're such a stickler for the truth, I think you should tell me all the bits you've so far left out.'

But I was saved from telling her about Wilma Curtess by the sudden and startling opening of the door, crashing back to the wall. Frank Givens was paying a social visit.

'First,' he said, 'I pay you a compliment. The work you did last night was good. When I heard about Judith, I already planned for the man to meet Nigel here. That may still happen. If it does, the man is dead.'

Nigel was glowering. I had cheated him out of a job. More, I had detracted from his sense of self. He was not just a bouncer, he was one of Big Frank's best soldiers. He looked hungry. He looked mean. He looked quite capable of eating the furniture if required to do so by his boss.

'You've changed since we last spoke, Frank. And so has Sonny Jim here. What's happened?'

'We've had word from the hospital. Judith has gone. Discharged herself. I want to know where she is. But before you say anything, let me warn you. You're a funny man. Okay. But I only ever laugh at misfortune. Got that?'

233

It was true he hardly seemed the same man. Even his clothes were different. He wore a pale dove-pink suit with silver threads in it, and sported a matching mauve handkerchief and tie.

'This lady will find it hard to understand what we're talking about,' I temporized. 'So I'll just see her to a cab.'

Big Nige laughed. Givens was ominously calm. He turned his gaze on Lydia.

'You're Mrs Nicholas, of course. This thing we're talking don't concern you. Pick up your bag and go.'

Perhaps he did not know she had come direct from Downing Street.

'You stupid little man,' she said with breath-taking asperity. 'I'll do exactly as I like, thank you so much.'

Givens examined his nails.

'Mrs Nicholas, don't make a fool of yourself. This is a business matter between me and the clown here. Go back to your stately home, or wherever you live, and get on with your life. Bury your husband.'

'The murdering bastard,' Nigel added. Maybe it was his way of showing he could follow the conversation. Givens frowned, and Lydia turned to me in bewilderment.

'Do you know what they're talking about?'

'Just do as he says. Pick up your stuff and go. I'll call you later.'

'I'll stay,' she said. Nigel giggled. He pointed a bent finger at her.

'You're husband's a big cheese, right? In the Government and that? He murder a black girl called Wilma Curtess, understand what I'm saying? Cut her belly open and chuck her in the river. Maybe he don't say nothing to you, like you have the amazement on you now and that. But your husband he's like a pile of shit, right? He kill this black whore, I'm telling you, know what I mean?'

'For which he was going to cop a charge of murder,' Givens murmured. 'Hence murdering bastard.'

Lydia looked at me.

'Is this true?'

Givens waved his hand.

'A hundred per cent it is true. If someone hadn't offed him, he would have stood trial. No question.'

Time for me to make a defiant gesture.

'What happened, then? Who did kill him? Did Nigel here get his wires crossed? He doesn't look too bright.'

'First off,' Nigel explained softly, 'I wouldn't have used no shooter on the guy, right? That would have been too quick and that ain't my way. Second, watch your tongue. Speak when you are spoke to.'

'Is it true?' Lydia repeated, aghast. 'About this girl?'

'I'm a businessman, Mrs Nicholas. I'm part of the enterprise culture. I vote for your husband's Party. But you can take it from me, it's def. Your boyfriend here is trying to protect your finer feelings. But he knows. Half fucking London knows.'

He lit a cigarette and turned back to me.

'Now then. You saw Judith yesterday. Where is she?'

'I don't know.'

'And Hilary?'

My groin began to crawl.

'Who's Hilary?'

Givens sighed. He nodded to Nigel, who picked me off the couch with both hands and tossed me into the hi-fi stack with no more effort than if I were a cushion. The whole lot came down on me, equipment, CDs, the lot. Nigel reached and picked me up again. This time he threw me against the far wall. There was a crash of glass as a framed print fell off its hook.

'Now pay attention, clown. I want to make this quite clear. When I catch up with those two, they're going to be sorry they were ever born. They're going to suffer. Can you hear me, can you understand what I'm saying?'

Nigel pirouetted and kicked me in the chest as I tried to

stand. But Lydia had been in a rough house or two in her more exotic days. She tried to jump on his back. There was a brief tussle before he had her standing on tiptoe, his hand under her chin, his fingers pushing the flesh of her cheeks into her eyes. With his free hand he ripped the blouse off her back; then, with a single snatch, her bra. He threw her back into the couch before attending to me a third time. I was trying to crawl up his leg, my ears ringing. Fists tight to my scalp, he ran me into the wall.

'Quiet,' Givens bellowed. Nigel stopped shouting and Lydia stopped screaming. I looked cross-eyed down my nose at the bright red blood that was pumping out of it in spurts. Givens kicked out in irritation to get me away from the cuffs of his trousers.

'You,' he ordered, 'will keep your face out of it from now on. I never want to hear your name again. If I do, you are in deep shit.'

Nigel picked me off the carpet and put his face close to mine.

'Give Mr Givens here some of your lip. I want you to. Then I give this woman here some bone, so for once in her life she feel it. Right here in front of you. She ain't never going to be clean again. You hear?'

'Why are you doing this to us?' Lydia shouted. 'What are you trying to protect?'

Givens wagged a stubby finger at her.

'Until Billie Curtess was murdered, I couldn't give a toss about you or your husband. Know nothing about you or this piece of shit on the carpet. I am a businessman, Mrs Nicholas. I protect my business. You come any closer, ask any more damnfool questions, do any more damnfool things, you wind up hurt. That is the way we people go about our business.'

He watched me trying to get to my hands and knees.

'You in particular. No more Judith, understand? I leave that white bitch without a nose and ears, I find her. You be out of

236

this flat by six tonight. Maybe this woman will take you in. I don't care. No more putting two and two together. When I find Judith, like I say, I explain the situation to her too. But you, now, are out of it.'

I made a lunge for him that he evaded easily. I fell on my face on top of the coffee table. Nigel laughed.

'This geezer is stupid. Better I take him out to Epping, break both his arms.'

He stamped on my instep and the pain catapulted me over the table. I fell in a shower of coffee mugs, ashtrays, the light that Judith had switched on and off all those years ago; and blood. Givens stood.

'You are a sensible and educated woman, Mrs Nicholas. You can see the broad picture. You have children for example. This person on the carpet is finished. He is out of it for good. So clean yourself, find a blouse from Judith's wardrobe, and go home.'

'Listen to the man,' Nigel crooned. He brushed the palm of his hand upwards over her breasts and giggled when she struck it away. Lydia beat on his face and chest with closed fists. Nigel just giggled some more. But Givens was sauntering towards the door. He didn't pay big money to his minder to find himself opening his own doors. Regretfully, the gorilla pushed Lydia away.

They left us hugging each other in the wreckage of the room. I thought of Waxman downstairs, hiding behind Leah, and knowing the bumps and crashes had not been me trying to teach Lydia the rudiments of basketball. I listened hard to hear if they stopped off at his door. They tramped downstairs, nattering. Lydia clung to me, sobbing. There was blood and glass everywhere and the sharp nip of electrical insulations burning out.

'My God.' Nicholas's widow laughed hysterically. 'How much blood have you got inside you? There's pints of it every-where.'

I slumped to the floor, her on top of me. Her breasts were wet with blood. It was caught up in gobs at the side of her face.

'It's like being in the damn movies,' she shrieked.

So it was. Givens had played a good scene with his pal Nigel. It was far too much like the movies. But he had got his central point across. He was serious. He might come on like a bad film, but he knew, I thought, he was getting his point across. I jammed my bleeding nose against the sharp point of Lydia's shoulder. If I was frightening her into unseemly laughter, it was a pound to a penny that Judith's face was scaring the living shit out of passengers waiting in the boarding lounge to begin a late season stint in the sun. In Athens for example, or that neck of the woods.

'What utterly clichéd villains!' Lydia shouted, rolling off me. Her hysterics gently subsided, leaving her staring at the ceiling, covered in my blood, and reflecting that only an hour or so ago she had been sitting with her knees together, looking into the Prime Minister's mad and unforgiving eyes.

22

David Nicholas was buried in All Saints Church, Perslade, on September 13th. The widow had expressed a desire for a quiet funeral and so a congregation of no more than two hundred saw him to his rest, attended by thirty photographers and two network television crews. The vicar was torn between elation and religious earnestness. Sitting in the family pew, next to the widow, her children and her parents, was Dickie Sampson, full of jowl and sleepy-eyed, the Chairman of the Party and a life peer. The Home Office was represented by the two junior ministers who had been David's colleagues. The Leader of the Opposition sent a wreath, much photographed by the Press. With that hideous sense of vulgarity that sometimes overcomes otherwise quite rational and good-hearted English people, the floral tributes were guarded by two melancholy children in Scout uniform. Most absurd of all – especially if you believed the papers and thought David had been done in by the IRA – a giant Union flag was flown from the church tower.

The lessons were read by a convicted murderer – nice touch – who had paid his debt to society, married his prison literature tutor, divorced her, and published a not very good novel touching these matters; and by Lord Smeaton, Home Office spokesman in the Lords. The noble lord was distinguished by a lack of chin, a child's haircut and a peculiar fluting voice more suitable to luring birds, or calling the cattle home across the lea. He looked about nineteen years old and was the only person present at all likely to burst into tears. The convicted murderer turned wordsmith was a different matter altogether. He scandalized the locals by mounting the pulpit in a leather blouson without tie, and jeans so crumpled you could use them to make concertina bellows. It goes without saying that he came from Liverpool and was a celeb on late night television. Dickie Sampson listened to his nasal twang with every appearance of pleasure. It was all a terribly English occasion, from the flowers to the hats. The language of the service was in the New English Banal Version.

So far as the cameras were concerned, Dickie and the Perslades stood side by side in their solemn rededication to the fight against terrorism. And by now we were certainly talking terrorism. The Prime Minister's spin doctors had been hard at work in that regard for two days past, with enough success to cause three harmless Catholics to be done to death in Northern Ireland by Loyalist bullets. In Leeds, there had been a serious affray outside the Irish Centre. The Prime Minister's stance had hardened. The words 'cruel assassination' had now been used twice publicly. Thus Dickie and that other slice of Old English roast beef, Lord Perslade, volunteered themselves for many photo-opportunities. Dickie shook hands with the Scouts. Perslade stuck out his jaw and glowered like Mussolini. But the Chairman of the Party was batting against country bowling, as he soon discovered.

'Rather good, this parson,' Dickie said very audibly, after the service.

'Bloody sound man,' Lord Perslade snapped.

'Good turn out for the boy. The locals very loyal.'

'Here for the telly,' Perslade explained, as if to a child.

'Are we goin' over the boozer after, or wha'?' the novelist murderer wanted to know of anyone who stood near him.

Lydia, as far as I could judge, was already higher than a kite. She beamed smiles on everyone and infuriated her children by ruffling their hair, along with other motherly, but also decidedly First Lady gestures. I was never nearer than thirty yards from her. I sat through the service with the postman, a sardonic gargoyle called Alf. At the Committal, he and I stood in the lee of a buttress, having a crafty smoke and talking Alf's politics, which were to gas the festering lot of them. He meant the upper classes.

'You'd be from London, I suppose?'

'Sort of, yes.'

'Been a few times meself. Did nothing for me. Press, are you?'

'No.'

'Scruffy enough for the Press.'

'It's the new style, see, Alf.'

He beamed his bright red nose at me.

'He was a pushy bugger, this one, and no mistake. Clever man, mind, but you can't always set store by that. A bit of a liability even, in their game. They say the Irish did him in.'

'Believe that?'

'I should think if anyone shot him it would be old Perslade.'

'Why do you say that?'

''Cos I'm barmy,' Alf said, with low cunning.

We straightened ourselves and stood to attention as the party that had gone to the grave suddenly came round the corner of the church, led by the vicar in flapping gown. As she passed, Lydia looked at me without expression. Sampson and his detective brought up the rear of the procession, their shoes crunching on the juicy, rain-filled gravel. The Chairman of the Party smiled at us and astounded Postman Alf by pausing to shake his hand. A helicopter wittered overhead.

'A right bloody bunch,' Alf muttered.

I drove back to a caravan site located at Battiscombe Farm and made a pot of tea. There was a portable television in the caravan but its frame hold was on the blink. Racing from Doncaster slithered past like a cascade of playing cards. My neighbours had drawn their curtains and were at it like stoats. Most of the other late holiday-makers were retired folk, walking about the sodden fields at a snail's pace. One of the redheaded Battiscombe boys was riding his trials bike through the little valley, leaving behind the acrid smoke of hundred octane fuel. It was all very relaxing, in its way. Intermediate Orchestra won the big race at Doncaster. A wasp tottered about at the window pane, dying of boredom or old age. I thought about the peculiar smell of sun-warmed varnish, and whether there was any real chemistry in the difference between that and the utterly different smell of damp carpets.

Lydia Nicholas came about seven. She had changed into jeans and a sweater. It transpired that the Perslades had asked the most notable guests back to the house, given them smoked-salmon sandwiches and champagne, a flustering touch, and then sent them packing. Lydia waited until her father had gone to talk to the deer, his invariable six o'clock habit come hell or high water, and then slipped away. She was extremely tense.

'You haven't heard any more?' she asked.

'No. Only you know that I'm here. How about you?'

'Me?' she protested, but looked uneasy.

'From Yanni, for example?'

She shook her head and plumped down too hard on the unyielding cushions of the banquette.

'The Athens telephone number doesn't exist. Maybe the address is fake as well. Maybe I'm too stupid for words. Or too trusting or something. You think all three of them are over there together, don't you?'

'It would be a laugh,' I admitted.

We drank lukewarm vodka and tonic. She peered into the glass, looking dark and vexed.

'What did you think to the thing at the church?'

'The thing at the church – oh, you mean your late husband's funeral.'

'Oh, do piss off. I'm not in the mood for it.'

'I thought it was all a jolly good show.'

242

She slugged back her drink and wiped her mouth with her wrist. My neighbours had drawn back the curtains and were dancing cheek to cheek to an inaudible radio. They looked like schoolteachers engaged in their first adultery. Miss was short and dark. Sir was tall and thin.

'This is a terrible place,' Lydia said. I saw that she was crying.

'Chin up, you don't have to live here. There are toads in the bogs. Horse-flies like condors.'

'Could that man Givens get to them, do you think?'

'The Terrible Trio? He'd have to find them. But after that I don't think he'd have any trouble. Big Nigel looked the part. And violence is international, like flower-arranging. It crosses language barriers.'

'Could you stop Givens?'

'Lydia, I am crapping with toads jumping over my shoes just because I'm no match for that sort of thing. Givens is no mug. When he says he has business interests, he's not talking about buying little terrace houses in Ilford and doing them up for a profit. He acts small-time, but that's his front. I think he's the real thing. Okay?'

'I thought he was an insufferable little oik.'

'Well, there you go.'

She stared out of the caravan window. The rain was tumbling down. My two teachers were sitting at the table, a litre of wine between them. Beyond, yellow rectangles of light indicated other caravanners serving up fish fingers and beans or, perhaps more adventurously, instant chow mein.

'You must realize what it is that's bugging me. I want to see him again.'

'The plucky Greek.'

'Yanni.'

'Yes, well, that's very romantic, Lydia. You should take a Mediterranean holiday, perhaps. Buy a reliable phrase-book and go off into the blue for a couple of years. Who knows? Stanley found Livingstone.'

243

'He lied to me. He seemed so simple and direct, so obvious – and yet he lied to me. Did he kill David?'

'Pass.'

'Oh God,' Lydia wailed. 'What does it matter? I can't spend the rest of my life being the grieving widow. I can't stay cooped up. I want him. I want the chance of him.'

'And what am I supposed to do about that?'

Lydia shook her head, as if clearing away insects.

'I don't want that whore to get away with any more, that's absolutely certain.'

'Is she getting away with anything?'

'Your friend Givens seems to think so. What is she doing over there?'

'What am I, a mind-reader?'

'Some poxed-up, overweight cow, humping around with her udders.'

I thought of David's coffin in the fresh ground, the rain seeping down six feet through the air-spaces. I was in no mood to fight Lydia about Judith. Hilary had flown to Athens, she to Corfu. This from Ted Gerson whom I phoned at his house every night. He showed no special interest in where I was. Not that it mattered – Battiscombe Farm, which had been Lydia's bright idea, might as well have been on Planet X for all Ted cared. While it doesn't take very much to tumble into drama and intrigue, it takes even less to tumble all the way back out again. Down here on the farm, the world of Frank Givens was practically unimaginable. I had all on to remember that we were talking about an errant bundle of molecules called Yanni who had skipped the country with millions. I mentioned this in a mild way.

'That's not the point. You haven't answered my question. Did he kill David?'

The rain had increased in volume, so that it rattled the roof and threatened the leaking windows of the caravan. I felt that terrible languor that comes from inhaling too much Calor gas and enduring too much loneliness.

'Maybe,' I said at last.

'And we can just leave it be, can we?'

'We? Who's we? Listen, Lydia, you would like to see him again. I would like to know that she's safe. That's very sweet of us both. But I have to say they seem – compared to you and me they seem – extremely resourceful people. They are following a plan. And enjoying the fruits of it, maybe. Or maybe they're double-crossing each other blind. Who knows? I won't say who cares, but why don't we call it a day? I have enough money for one more week in this dump. By then my hair will have turned white. You're not talking to Sam Spade.'

Lydia sighed. She extended her hand in a sudden manly gesture.

'You're right,' she said. 'It's all hopeless.'

Though I had been asking for it, the chomp of the axe cutting through the tangled knot was painful to my ears. I stood, hoping to embrace her at the very least. She read my intention.

'Maybe if we'd met some other time,' she murmured.

'Ah yes, but then you would have set the dogs on me.'

I walked her to the car with my coat held over her head. The rain was coming down like a film tempest, and the grass was slippery. She got in the car and stared at me a brief moment. I must have looked eminently disposable – drenched to the skin and shivering with cold. I thought she was going to say something, but all I had from her was a tight little smile. She started her engine with a customary wasteful roar and then lolloped cautiously across the caravan site. Her tail-lights blinked on and off. Maybe she was signalling goodbye. But it was more likely she had forgotten for the moment how to find the main beam.

Waxman was murdered in London at almost exactly the same time. He was taken to the roof of a multi-storey car-park in Hammersmith and flung over the side by person or persons unknown. Abutting the car ramps was a Victorian stables that had been converted into a design studio by a partnership of four young gays. It happened they were all there and in conference when the accountant hit the roof above their heads. He died before the fire brigade could reach him. They brought him through a skylight and laid him on the office floor, drenched, wide-eyed, and smashed up.

It put a new complexion on things. Ted and I met in the pub in Earls Court next day, after I had seen news of Waxman's fall slide past on the caravan telly.

'How is Leah?'

'Hospital. Shock. He sent her to her sister's in Romford. He knew it was coming, in some form or another. She saw it on the news, like you.'

'What about his wheelchair?'

'What about it?' Ted repeated glumly.

'It wasn't there?'

'Where? At the car-park, or in the flat? It wasn't anywhere. It was gone, along with the accounts he was doing for Givens, and anything that even remotely resembled a diary, a notebook, or anything at all by way of a business record. They're waiting for Leah to help them make an inventory of what's missing.'

'What does Givens say? Did you try him?'

'You'll like this. He was in Paris, setting up for a charity concert. The heavy – Nigel? – was with him.'

'They're alibied.'

'Six different ways.'

I studied him. His expression was calm and neutral.

'Does it tie in?'

'Tie in with what? It stinks the place out. It should tie in with something?'

'You know damn well it does, Ted.'

He ignored me. We sat watching the local screamers pouring blackcurrant into their Guinness and talking about yesterday's match at Loftus Road. QPR had been hammered by Everton.

A disabled accountant flung off a roof here and there was nothing to the point. It was somehow un-English, moreover, and because of that, unreal.

'What do you want me to say?' Ted asked, relenting. 'It was crude. It has got up people's noses. Mr Givens and his affairs are going to get put through the mincer.'

'You can promise that, can you?' I asked bitterly.

'It's Serious Crime Squad business. They're swarming all over it. And the Press are intrigued. But it'll never tie into the Nicholas murder unless something goes badly wrong with the machinery. Your trouble is you know too much.'

'That was his trouble.'

'Yeah, maybe. You're worried about your girl.'

'About Judith.'

'I can understand that.'

He picked up his whisky and sniffed. His pale eyes suddenly flicked to my own.

'If she's on Corfu, there is plenty to worry about. But what are you going to do about it? You want to worry more about yourself. I'm talking about the Yard. They may be all bent out of shape by the politics of this Nicholas thing, but they can read and they are still police officers. You keep turning up like a bad penny.'

'Does Judith deserve to be killed?'

'We don't know, do we? We just don't know what really bad shit she's been dealing people. Or do we?'

I shrugged.

'Look,' Ted said, 'I'm going to tell you the truth. There is a murder investigation still in progress on the Nicholas thing.'

He held up his hand to stop me from exclaiming.

'Don't get excited. Not me – I'm out. But you can't corrupt everybody. The DPP's office has yet to frame charges against the three Irish. There's a hell of a row about that with the Cabinet Office. You can imagine. The boys in Wiltshire are digging their heels in, too. The timing stinks. The forensic on the bullet is inconclusive.'

'How can it be inconclusive?'

'No gun,' he murmured.

I stared at him in blank amazement. Over at the bar, football had given way to the other main topic, sex. A very beautiful and assured young blonde was permitting some boisterous young wallies to peep down the front of her tee-shirt, the better to inspect her all-over tan. Ted pushed his chair back.

'Let's talk outside for a bit,' he said.

We stood on the corner, grit flying into our eyes. Ted examined his pipe and put it away in his jacket pocket. Because it was Sunday, he was unshaven, and the bristle at his neck and chin was white. He looked tired, as though doggedness was proving a failing virtue. Sharp lines creased his mouth and chin.

'The Irish boys are shooters, no doubt about that. But the bullet doesn't match the pistols they had when they were arrested. There are other problems, but they don't concern you.'

'Then they didn't do it.'

'We can't say for certain that they did,' he corrected. 'Come on, be grateful I've told you even this much. And it is also very true there are enough hooks and eyes left in that enquiry to link it to the thing that happened last night. Once someone assembles the full cast of characters.'

'You for example.'

'No,' he said heavily. 'Not me. Let's walk.'

'Walk? Where?'

He rounded on me with exasperation.

'Walk, for Christ's sake. For the exercise. For the lack of something better to do.'

We set off down a row of villas, every fourth or fifth one with a drunken estate agent's board looming out of the ugly little gardens. I realized he was preparing to make a big statement. He walked with his hands in his pockets, head down.

'I was only ever interested in Nicholas alive. I've been watching him for nearly three years. He did that black kid, you know. I'm sure of it. But believe me, he had some pull. You've seen what happened once he was dead. I'm a leper for even daring to suggest he was ever anything but Mr Nice Guy.'

'What are you trying to tell me, Ted?'

'I get off here, is what I'm saying. I can't help you any more.'

He did not like saying it. We turned right at the bottom of the road and picked our way over pizza boxes and lager cans skidding up and down in the breeze. One or two men were cleaning their cars. Dogs roamed in packs. All these houses were owner-occupied, and some looked quite elegant. But they were not the houses of proud citizens. What was worth having was exclusively behind the front doors. The street was just a meaningless tract of concrete.

'Can you do that? Can you get out, just like that?'

'In a famous phrase,' he said, 'it's my arse now.'

'This is sudden.'

He would not take my eye, but walked steadily on with his head on his chest.

'You're right. It is sudden. I'm out. I think you should jack your own hand in, too.'

'And wait to see who wins the general election?'

'Very funny. I don't like this, but I have to watch my back. Maybe it'll all come out. That's what the police are here for, eh? But my part in it is over.'

'You're serious?'

'It's a matter of priorities,' he said. The sardonicism floated away on the wind. I was utterly confounded. It seemed incredible to me that someone I knew as well as Ted Gerson should back off. The beer rose back up my throat as sweet bile. We walked the last quarter-mile to his car in strained silence – far too far, far too silent.

He had driven in especially to tell me this, and would return to the plain brick house with the sagging wooden garage, the work shed and the neighbours with their cans of lager and their snuffling grandson. There, at least, there were wisps of an older England – an ancient and cherished oak in the middle of the road girded with hoops and railings, wild flowers in the woods and trees, even flints in the fields of the men like him who had first settled there not years but centuries before.

We shook hands at the side of the car. He smiled shortly, reached, and pinched up the skin of my cheek in an affectionate gesture. I felt more choked than I dared show. He got in the car, started it up and pulled out without a backward glance. Within a few seconds, London had swallowed him.

But then, he had somewhere to go. He had, more than I, somewhere to hide. I walked back to the pub for last orders, to think about where I might go to.

23

Even in the late season, Corfu is a bad place to be. I sat at a tin table in the Old Port and watched the dazed and exhausted Corfiotes exact the last few grubby drachmas from a thinning crowd of mainly North European and mainly British holiday-makers. There was suppressed resentment in the air, along with the stench of horse piss and the grit blown up from the shabby square and its tired trees. It had been a summer of unusually persistent electrical storms on the island and – perhaps as a consequence – there had been bad medicine among the package tour braves. The police had imposed an eight o'clock curfew in most places in the south of the island, to limit the damage done by jolly pink giants kitted out in Union Jack shorts, and their plump little sugar-mice girls. There had been four deaths since the season opened. Heads had been broken, cars had been wrecked. Threats had been issued and vengeance vowed. At the airport they were getting back on the planes with nothing but their soiled and dusty shorts, broad slashes of mercurochrome ointment as campaign medals – no luggage, no money, no presents for Mum and Dad, no pleasant memories. Middle-class punters with sail bags, who had been safely out at sea and only smelt the island, looked on with terror. The departure lounge was a lake of beer from Dortmund in which lay the unemployed from Manchester and Glasgow. They were buying ouzo and drinking it out of the neck of the bottle.

I spent three days looking for Judith in the slightly more

salubrious parts of the island, only to stumble by accident across Hilary at the Old Port. He was wearing his famous pearl-grey belted slacks and cyclamen shirt, topped by a straw trilby. When I set eyes on him he was walking down the gangplank of the car ferry from Parga. It was worth three days in the hell-hole of Europe to see the dismay flood his face. He made his way towards me, a dinky little bag on his shoulder, and sat down at the table. But not before dusting the chair with his hand and scowling at the grey crumbs of bread and cheese beneath his feet.

'I might have expected it,' he said.

'Where is she?'

'Even if I knew, would I tell you? You are not exactly the person she is most wishing to meet. She is certainly not sitting by some casement waiting to let down her hair like Rapunzel. In fact, if I were you, I'd go home now. Cut your losses.'

'Keep blustering. I enjoy watching you trying to think on your feet.'

He raised his straw hat to me.

'Are all these beer bottles yours? Rather a vulgar display of grief and unrequited emotion.'

'Is she on the island?'

'Here I can be quite definite: no. And what brings you here, apart from a gift for being in the wrong place?'

'I've found you, though, haven't I?'

'By purest chance.'

'I want to see her, Hilary. Now that you're here, I shall.'

'I think not.'

'How is Athens? How's Yanni?'

'Fine,' Hilary said breezily.

He peered round. A grizzled old lady dressed in grey and black stood at his elbow, regarding him balefully. He asked for a beer, changed his mind and ordered a Sprite, changed it further and asked for a café cognac. The waitress stood watching him, stock still, only her whiskers twitching. Hilary took off his straw and laid it on the table. He seemed to be blushing. In time, the old lady moved off, her flip-flops slapping. We were talking a good ten minute wait here. Hilary looked at me and grimaced.

'I suppose life must have its coincidences,' he muttered.

'Not really. I meet the ferry every afternoon. I have a baggage handler at the airport who meets the Athens plane.'

'There isn't one,' Hilary said.

'The Fokker Friendship that flies in every day for people with serious money in their pocket. That's people like you. What's the matter, Hilary, haven't you got your cut?'

'What a fevered imagination you have. I'd forgotten.'

'Want to know what finally persuaded me you were a bit of a scamp after all? The fate of Wallace, your faithful Girl Friday. You left her for dead.'

'She isn't, though,' he flashed anxiously.

'How would you know?'

The damn straw hat was troubling him. He put it on and took it off again, experimentally. He laid his hands on the table, palms down, and examined their mottled backs as if trying to divine the future. The sun and the sea had reddened his skin a little. He looked what he was: the prosperous and faintly dismayed Englishman abroad.

'Very well,' he said at last. 'What do you want?'

'I want to see her. I'm not letting you out of my sight until I do.'

'Oh well, as to that, I rather think the circus has already left town.'

He tried to make it a snigger. I reached suddenly and crushed his hand in mine.

'Listen to me, geek. Waxman is dead. He was chucked off a roof in London. Remember Gerald? I'm sure you do. They threw him away like an empty lager can.'

253

Hilary shrugged as lightly as he was able.

'That sort of thing is frowned on, I always understood.'

I crushed his hand harder. He let out his breath in a wince of pain. He had made no effort to protest that he didn't know who the hell I was talking about. He tried to look about him insouciantly. But his face was growing paler.

'You're in trouble, both of you. I met Frankie Givens. He's upset. Enough to chuck Wheelchair Waxman off a five-storey building. Now let's cut the Alec Guinness in Havana crap. I think Frank is going to come looking for you.'

'Oh really!' Hilary exclaimed. 'It's like the Chinese theatre, where the warrior fights an invisible bogeyman in the dark. Do spare me the drama. I haven't the faintest idea what you're talking about. Let go my hand.'

'I want to see her, Hilary.'

'But does she want to see you?'

Then he knew where she was, I reasoned, or could communicate with her. I let him snatch his hand away.

'You're no good at this,' I said. 'I don't want to persuade her to come home. I don't want her to go down on her knees and beg to be forgiven. Least of all do I want to hear some sad story of how Yanni has chiselled you both. I just want to see her once more. For the last time.'

He stared down the dock. A thought occurred to him.

'How did you get the money to come here?'

'From your second cousin,' I said brutally. 'She has pots.'

Hilary glanced back at me. Spots of sunshine the size of coins were thrusting through the vines overhead and dappling his shirt and slacks. They danced gently on his cheek and nose. He looked old and frail and clownish.

'I read about Gerald Waxman in the English papers,' he said.

'Then you know there's a wave of shit heading your way. You're a little tired old painter far from home. You're going to take me to her.'

'I don't think so.'

Down at the end of the quay the boat to Paxos was loading. The crew carried on tomatoes, fish, pastries, beer. Three German couples with shaft-driven motor cycles sat defiantly in the centre of the deck, being walled up with restaurant orders. The skipper looked mournfully on all this. In addition to the Germans and the boxes of provisions, he had to lade a car with Greek registration and four immense coils of plastic piping. The weather-beaten old tub was moored up stern-first, the Gardner engines on tick-over.

'Come on, Hilary. Be your age. If you're on your way to see her now, what's the harm? If you're on your way to see Yanni, he can tell me where she is. But in any case, I'm not going to let you out of my sight. So where is she?'

The answer was, of course, Paxos. We bought tickets and after much scrutiny from the bored and truculent tourist police, who counted the deck passengers three times, we cast off and headed out to the south on a three-hour journey. A brisk offshore wind from the Albanian coast chopped up the seas. Hilary was in a fit of sulks. He went to sit in the dusty lounge, and began ordering a string of Metaxa brandies. I sat up in the bow of the boat, wetted by the cross seas and shaking with the emotions of the timid hunter. All around were flotillas of sail, much like the flaky paint of the old GWR carriage from what seemed long, long ago. I wondered yearningly whether she had ever seen them and made the same connection.

Not to be denied her worship, even for three hours, an Australian girl took off her tee-shirt and lay back among the boxes of Dutch-caught flat-fish. The judder of the engines was transmitted through the deck to her generous and careless body. Her forearm shielded her eyes: she lay with the patience of the young, letting the sun strike her. Her nipples floated like delicate pink paper roses. Some of the time she lay with her fingertips covering them. It was hard to believe there was a care in the world that could touch her. One of the deck-hands sat near by, entranced, smoking and glancing at me shyly from time to time.

We berthed first at Gaios. Hilary seemed uncertain what to do, but had the problem taken out of his hands by a surly old man in a battered Toyota, who opened the door for us to enter, while at the same time conducting a conversation with the ferry captain fifty yards off. The plastic seats were hot as griddles. Hilary shook his head unhappily. He was flushed with drink.

'You'll make it quite clear I had no choice, will you?'

'You are – as always – fragrant in your innocence, Hils.'

'Oh piss off. Is this a cab or what the hell is it? What is happening?'

The driver was loading the boot with trays of tomatoes and crates of Stella. On the seat next to him he piled label-less two-litre cans of something or other, wedged in with flat boxes. Finally, he presented Hilary with a tray of cream cakes to rest on his knees.

'The Villa Marguerite,' Hilary commanded.

The old man stared, picked some blackened debris from his nose and spat. We set off from the dusty quay as if pursued by a hundred-foot tidal wave, or racing towards the last gallon of petrol to be sold in the world. The Toyota wheels bit hungrily on the beginnings of a metalled road, bouncing Hilary's cakes clean off their tray and back again. We raced uphill between stunted acacia, the sea already darkening to a Homeric claret below us.

'Jesus Christ, he's going to put us into the ravine,' Hilary shouted, so echoing the remark made by every foreign devil tourist to ride in her since the cab had first been ferried across on the *Kamelia*, and blessed in the square at Gaios by a bearded priest. Using the horn as a weapon of war, we careened round blind corners and leaped over the crest of hills. Trucks, cabs and petrified scooter drivers flashed past in a blur. The old man drove with one hand, the thumb of his free hand raking round inside his nostril.

'They're all like this,' Hilary complained. 'They're all maniacs. Slow down, will you?'

Instead, more horn, more grinding and squealing of shock absorbers. At the very top of the island, as far as the road went, the driver slewed to a halt before a dusty and lacklustre restaurant-bar, tooting furiously. A beautiful young Greek girl sauntered out, opened the door to Hilary's side, and took away the tray of cakes with a faint smile. Our driver got out and shook hands with an old man or two. He bellowed out news of the Battle of Salamis, or perhaps details of the suicide of that old raver Socrates, and serve him right.

'Oh Jesus,' Hilary said in disgust. We clambered out, the backs of our thighs stuck to the seat with sweat. The cabbie wheeled round. He affected to be surprised and astonished by our very existence.

'The Villa Marguerite,' Hilary shouted.

The driver pointed. He intended only to indicate a path through the olive groves. But there, standing with a plump arm shading her face from the last of the sun, was Judith.

'Look what Hilary's brought you,' I said, my voice shaking for some reason.

Very close up, within kissing range, I saw she was crying. Her face was still muddy with bruises. She held out her hand in an absent-minded gesture.

'It's down here,' she said.

From the verandah there was a fine view of the sea, now a deep ultramarine. In the very distance, a purple and indistinct smudge marked the mainland. A few yachts making to anchorage in Monganissi set off the scene obligingly with wings of white. We sat watching the light fall from the sky. The verandah rail, the table, the arms of the chairs, were still quite warm to the touch. I held my ice and ouzo to my cheek. Judith half sat, half lay, a faded cotton sarong tucked to her armpits.

'Is that where you swim, down in that bay?'

'Now that the Italians have gone home, the whole place is practically deserted. You can walk all over this side of the island through the olive groves. There are four little beaches within reach. It's heaven.'

'Lucky old you,' I said.

'That's right,' Judith said heavily. 'Lucky old me.'

Hilary had gone for a diplomatic nap. The cicadas chattered. Somewhere in the olives a donkey groaned in an ecstasy of unhappiness. Far away, you could hear women calling to each other. I took her hand by the very tips of her fingers.

'It's no use,' she said. 'I'm a hopeless case. You wishing me different can't ever work. Say I only had one leg. Could you wish me another one?'

'A difficult challenge.'

'I knew you would come. I dreamed about you coming. And dreaded it.'

'You took some finding. I came to say I love you.'

'No,' she said sharply.

'That's all. I don't plan to do a damn thing about it. I came to tell you, nothing else.'

'You hate me just as much as you like me.'

'Have I used the word like?'

'We can't go off into the sunset together, if that's what you want.'

'Judith, listen to me. They killed Gerald Waxman.'

She sat bolt upright, her eyes wide.

'He's dead?'

'Very. In very suspicious circumstances. You hadn't heard?'

She waved her arm at the olives round us.

'Here? How would I know anything like that? Who killed him?'

'Three guesses,' I said, watching her carefully. She managed to look as though three hundred guesses would be too few.

258

'Remember me telling you about the leaking boat? The Government rowing in the leaky boat? This is it. I mean this is the big moment, when the water's coming in faster than they can bail it out. Gerald was chucked off a roof. That's not going to go away in a day. All the little pieces are coming together.'

She shook her head, as if troubled by flies.

'Who killed him?' she repeated stubbornly.

'Why was he killed? – that's going to be the question. And little by little –'

'Yes, all right,' she snapped.

'I came to find you because you are in danger. I mean real danger. I'll leave tonight. I'll sleep at the taverna and catch the ferry tomorrow morning if that's what you want. I'll go home and wait to read about you in the paper.'

She stood up and pulled a sweater round her shoulders. There was a little oil lamp on the table, which she lit.

'Know what it's like, being me? I can't think. I feel, I have these huge feelings, but I can't think them through. I can't face myself. I never will. I read, I sit here trying to get it straight in my head – but it's like everything else that's happened to me. Nothing is nailed down. Everything's at a distance. Can you imagine what that's like?'

Huge tears were rolling down the side of her nose and into the corners of her mouth.

'Tell me,' I said, my heart a bloodied rag.

And so, on the terrace of the Villa Marguerite, it all came out, as far as human predicaments do have shape or can be explained. As it grew dark, the little lamp flickered between us, caught by an onshore wind that smelled not of the sea, but of the dusty groves. Paxos is the very place on earth for such moments. A little reef of limestone, terraced and planted with olives four hundred years ago, couched in shallow, tideless seas, within sight of the mainland but indifferent to it. The wind rustles the crackling leaves, the little flame flickers. You have only to be on the island a few hours to realize how utterly small and insignificant is life measured by human ideas of time. You might as well be Venetian: you might as well be the Egyptian pilot sailing down the east coast who heard to his amazement the rocks and groves weep the message that the Great God Pan was dead. What Judith told me was cast immediately into the same darkness: it was past, and there was no way of recovering it, nor of living without the consequence.

When Judith moved into her flat, she and Waxman struck up a friendship. Leah's suspicions were well founded: Waxman taught himself to climb the stairs and soon to haul himself on to the bed with his strong arms. It was very simple: he had recognized David Nicholas. There had to be room for him, too. He liked the idea of having a whore for a neighbour, especially one so well connected, to whom he could talk about books and concerts. Sometimes he would lie on the bed and watch her dress to go out, or come from the shower with her hair towelled and turbaned, restless and at a loose end. He was there because he had recognized her lover and his mouth must be stopped. It was thrilling, to be part of Judith's cabinet of secrets. And in his own way, he was discreet. He never overbid his hand. The sexual favours he got were the proceeds of mild blackmail, or a way of assuring his discretion – but he was also astonished to realize she liked him for himself, for his own sake.

It cost Judith very little to find out who the accountant's principal client was, nor why Givens needed to launder money right across London. She had a secret: so did Gerald, and they exchanged them. He knew all about Givens's operation – once a year, he was a practical part of it.

'You should have looked at Gerald's wheelchair more closely,' she said. I blinked.

'The trips to Vegas!'

The trips were financed by bonus payments made by Givens. To begin with, the Waxmans were genuinely overwhelmed.

'I would do this for you,' Givens told Leah at a charity boxing match at the Café Royal, 'if your brother lived in Timbuktu.'

Maybe Gerald checked where Timbuktu was, and the comparative price of an air fare there. The second time he went to see his brother-in-law Harry and meet and greet some of the greatest in the business, he put the wheelchair on the bathroom scales in London and again just before he left for the airport in Vegas. There was a difference in weight of five kilos. He couldn't tell Leah, but it was too exciting to keep to himself. Who better to tell than Judith?

'And you told David.'

'They met. They talked things over, what to do. Gerald kept a diary of all the people he met on the Las Vegas end of it, including his crazy brother-in-law. He got himself photographed with everybody. It was a dossier: he worked incredibly hard on it. It was his insurance against any trouble. He was bringing in coke worth a quarter of a million for Frankie, every trip: he needed an edge. David was fascinated with the problem.'

'David was an idiot.'

'Yes,' Judith said, as though isle-strewn Ionia had opened her eyes.

'Okay, let me guess. He talked Waxman into keeping it with the rest of his stuff in the security vault.'

The Waxman dossier, nestling cheek to cheek with David's collection of pornography: what a set of incredible clowns they were, David, Judith and Waxman. She spoke about the investigations Gerald had made as though they were some kind of atomic device, with the clock counting back to Armageddon. But how much could he actually have found out, squidging round Vegas in his chair, Harry Hartsilver's dumb brother-in-law, who couldn't stop talking, or singing Mel Tormé in the elevators? Judith seemed to imagine there was mighty ju-ju in the diary and a few photographs.

'You think people just walked up to him and said "Hi! I'm one of the big operators out here and if there's any way I can indict myself, you go right ahead and say"'!'

'I don't know what he knew,' she sulked.

But I was on song. I had forgotten how angry it could make me when her chin went down and her eyes took on that defensive look. I pushed her.

'You think Waxman said "Okay, Mr Braccio, that's fantastic. I'd like to take your photograph in some compromising circumstance of your own choice. You think of a way of stitching yourself up, and then I'll take the snaps to Boots when I get home. But first, go get me a pina colada and something for my wife. Oh, and have Sinatra come over to my table."'

Judith's voice was small and patient.

'He was carrying five kilos for Frank Givens, once, sometimes twice a year,' she said wearily. 'I don't know what he wrote in the diary. What else did he need to write, for God's sake?'

'He showed it to you, though?'

'The book itself. Some loose pages. Names. Phone numbers. The kind of photographs they take in hotels. Of people eating.'

'Or seen sharing a joke.'

She looked at me as though I was missing the point. She had already said what needed to be said: Waxman had lodged a virtual confession of complicity in drugs smuggling with David. I capitulated, but only a little.

'Okay, he talked it over with David, and David was fascinated with the problem. I can picture that, Judith. A Home Office minister having an interesting chat about a drugs ring in a tart's flat – that makes great sense.'

Again, Judith shrugged the sarcasm away. Little white moths were flying in frenzied circles round the lamp. I had read somewhere quite recently that moths make these suicidal dashes at flame because the wavelength of the light corresponds exactly to the sexual emanations from their mates. The moths were burning up for sex, and could not help themselves. Or was it love?

'All right,' I said. 'What did David do?'

'He handled everything. I don't know how he did it, who the go-betweens were, but suddenly we have this damn drugs baron paying us hush money.'

I stared.

'How much?'

'Five hundred a week.'

I rubbed my bare arms and huddled deeper into the chair. Hilary had woken and was pottering about inside the villa making tea.

'What are you thinking?' Judith asked dolefully.

'It was cheap at the price,' I said. 'You think he was letting you rip him off without getting something in return? Your pal David was so bent he probably thought it was the play of market forces or some evil shit like that. But Givens had a Minister of State blackmailing him. How many drug dealers can boast that? You think he couldn't call in the cards any time he liked? How long did this go on?'

'About a year and a half. David said it was untraceable money.'

'David was a raving lunatic.'

'It was a way of keeping Gerald and me safe. Putting it into David's stuff at the security vault was a way of insuring ourselves.'

'Givens would have swatted you like flies any time he liked. He's made a start already. Wheelchair Waxman is in the fridge with a tag on his toe.'

She put her head in her hands, sobbing. I rose, and hugged her to me. The moths flung themselves at the glass of the lamp.

'The three of you were partners?'

'Yes,' she wailed.

'You split the money three ways?'

She put her arms round my hips, her face buried in my belly.

'Two ways,' she whispered, muffled by my body.

'Let me guess who was left out.'

'I didn't want it in the first place.'

'It was enough for you to risk your life, was it?'

We walked up to the taverna through the scented dark. Every so often I kissed away her tears. She wore her sarong as a skirt and had pulled the sweater over her head. Her breast burned warm against me. It was painful coming into the light. The beautiful young Greek girl glanced at us with sympathy and selected a table for us against a sagging reed screen. I guessed she ate at the taverna most evenings – they liked her and she responded with a quiet and a politeness that made her even more tender and vulnerable. We ordered *sofrito* and a bottle of the over-sweet white wine. Just in the few days she had been on the island, her skin was burned a rich brown. She pushed back the sleeves to her sweater. Her hands were shaking.

A possibility suddenly occurred to me. Waxman takes half the money and gives it straight back to Big Frank, who pats him on the head and congratulates him for a clever scam. For only half the money paid across, Givens has a junior Cabinet minister on his payroll. How can David put the bite on anybody if Wheelchair Waxman confesses simultaneously to carrying dope and partnering an MP in a case of blackmail? With this scenario, Judith is where she always is, trying to get an edge, but being fooled by bigger crooks than she can imagine.

'Do you like it here?' she asked me, meek as asparagus. I wrenched my mind back to her. We clasped hands across the table.

'I love it,' I said. I brought her fingers to my lips. Judith nodded to the kitchens.

'The Greek girl is called Anna. She's engaged to a man who's working in Bielefeld. She wants to go and live there.'

'And start a kebab house.'

'A family,' Judith corrected mournfully.

One fateful evening, Yanni announces he is going to do the vaults. Mischief! Neither David, Judith nor Waxman have any idea he is going to make a special point of robbing David's box. When, in time, David learns the truth about that, he has two options; he can go to Givens and tell him frankly and openly that the famous dossier is now at large in the community, or he can try to keep this news quiet, no matter what the cost. The alternative – Givens finding out for himself – might well cause unpleasantness all round.

'After Yanni did the vaults, what happened?' I asked her. The question seemed to her to have come out of the blue, as if there were no crisis, as if I were merely enquiring who won the Derby in 1976.

'What happened? How do you mean, what happened?'

'Did David call a meeting, to discuss what to do next?'

'He may have done. He may have talked to Gerald. I don't know.'

'So though you hadn't taken any of the money, you were there in the trenches with them, and it never occurred to you to ask what had happened to the damn dossier. Maybe I worry too much about you, Judith. Maybe you lead a charmed life. Maybe innocence is bliss. Or maybe the tooth fairy took pity on you as a child and has hung around ever since.'

We drank coffee at the rickety table. When she first came to the tiny village, they enquired about her bruises and she told them she had been in a car accident. As we sat holding hands an old man came in and presented her with a hen's egg, to much cheerful badinage. One of his eyes was white as marble. His cotton cap was mottled with water stains. Judith pecked

265

him on the stubble and his hand touched her gently on the ribs, high up. He looked at me with sly pleasure, before being shooed away by Anna.

I suddenly realized Judith was watching the road, or more accurately she was listening for cars coming up the hill. She caught my eye and placed her egg in the tin ashtray.

'One day he'll come for me,' she said. She had no need to name the man who would come and transform everything. I wondered who would reach her first – Yanni or the implacable Givens.

'Have you seen him since you got here?'

She shook her head, her lashes thick with tears.

'He's on the mainland. I don't know where.'

'Has Hilary seen him?'

'No.'

I thought of Ted Gerson's question.

'Just exactly what is Hilary's part in all this, Judith? Why is he here?'

She put her head on the table and wailed.

'I don't know. I don't know what is happening or how it will end. I'm terrified. Seeing you has only made it a thousand times worse.'

'Then why not take comfort from familiar circumstances?' I asked, and was rewarded by an anguished snort of laughter. She reached for my hand and held it with the grip of the drowning.

24

Going back through the olives, I caught her up and turned her round to face me. After she had made a little pretence of incredulity, a dumbshow of amazement, we kissed. A little way below us, and to the side, the oil flickered soft and yellow on the villa verandah. Now that the night was cooler, there were rustlings in the dark and sometimes alarmed scamperings, as lizards took flight from the emaciated grey cats I had seen earlier. Judith slumped against me, her chin in my neck.

'You were always the best thing in the whole business,' she whispered – hardly a rich compliment, even supposing for a moment she was being honest.

I pulled her down to sit beside me on a little terrace of limestone. Olive number 27 was at our backs, the figures painted on to the twisted trunk with neat whitewash. I held her hand, bouncing it a few times on my knee. Her soft breast pressed against my arm. She leaned her head on my shoulder. I tried to swim my way through a flood of old emotions.

'How did you find this place? I mean what made you come to this particular village and the Marguerite?'

'It's Yanni's. He owns it. He bought it with gambling money years ago, before I met him. He always kept a photograph of it in his wallet. He showed everybody.'

'Who's everybody? Mention a few.'

'How do I know,' she moaned. 'I don't care any longer.'

'Well, if you want to save your life, start caring.'

Her eyes had taken on that curious blank look, as happens

when you try to scold a cat for misbehaviour. Or perhaps cats look like that all the time and you only notice when you want them to show a little emotion. Judith stared me down in the moonlight.

'Let them come and kill me. I just don't care any longer. You keep trying to tell me I've been used – do you think I don't know that? People like me never win. I may as well lose completely.'

'Like Billie.'

'Yes, like Billie. I'm no better off than she was.'

'That's rubbish,' I contradicted helplessly.

She had come to the island and his villa in the hope of finding him there. The first night, she slept on the verandah, with her suitcase for a pillow. Next day, she saw a figure coming down the path from the road and ran to greet it. It was Hilary. He had crossed from Parga and though he had not seen Yanni face to face, he bore a message. She was to stay put and wait. Everything would be well. Yanni would take care of everything.

I thought about this, listening to the wind soughing gently in the grove all about us. Judith leaned against me like a drunk. Down in the villa, a shadow momentarily crossed the lamp. Far away, a scooter laboured up the metalled road from Gaios.

'It sounds crazy,' I said, 'but I'm glad I found you. I hope he comes.'

'No you don't,' she muttered into my chest.

I hugged her, my arms and skin remembering anew her weight, her solid flesh.

'You're a glutton for punishment,' she said, dull.

'I'm trying to be a loyal friend. I didn't come to get in your hair, I promise. But I can't leave without saying this – I think you should leave, get off the island.'

I might as well have been talking to olive number 27. Her arm lay across my lap, inert. Her hair stuck to my lips. I could smell suntan oil on the nape of her neck. Whatever had obscured the lamp on the terrace had moved away. The strains of some keening Greek love song rose from inside the house. It was a radio broadcast, drifting off altogether and then coming back again, very low.

Maybe I wasn't even thinking of saving her life: what weapons did I have to defend her with, who would not defend herself? Maybe I had come all this way only to save what shreds of self-respect and independence she might have left. Waiting for Yanni was much like waiting for some final blow in the face – not killing, but brutal. Above all, from her point of view, heartless. Judith stirred.

'Come and swim,' she suggested vaguely. 'I need to do something. I'm going mad. It was rotten of me never to say I loved you back. It was cruel. But I couldn't help it. Come down to the beach. Please. To please me.'

The path zigzagged through the olives and meandered past thickets of sloe. We stepped out on to a tiny crescent of white stones that shelved steeply to the inky sea. A power launch swung at anchor forty yards offshore.

Judith pulled off her clothes as if dreaming. She stood for a moment looking out at the water, her arms joined over her head in a kind of luxurious ease, her breasts raised, one hip thrown forward. The moon lit her lovingly. She turned to me.

'You can't imagine what it's like,' she whispered sadly. She picked her way down to the sea and waded in, phosphorescence sparking all the way up her thighs. I undressed and followed. She turned to watch me, her torso twisted round on her hips, her hands between her legs. Then she threw herself out into a silver and gold plunge.

We swam half a mile to the point, side by side and silent save for the splashing of our arms. She was a strong swimmer and water was her element. All the same, I was watching her out of the corner of my eye, for I truly believed her capable of raising her arms and disappearing under the little inky waves in an ecstasy of self-abasement. When we reached the rocks that marked the end of the promontory, she rolled on her back like a dolphin and lay looking at the juicy stars.

'If this were all there were to life, then I could love you to the end of time,' she said dreamily.

I laid my fingers along her cheek. She rolled again, her breasts floating free of her ribs, and reached for me with her arms. We embraced. Her skin was slick and cold and made the inside of her mouth seem scalding hot. I kissed her neck, her shoulder. Judith smiled. Her hair hung in rats' tails. Her lips were salt. She wound her legs round me.

'Your cock,' she murmured, with childish pleasure.

There was something bobbing in the water at her back. She turned in a momentary panic – we both panicked – and thrashed away from the object, supposing it to be a jellyfish, or maybe a Portuguese man-of-war. I peered into the sparking phosphorescence.

Floating brim down was Hilary's straw hat.

I swam to the power launch and reached in to touch the engine casings of the twin Evinrudes. The metal was warm. Judith was scrambling up the stony beach on her hands and knees. When I got back there myself, she had already pulled a tee-shirt over her head.

'Go away,' she said, in such an ordinarily pitched voice that I shrank. She threw my clothes at me.

'I want you to go. There's a room at the taverna. They'll put you up there. I don't want you here any more.'

'Don't be a fool,' I said. 'He won't let me go now.'

'Who? Who are you talking about?'

'I'll give you three guesses.'

'I don't know what you're talking about,' she said. 'Hilary went for a walk along the headland. Anything. His hat fell off, or blew away. What does it matter? I just want you to go.'

'We'll go back to the villa,' I said, trying to adjust my eyes to the dark of the grove behind us.

'No,' she shouted, and got back an echo from the cypress-strewn rocks. When I reached for her she knocked my hand away. In the same instant my eye caught a movement of something white.

'Don't be silly, Judith,' a pleasantly low and caressing voice said. A figure stepped from the shadows. He smiled at me.

'Put some clothes on, my friend. You will feel more comfortable. And then join me up at the house. Judith, wait with him.'

'Yanni,' she whispered, like a child greeting its father.

'You too, Judith. You must put some more clothes on.'

'Where's Hilary?'

'Up at the house,' Yanni said.

It was much darker and cooler in the groves – the waters of the bay had been warmer than the air. We shivered as we toiled after Yanni. I held her hand and half dragged her up the path. We meandered this way and that, striking out in wrong directions. Judith shook her hand free and pushed ahead of me. The last hundred yards to the villa were on a substantial track of dusty white grit, and when we struck that, I looked up and saw Yanni on the verandah, watching us come. When we finally mounted the steps, he was there to greet us with all the politeness I had heard described of him. He shook my hand in the Mediterranean fashion. He kissed Judith on the cheek and suggested she go straightaway and shower, wash the salt out of her hair. Then perhaps she could make coffee for his guest, yes, coffee would be nice. Be sure to dry the hair carefully. Swimming at night was fun, but it was easy to catch cold. And salt makes the hair sticky. He shooed her away.

We sat down inside the villa, on cane armchairs stuffed with pale blue printed cushions. We drank Courvoisier from balloon glasses. I felt it was all exactly as he had planned, this villa, life lived to his choice in things. In some absurd and irrelevant way, before we went any further, he wanted my approval of the furniture and the hideous tiled floor, the breakfast bar and the paintings of plump nudes representing Aphrodite. An ancient old French musket hung on the wall in pride of place. He had pulled it from the sea, one summer's holiday, scuba diving.

He was even bigger than I had imagined. He wore a great pair of white cotton trousers, topped by a black Princeton tee-shirt. His arms bulged with muscle. There was a repose in him, not of a major bank robber and fugitive from justice, but (say) a carpenter, or a jobbing builder. He looked like someone who had worked out of doors all his life. I thought of his neat tool box in the garage at Brookman's Park.

'Hilary resting, is he?'

Yanni smiled.

'May I ask you a question? What have you got from all this? I know something about you, not much. You are a good friend to Judith. You swim well, you think quickly. You are not afraid of me. All these things are friendly to my purpose. But I ask out of curiosity.'

I shrugged and reached for his cigarettes.

'You know how it is. Got to keep moving. Can't stand still. One thing leads to another.'

'If you have a chicken, you have eggs,' he suggested.

'That sort of thing.'

He paid this remark elaborate respect. But all the time he was pondering, his eyes never left mine. When I had leaned forward to get his Marlboros his weight had shifted casually. He kept his legs tucked under him, wide awake and dangerous.

'This island is very old,' he said at last. 'The people here have seen many different things, many different flags. Not until 1864 was it joined to Kérkira and spoken of henceforth as Greek. In your country, one thing does lead to another. But I don't know that the people of this island would be at all interested. They see the chicken, they expect the egg. They don't run after things.'

'This is strange, Yanni, coming from a bank robber.'

'I am different.'

272

'You're certainly not famous for sitting on your arse, waiting for the eggs to hatch.'

He laughed.

'You like this villa? I had a big win, unbelievable money, at roulette. The next day, it was Gold Cup day at Ascot. I have a fancy, a big horse, an ugly damn horse. I managed to lay ten grand at 12–1 on the rails and I was so nervous, I can't watch this race, I put my hands over my ears even. When she win, the horse, I am sick right there in front of all these rich English. You like this story?'

'Let's cut the crap. Where is Hilary?'

Yanni looked at me with unshakeable calm.

'He is in the boat, my friend,' he said softly.

Judith came into the room, wearing a billowing blue skirt and a pale pink baggy tee-shirt. She had made-up her eyes and drawn back her hair from her neck. Yanni blew her an appreciative kiss.

'Pink against that skin is good. Now you look as I remember, beautiful Judith.'

'I'm frightened,' she said.

It was a phrase she used often, and one that pointed back all the way to the child in the bedroom at Bracknell, Dad with his finger to his lips. It was an expression of the truth, but also a faintly disgusting little-girl provocation she would never rid herself of. Yanni looked at her carefully for a few moments, choosing to read only the literal truth of the remark. She had looked for Hilary in the bedrooms and not found him. His expression was unsmiling.

'It is right to be frightened,' he said at last. 'While you are at the taverna, I am listening to Greek news broadcast. In London they are connecting the death of Mr Waxman with the killing of David. Someone has been very clever. I think he is a young man, don't you? A clever young journalist with a good brain, a nice girl, nice flat. And now a big story! These two men, so apart in so many ways, both murdered – and there's a connection!'

273

'What did Greek radio make of it?' I asked.

'There is a political crisis in your country. There is whiff of scandal. Maybe there is cover-up.'

'Okay,' I said. 'Now answer this: why is Hilary dead?'

Judith made a little mew of horror.

'He can't be,' she whispered.

'He's in the bottom of Yanni's launch, apparently. And it's not much of a guess to say he's not there to sketch by moonlight.'

'He's not dead,' she wailed stubbornly.

'Now you just make her more frightened,' Yanni chided. 'Don't do this, please. She is making us coffee. Judith, have you forgotten? But first, both of you – I am not here to pay a pleasant visit to old English friends. You try anything stupid, either of you, you are going to be sorry, I promise.'

She stared at him, confused by his tone of voice.

'Make some coffee,' I said.

He was watching us with all the assurance of a big man, a frighteningly alert and powerful figure who could leap from the chair and break someone's back in a second. Judith seemed to understand this at last, and went behind the breakfast bar.

'Hilary is –' Yanni searched his English vocabulary. '– I want to say he is speaking contemptuously, but that wouldn't be quite right.'

'He is arrogant,' I suggested. Yanni considered.

'You think he is feeling arrogant because I am a lazy Greek? Maybe. I never meet anyone like him in England. Not quite like him.'

'Perhaps you can tell me where he fits into the story?'

'For sure,' Yanni proposed archly. 'He killed David. I pay him a lot of money to do it.'

In the kitchen, Judith dropped a mug.

'That doesn't sound too likely,' I said shakily, wondering how to keep the initiative and prevent him from swamping me. He regarded me with mild amusement.

'Now why do you say that, my friend?'

'Hilary couldn't open a window without difficulty. Hilary is a damn water-colourist.'

He laughed.

'Life is strange. Don't you English say something about truth being stranger than fiction? When I first come to your country I am carrying boxes of oranges about for a living. Then I meet a whore and marry her. I live off her back. All this time I am nothing to the people of England. I am like the Invisible Man. This is very strange experience. I ride around on the Tube reading Greek newspapers, meeting no one, talking to no one. Then, all of a sudden one day, I got two women wish me to kill the same man.'

Judith leaned forward on the workbench. There was a nursery splashing sound. Yanni bit his lip, surprising me with a look of genuine contrition and embarrassment. Judith held up her skirt and wiped her legs with a towel. She threw it into the puddle at her feet and stood on it.

'I never meant you to kill him,' she whimpered.

'But, poppet, I didn't.'

'Neither did Hilary,' I said. Yanni's glance flicked back to me.

'Imagine the situation, Englishman. Judith would like him dead because she feels dirty, and she feels betrayed. After all these years, she is coming awake. The black girl David killed did this for her. And Lydia would also like him dead. They never met each other, but they each tell me this. They think I am like a god, that I can do anything. This is strange for me to understand.'

He laughed.

'I go back to my old ways, take the Central line to Epping and then all the way back west. I have friends in Germany, in Westphalen – maybe they can help. For sure they can help, if I wish. Make this business for me.'

'It was Lydia who suggested Hilary, was it?'

He pointed a finger at me.

'You're smart. But not so smart as you talk.'

Judith was moving away from the kitchen. She looked ready to run for it. Yanni rose to his feet with electrifying speed.

'No, darling,' he said. 'Bring the coffee.'

'But I'm wet.'

'Don't be a child. Do as I say.'

He turned to me.

'And you. Please don't make no trouble.'

'Let her go.'

'I don't think so. Remember, I don't mean any harm to anybody.'

'Then what is Hilary doing in the bottom of your launch?'

'He is being dead,' Yanni said, with the facetiousness of the millionaire.

'And why is that?'

Yanni sat down again, haunches on the edge of his chair, feet tucked under him. He rubbed his bare and bulging forearms.

'I rob the vaults. The night of the robbery I stay with Hilary. And the next night also. There is much work to be done. I need a quiet place, somewhere to think. And lovely Judith has told me this one time about a wise man who lives in the woods. I make a note, remember.'

Judith arrived with the tray of coffee. Yanni nodded towards the table.

'Put it down, petal. Don't sit on the cushions if you are wet. Sit on the floor. This will soon be over. No more tears.'

'Oh Yanni, please,' she implored. His frown, his mere frown, was enough to make her hand shake. He watched the tray all the way to the table. He was formidable all right; I knew I could never take him while he sat there coiled like a spring.

'I find Hilary's house in the wood,' he continued. 'The situation is all round very good. At first he is not too pleased to see me, but soon there is a lot of money on his carpet – money, jewellery, gems. But I mean a lot. We drink some wine together. We sing some songs. I give him more money than he can ever need in his life. Then we talk a lot about Judith.'

'Later on, he planted some of the stuff out by the reservoir.'

'That was my idea!' Yanni exclaimed admiringly. 'I suggest to him, yes, that he and Judith can stitch David up.'

'But in fact it was Judith that went out there. Dumped the stuff and when it was discovered changed her mind.'

Yanni laughed.

'My little Judith! But the idea was good. She spoil it for herself. Hilary – Hilary would rather see him dead. He tells me what I already know, that Judith would also like to see this man dead. I have two Tesco bags of gear spread out on Hilary's carpet. But I am not thinking death and retribution.'

'You need to use him as a go-between when you need to contact David, to get out of the country,' I suggested.

'Yes,' Yanni smiled. 'Such beautiful manners. A painter, an artist. The kind of person I would like to have been myself. In my own house, you know, I have books on antiques, on Titian, Rembrandt. I always like these kind of people. Tintoretto is a favourite.'

I must have been looking at him as though he were indicting himself for gormlessness: he stroked his chin with the first signs of uncertainty. Judith was watching us both.

'Then why is he dead?'

Yanni shook his head, as if in wonder at that himself.

'He is greedy. He already has the money, but he wants more. Not just money, but things I cannot give.'

'Love,' I suggested.

'Strength,' Yanni corrected. 'Maybe. I don't know. Maybe love. He wants me. They all want to find something in me. But what?'

'Want to know what I think? I think you're full of shit, Yanni.'

His eyes dwelt on me thoughtfully.

'Here, on this island, I could give a diamond to a peasant, or pay for a meal in gold. Once the fist has closed: silence. You could tear out the man's heart before he told you any more. Tie him in a sack, throw him to the fish, he say nothing. What is me and what is him are separate things. I never told Hilary to kill David. He is dead now because he was stupid then. Death is best greeted when you are old and in bed and you don't quite recognize your visitor. Death is like an old uncle who don't come to the house too often. Any child who sits in the olives and scares birds can understand that. You are here because Waxman has been killed. And Mr Waxman is dead because some people are very, very angry. It's more business than I need.'

'Then why kill your partner? Why now?'

'Because I don't need him,' Yanni said simply.

'Maybe you came here to kill Hilary and Judith and found one more person than you'd bargained for.'

He stood up unexpectedly. From the cushions of his chair he had produced a huge and unwieldy Luger, fifty years old but in dangerous working order.

'Maybe. But why ask more questions?' he murmured reasonably. 'It all comes to nothing in the end. Hilary is dead because he make a mistake. Maybe you and Judith can live. I don't know. But now we must have some coffee together and go a little sea journey. We make a little adventure.'

Even then, even in the launch, I think she believed Yanni had in fact come for her, that somehow all these troublesome words – the talk, the explanations, the arguments – would melt away. Even with Hilary dead in the bottom of the boat, his jaw gaping open, his eyes reflecting the starshine, she would jump clear of disaster into the arms of the big guy. Or maybe I was doing her a disservice, of an awful kind. Maybe she was already half in love with death. She lay against the white fibreglass bulkhead, her arms hugging herself against the surprising cold of the night air, her face in shadow. Hilary's body rolled from side to side at her knees. The twin Evinrudes purred as we motored without navigation lights through the Panagia channel, the lights of Gaios winking at our passage. Yanni managed the boat and the Luger with smiling ease. At his invitation, I had brought the brandy with us, and he and I drank from the neck of the bottle.

'Be assured, my friend,' he said, keeping his voice low, 'I am not going to kill you. I would risk too much. Hilary was an accident.' He nodded to Judith slumped in the bow.

'Also, I need to make her see that people are alone in life.'

'She knows that.'

'I think not.'

'You won't get away with this, Yanni.'

'Who can say? Anything can happen. Now, no tricks. You see this little boat at anchor ahead of us?'

We were in the lee of St Nicholas Island, and by peering forward I could just make out a dark shape. If it was a boat, it seemed unnaturally low in the water. The sight of it made my blood run cold. We had not happened across it by accident. Whatever else was happening, Yanni was not improvising. He dug the pistol barrel into my ribs.

'I bring us alongside,' Yanni said, 'and you will please pick up the rope you find trailing from the bow and tie it on the cleat here.'

'You can do all that. I'm no sailor.'

Yanni smiled in the darkness.

'Make a mistake, the gun goes off.'

He throttled back, and the launch slid towards the sullen little fishing boat. I leaned out over the transom of the launch and picked up the painter. Yanni grunted approvingly.

'Now tie her off to the cleat. Judith, come awake, please. What we do now is to transfer our friend Hilary into this little boat.'

'I can't touch him,' Judith mumbled sullenly.

'Yes, you can,' Yanni said. His voice was sharp.

'I don't want anything to do with it.'

'Judith, try to understand. I am where I want to be. I am exactly what I want to be. From now on. I am not considering what you think, or what you want. But if you want to live, do as you're told.'

'Help me put him into the other boat,' I said.

I picked up Hilary by the legs and swung them over the gunwale of the launch. She made no move to help. I reached over and dragged her to a sitting position by her shoulder.

'Come on, do as he says. It doesn't make any difference to Hilary, he's dead. Help me get the body into the other boat.'

It was not as easy as it sounded. Once we had started, the launch began to rock crazily. If I had been going to take Yanni, it would have had to be right there. I was furiously trying to think. If this was all pre-planned, perhaps he expected to be dealing with two corpses. This much at least was improvised. As if waiting for me to finish working this out, he sat in the stern sheets, the Luger pointing directly at Judith. He knew I would not risk her life for mine. So she and I tugged and heaved, pushed and cursed, until Hilary rolled into the bottom boards of the little fishing skiff with a faint splash.

I pulled Judith down on top of me and hugged her.

'It's all right,' I whispered. 'Everything's going to be all right.'

'Judith. Untie the painter, please. The rope, the wet rope from the other boat. Pass it to me.'

He realized he had made a small mistake. When he had the painter in his hand, he hesitated fractionally.

'Yes, please, Judith. Come back towards me.'

She crawled across the bottom of the launch and flung her arms round his knees. Did she even then believe she was going to be forgiven, asked to sit beside him, asked to train the pistol on me while he got them both out of it for ever and ever? She clung on to him, sobbing, kissing the fabric of his slacks, rubbing herself against him like a cat. He tolerated her embraces for a few seconds and then pulled her up by her hair. I tried to move my legs under me so that I might spring. Yanni looked over her shoulder.

'The barrel is pressed between her breasts,' he said. 'Don't be a fool. I won't hesitate.'

His fist tightened in her hair.

'Reach out over the end of the launch and pull up the anchor rope,' he ordered. She looked at him muzzily. He jerked back her head in impatience.

'The boat Hilary is in,' I said. 'Feel around in the front and find the anchor rope. Do as he says, and pull it in.'

'You are a sensible man,' Yanni said.

When she had pulled up the heavy round stone that served as an anchor, he pushed her back towards me and swiftly tied off the painter. She tried to crawl back and he kicked her flat to the boards. I dragged her clear and pinioned her arms. She was panting with rage and despair. There came into my mind the night she had bitten through her lip and torn at her breast with her nails.

'Let him save you,' Yanni said. 'Don't fight him.'

'You evil bastard,' Judith spat.

'Yes,' the Greek said. 'Unfortunately.'

Still with the Luger trained on her, he opened the throttles and we began pulling clear of the shadow of the rocks, towing the little skiff behind us. We butted out on full power, through a short sea. A wind that was hardly noticeable in the tavernas and bars of Gaios was, out here, like a dangerous beast. Spray started to come in. I kissed Judith's cheek and tried to warm her with my own body.

The two outboard motors were at full revs, but the tow we were making made the launch extremely sluggish. Yanni sat by the short tiller, his bulk silhouetted against the sky. He cursed once or twice in Greek as we rounded Monganissi with painful slowness. I hugged Judith, my teeth chattering. Our clothes were wet through. Yanni finished the brandy and flung the bottle into the sea.

I estimated we were standing off shore about two hundred yards. We were rounding the bottom of the island and beating up to the west. The hull of the launch began to boom. As we crabbed our way north, Yanni beckoned me to him.

'All I ever did was to rob a security vault. That was my only purpose.'

He was having to shout. I glanced out. Paxos was a menacingly high profile off to starboard. There was not a light to be seen anywhere along the shore.

'This is the west coast of the island. Big currents, very dangerous. The cliffs are very high. Only the big caiques come here. Only the best of our sailors. And never in this weather.'

Even on full power, we stood in danger of broaching. Yanni slipped the Evinrudes into neutral and swiftly untied the skiff and cast it off. I watched him like a landlubber. The bows of the launch, now that it was under no power, were flipping up like paper in a breeze from a window. The hull boomed as each wave hit us.

'You can save her,' he shouted. 'You must! You were strangers to the island, newcomers, and you took a little leaky boat and ventured where you should not go. Poor Hilary died. But you can live. Look at me!'

I turned my face towards him and he smashed me with the butt of the pistol. I fell back into the bottom of the boat, seeing stars. When I got to my knees, Judith was already overboard. I saw her head bobbing and heard her scream in the dark.

'I don't want her to die, English,' Yanni bellowed. 'But I don't want her with me. All I ever did was rob the rich. All they ever did was rob the poor. Anything else is none of my business.'

When I rushed him, I had the advantage of coming from a

282

crouch just as he rose to pitch me overboard. I hit him just above the knees, he staggered, and we went over the side together. We kicked at each other in fury as the water closed over us. In falling out of the launch, I had grazed my shin back to the bone, and the agony of it gave me demonic strength. We flailed at each other. When I broke surface, he was already five yards off. All around were jellyfish the size of footballs, dislodged by the storm. I heard Yanni curse and, further off, Judith screaming. I felt the sting of a jellyfish like a lash with an electric wire. The current was dragging me south, and on it there floated not tens but hundreds of pale pink globes. I turned, kicked off my slacks and shoes and began to swim back through them towards where I imagined the launch to be. We were, just as he had planned us to be, a little maritime misadventure.

The launch was empty. I hung on to the side, kicking out in terror as the soft globes slid past. For five minutes I tried to find the strength to climb over the freeboard. The engines patiently idled. I gave up counting how many times I was stung. I managed to pull myself to the bow of the launch and throw out the anchor. The little craft came round head to wind. Choking, I heaved myself over the side and tumbled in. In the middle of my back was the pistol, and one of Judith's sandshoes. Coughing up salt water, I crawled to the bow and lifted the anchor.

I found the little waterlogged skiff almost immediately. Hilary was no longer in it. For half an hour I circled and called as the west wind blew the seas up higher and higher. There was no answer from either of them. I stood in the launch and bellowed my lungs out. Along the shoreline, at the base of the cliffs, the waves were crashing white and spiteful. The limestone cliffs rose sheer towards the stars for six hundred feet or more. On the far side of the island, less than three kilometres away as the gulls fly, the bars were still open, people were still dancing or shouting drunk. There, ketches lay at anchor, sailboards were stacked up neatly in the fragrant dust of bushes, nothing more dangerous than discarded suntan bottles floated in the water. They were listening to tapes in the villas, or making love. There was nothing like this. If I found Yanni, if he had not slipped back under the waves like Poseidon, I would kill him. I would split his head and send him to the bottom. A hundred times I steered towards a shoal of jellyfish, shouting and raging.

Just before reason told me to give up, I found Judith, floating in the water. She had taken off her skirt, but her pink tee-shirt had inverted like an umbrella, covering her face and leaving her flesh bare. As the launch slipped up towards her, I cut the engines and reached out for her, yearning towards her, willing her to be still alive. I locked my arms round under her armpits and pulled with all my strength on her body, shouting and raging at her to be alive with the passion of sex, the wild language of love and possession. Her head moved in the dark, the hair streaming out from it. All the abundance in her, all the huge brute persistence, the endurance that had carried her here, the force and vitality that shed her from her mother's womb and sent her wailing into the world, competed with me and the sullen mindless sea. I held her up, her back against the bucking launch, my arms tight round her, and rained kisses on her, as the sea started to slop into the boat and the rain rushed in squalls over us.